A NEW YOU

BY HILARY BROMBERG

OSCURA PRESS

A New You

Oscura Press
Tijeras, New Mexico
http://www.oscurapress.com

Foreword

Our mission at Oscura Press is to bring to light extraordinary literature written during the Second Dark Age. This sad time—dating from Late Postmodernism until the Great Devastation—saw what seemed to be the death of literature. A number of factors contributed to this decline: corporate hegemony, collusion between government and industry, and technological advances that led to the ubiquitousness of mass media. An unprecedented level of mass control was finally possible, and certain industries, particularly technology, advertising, entertainment, and of course pharmaceuticals, exploited every possible human weakness for financial gain. Quite simply, Aldous Huxley's *Brave New World* had come to pass.

It was only in the aftermath of the Great Devastation that the survivors were able to look upon the world with clarity. Mostly by necessity, people were forced to live unmediated lives again. It is in this spirit that we bring you *A New You.*

Oscura Press is pleased to release this astonishing document to the world. The unpublished manuscript was discovered in a bombed-out corporate campus, at the bottom of a large bag of shredded papers. We are unable to track down any information about its author, but we can say with certainty that *A New You* is one of the most significant works of Second Dark Age literature. Its literary influences were written during the previous century—it owes much to works such as *Death in Venice, The Immoralist,* and *The Yellow Wallpaper*—but its scope and intent place it firmly in the age of mechanical reproduction.

A New You is a dark dystopia, a *Brave New World* for the Prozac/Botox/iPod era. It's about surveillance and self-mutilation, abstract art and concrete longings. It's about what happens when we spend our lives interacting with images instead of people. It's the story of a young artist who gets a corporate grant to stay inside a locked room for a year and project her work onto the web. We follow her obsessive voice from an enthusiastic beginning to a horrific end, through an ill-fated romance and a progression of physical transformations that turns her into a fantasy object as she gradually slips into madness.

A New You is not an easy read. It is graphic and bold and unrelenting, and its hypnotic prose will draw you into the narrative even when you'd rather hide your eyes. But we must not look away, even though we may flinch. Another Dark Age could fall upon us if we're not careful, and *A New You* is a warning, unfortunately unheeded in its time. It is an important work that must be read by every survivor of the Great Devastation, or we shall be doomed to repeat ourselves. Next time, there may be no survivors left.

September 11, Year 24 AGD
Tijeras, New Mexico

*A time came when none of us could use
the figure without mutilating it.*

—ROTHKO

January

THE ROOM WAS WHITE. She hated white, except when there was snow. But that was how a canvas started, and she did love to paint on canvasses. And so, she found herself in this room, surrounded on all sides by canvasses that she could paint in any way she wanted. She would be living like this for a year—the grant stipulated that as long as she projected her room onto the World Wide Web twenty-four hours a day, she'd be able to order paint and food and anything else she wanted and she wouldn't have to do a thing but live. She was perfectly comfortable living in this manner, and she considered herself quite lucky to have gotten the grant—she knew somebody who knew somebody and it all worked out just as she wanted. Things had always seemed to work out as she wanted, and now she found herself in this blank-canvassed room with no obligations to anybody and the entire web at her disposal. She craved beauty, had always craved beauty, and now she had the chance to devote herself so purely to its creation. She liked things pure. She liked them abstract. Her dream was to create images so transcendent in their beauty that they would thrill anybody who came upon them. And not just thrill—thrills were easy and forgettable. She wanted to move, to change, to invent a new language of images and use it to transform the world. This was what she'd told the people who had given her the grant—they seemed quite pleased with the idea: a woman in a room alone creating images for all to see. The only stipulation was that she had to stay in the room for the entire year with no visitors. And she had to leave the lights on and the webcams running all the time. But this was fine. She rarely craved company—other people were a mere distraction from the important work she had to do. And she hated natural light and in fact any facet of the outdoors—sunlight felt too harsh upon her skin and nature made her sneeze. She could order anything she wanted from her lovely little silver computer, and the purity of isolation would do her quite a lot of good. A person needs to concentrate if she's to produce anything of value. A person needs to be able to sit in silence day after day in order to get into the deepest places. And as for the problem of being seen by everybody who visited her website, she actually rather liked the idea of being seen—it made her feel alive. She had grown up praised for everything she did, which added up to a lot of praise over her twenty-one years of life. To have everybody see her creations, to be famous—that was the goal held before her all her life, and here she was so close to attaining it. The praise would be raining down upon her and she'd feel complete. And what about the cameras watching her as a person, as a body moving in a room? No matter—it was only her mind that meant anything—her body was just a conduit for the products of her mind. And plus, in the very center of the canvassed room there was a smaller cube, just six-and-a-half feet tall and wide and made of frosted glass so nobody could see inside. They'd put a little tub in there, and a toilet and a sink and lots of mirrors. There was also a soft place on the floor where she could sleep, and a trap door for deliveries and emergencies and for throwing her garbage away. She would use the cube for mundane matters and she would only present herself to the public as she wanted to be seen. Complete control over herself and her surroundings. And she could paint as much as she wanted, for an entire year. She was so happy to have this opportunity to really work and grow and live. She wondered if she could apply for another year here after this one was done.

February

The room was a clear pink. The paints had finally arrived, and she exuberantly covered every inch of all the canvasses with ground. How wonderful it felt to move the brush through the room—she loved the wide sweeping movements she could make when she was only putting ground upon the canvas—so different from the deliberate little strokes she made when she was painting for real. But maybe the ground could be considered a painting of its own? A painting that was not just about the presence of pink walls all around, but about the gestural dance that she was doing as she finally took the walls from their sterile whiteness to this radiant new hue. She leapt from end to end and smoothed the tinted gesso on the walls, not caring about dripping on the floor because she was painting that as well. The brush was wide and the bristles soft and the gesso spread like heavy cream as she caressed the canvasses. She got the idea to take a brush in each hand and wave her arms like she was holding semaphores as she moved and covered and dipped and dribbled gesso everywhere and giggled as she slipped along the floor.

As the water ran pink into the little tub she thought about why she'd selected this particular shade to tint the gesso with—she liked to work by instinct and then analyze and then let the impact of the work take form inside her mind before she took another step. Something about prisoners. And bubblegum. And oh yes, an article she'd read some time ago about a color called Baker-Miller Pink, named after some gracious wardens who allowed a researcher to paint a prison cell bubblegum-colored and see what happened. And what happened was that the prisoners grew more docile and stopped attacking one another quite so often. And if she recalled correctly their heart rates went down and their friendliness went up, they started singing lullabies to one another and the researcher declared that from then on he would devote his life to touting Baker-Miller Pink. She certainly agreed that color had important psychological effects, but she wasn't certain if she actually felt any calmer since the room was pink. She did know that she felt much better since she'd had a chance to move around, to dance, and she wondered if she was making any progress towards her new language of images. Certainly there was a precedent for this sort of thing in Action Painting, but the ambidextrous semaphore gesture, combined with the prisoner-pink hue and her elected confinement in this place made her think she might be onto something. An interesting conceit, blurring the line between painting a room and painting *in* a room—what was it, then, that differentiated an artist from the guy who comes and paints your bedroom beige? She'd abandoned representational painting years ago—could pull off photorealism as well as the next person who'd taken far too many art classes, but she had become convinced that abstraction was what it was all about. She liked to read about science and draw her ideas from there—so many fascinating concepts for the taking within the worlds of psychology and neuroscience and linguistics and physics and math. She didn't always understand everything she read, but she figured that nobody else really did either, and anyhow she was an artist and didn't need to trouble herself with exact detail—according to Derrida you could interpret anything however you wanted and that was perfectly okay. Her senior thesis project—the one that got the grant people to notice her—was an installation inspired by an article she'd read entitled *World's First Brain Prosthesis Revealed*. It told of researchers at MIT who'd developed a silicon chip that could stand in for a hippocampus, the part of the brain responsible for putting experiences into long-term memory. The researchers hadn't tested the chip on slices of rat brain yet, but they had high hopes because they'd been working on it for ten years now, and they saw no reason why it wouldn't work on live rats and monkeys and people who had trouble remembering things. The article caught her attention because she'd never heard of a hippocampus before and she loved the sound of the word and the idea that you could replace the hippocampus with a chip—this way, she figured, you could program your brain to remember anything you wanted. When she learned that the word hippocampus was Greek for seahorse, so named because the anatomist who discovered it thought that it resembled one, she suddenly visualized the entire installation and shuddered at what she'd seen. A small room painted all around with the ocean and the sky above. And floating atop the water were hundreds of stylized seahorse shapes, black and bloated and clumped and clearly victims of an ecological disaster. The room was dimly lit, and it held only one person at a time, and when you walked in you heard a disturbed and urgent whispering from the walls: *I can't remember, can't recall, I can't remember anything … I don't remember, can't remember, cannot tell you anything at all.* And she sprinkled rotting seaweed in the corners of the room and entitled the piece *The Drowned Seahorse, or World's First Brain Prosthesis Revealed.* When she was interviewed about the installation, she talked enthusiastically about a future where nobody would ever forget anything.

She scraped the remains of the pink paint off of her fingernails and swaddled her head in a towel. The ground would take some time to dry completely, so she decided to search the web to see if her work so far had been original or not. She sat cross-legged on the soft place within her cube and cradled the little silver computer in her lap. She'd been online since she was a child and could spend hours surfing the web without blinking. First a visit to her website: the cameras seemed to be working nicely, you could see quite clearly that the room had now been painted pink, and if you clicked on the button labeled *Archive* you could see a recording of any time till now. There was no sound to accompany the images—she'd elected against microphones because she didn't want to disrupt the purity of her art with the sound of her footsteps or her breath. She watched a few minutes of herself leaping around and twirling brushes in the air, then turned the image off, embarrassed. She looked terribly fat in the paint-splattered pants she had on, and her arms did not look thin from any angle. She cringed at the thought of people seeing her this way, and resolved to do something about her weight. They'd bring her any type of food she wanted, so it was really up to her to determine how large she wanted to be. Fatwatchers.com, eslimming.com, doctorgourad.com, doctorhudnut.com, thevoid.com, loseweightnaturally.com, loseweightnow.com, and the gesso was dry but she still had so much to learn about how she ought to be eating that she sat in front of the screen reading until she fell asleep.

The next morning she felt miserable. She'd eaten an entire bag of gummi worms while looking for information about the proper way to eat, and so resolved to give up candy for the day. And with that resolution in mind, she began her original task of researching the history of Action Painting. Links led to links and then to a page that really caught her imagination. It was entitled rob-otics.com, and it belonged to an artist named Rob who used little robots to paint. The robots were driven by neural networks, just like the human brain, and their wheels released paint as they danced over canvas. Rob seemed to know quite a lot about how the human brain worked—he had an entire section on his website detailing the theory behind his robots: they were built with simple sensors that detected motion and light and sound, and these sensors fed into a computer brain that changed and learned with experience, just like the neurons in a human brain. The robots started out moving quite randomly, but eventually learned to avoid bumping into one another and even developed what looked like moods and personalities, which of course raised important questions about innateness and consciousness. Rob seemed to have been very successful with his robots, or Rob-ots as he called them—she read his whole biography and felt quite jealous— he was always having shows and performances and had even appeared on television and in a short documentary film. In the images section of his website there were many pictures of Rob staring intensely at robots, Rob pointing confidently at a diagram of a neural network, Rob looking suave at an opening standing next to several beautiful women. She wondered if Rob was single—he didn't say anything about his personal life anywhere on his website, and he didn't seem to be standing next to any woman in particular in the pictures. She found an interview of him from *Modern Cyborg* magazine in which he said that living with someone isn't easy with a bunch of robots running around, but the article was from a few years before, and his statement was ambiguous in any case.

She couldn't stop thinking about Rob as she dressed to go outside her cube and paint. What if he was watching her? She put on some control top stockings and ignored the way they ate into her waist. Short black paint-splattered skirt and worn black t-shirt and she was ready to present herself again. Two brushes, smaller this time, and a batch of light green paint to contrast perfectly with pink. She wanted to keep playing with the semaphore idea, but with gestures that were much smaller and more deliberate, and her hands began to move in abstract patterns that were mirror images of one another except that the right side was wilder and less precise. Was this what her brain looked like inside? She'd drawn these intricate arabesque patterns instinctively for years now—fluid and recursive and mysterious even to her—all she had to do was put mark-maker to surface and the designs would fall out before she barely even realized. She would sometimes even draw them in the air with her fingers, conducting a visuo-spatial orchestra for nobody to see. But now there were people watching her—how many, exactly, she didn't know—so she put the brushes down and began to trace out arabesques with her index fingers against the surface of the walls.

When she looked at herself on her website she was pleased to note that the skirt and stockings made her look more attractive. No matter that the elastic left a deep red welt around her waist and felt a bit constricting—she looked slimmer in her images, and that was what she'd wanted to achieve. But slimmer was not all—she was amazed to see that she'd fallen into some sort of a trance while she was painting arabesques in the air. Primitive and rhythmic and completely uninhibited she let those patterns move her body all around the room. Had she taken Action Painting one step further by eliminating the paint? Or had Fluxus already done this years ago? Once the postmodern barrier had been broken there was nowhere really left to go. Nothing was sacred or surprising or new. But she wasn't going to let that stop her from creating art—she had to just listen to her urges and forget about the rest. It was interesting to watch the differences between her hands as they mirrored one another through the air—her right hand was so much more expressive and moved raw and dramatic and her left hand moved with such delicacy and control. She'd felt that difference while she was air-painting and it was incredible to watch. She wondered how the pattern-making was related to language—it felt so much like writing when she made these abstract movements—were her arabesques a sort of language that she couldn't yet decipher?

Maybe Rob would have some insight into this. She looked into a mirror and remembered those beautiful women by Rob's side in the pictures on his website. She decided that her eyebrows needed to be narrower. She'd heard that you weren't supposed to touch the top arch of the eyebrow but only pluck from underneath, so she went to work along the bottom edge, flinching from the sting as she ripped out each little hair. The area was reddened and puffy when she finished, but she definitely looked more glamorous than she did before.

Rob had put an email address on his website, so she figured she could get in touch with him that way. Anybody that interested in technology would check his email fairly often, she reasoned, so if she sent a note he'd definitely write back quickly. She sat in the little tub and shaved her legs as she composed a note in her head, a note that would get Rob to notice her. Her skin was pale and sensitive and chafed quite easily, so she had to be very careful how she shaved. Deep soaking first in water and then gobs of cream—she smoothed it on and methodically slid the razor along her leg trying not to skin her ankles as she'd done so many times before. Her hair was dark and grew back quickly, so she had to shave her legs quite regularly if she wanted them to look at all attractive. She recalled a time in junior high school when she'd gotten teased for having stubble around her ankles—after that she'd never missed a spot. A dot or two of blood on the rough parts of her knees—not bad—and she kept going over and over the note to Rob. It couldn't be too formal or too coy or too forward. She had to leave just the right amount of mystery while letting him know enough to make sure he'd be interested. Anyhow, she only wanted his feedback about her work as a fellow professional, and she didn't know why her head was always going off into these silly fantasies. Enough. A simple email then, just a note to let him know she liked his work and was currently working on a year-long project that could be viewed remotely if he wanted. A friendly introduction, nothing more. She sent it off and went straight to bed because she couldn't stand to wait awake for an answer.

March

The room was gray and smelled of rot. She'd gotten tired of the pink. And not a word from Rob. She stood over the little sink and stirred the henna thoroughly, incorporating warm water into the green powder until she had a mud-like mass at the bottom of the bowl. The putrefying vegetal smell was overwhelming in the little cube—the outer room was ventilated to prevent her from going crazy from the fumes of acrylic paint, but the inner cube hadn't been designed with ventilation in mind. No matter, there was something primal and reassuring about the scent of henna—she'd never dyed her hair before, but it reminded her of something that she couldn't quite define, something from outside. She leaned over the sink and took handful after handful of the soft warm paste and pressed it into her hair, which was long and hung clumped against her face as she tried in vain to shake it away without spraying henna everywhere. She really could have used another pair of hands—she had no idea how difficult it would be to squeeze henna into every lock of hair while keeping hair out of her eyes so she could see what she was doing. Her hands were both filthy with the stuff, so she couldn't touch her face to get the clots of henna off. She realized that she should have kept one hand clean while she applied the henna with the other. A bit got in her mouth and it tasted like dirty spinach. She watched helplessly as her pristine little cube got splattered with henna despite her best attempts to remain self-contained. But she persisted—washed one hand awkwardly and scrubbed her face clean and squeezed up underneath her hair in order to make certain that she'd gotten every piece. And when it was complete she saw herself in the mirror and startled—fat green tendrils hanging down all around and she remembered when she'd been picked to play Medusa on Mythology Day in seventh grade; at first she'd been embarrassed but then she did some reading and realized that she sort of liked the part of the myth where she got to turn men into stone with her large hypnotic eyes. She'd sprayed green dye into her hair and twisted in some plastic snakes and applied iridescent green eyeshadow and heavy black eyeliner and coat after coat of mascara until her eyes were more intense than she could ever have imagined. She'd practiced that makeup at home every night for a week before Mythology Day, alone in her tiny bathroom while her mother was reading the newspaper and her father was reading her sister to sleep.

Her neck began to ache as she rinsed the henna again and again and green clumps kept on coming. Eventually the water ran clear, but now her hair was all stiff and tangled and desperately in need of conditioner. She reached for the bottle of Frizz-Be-Gone and poured it liberally onto her head. Worked it in and through and finally her hair began to soften. Rinsed again and scrunched the excess water out of her hair with a towel and when she looked at the bits that were beginning to dry she could see a definite reddish glow. She plugged in the blowdryer and was soothed by the warm air. Why hadn't Rob sent her any email? It had been weeks already and every day that went by she was sure that he had to respond, but then he didn't and she didn't know how to feel. She figured there were only three possibilities. He hadn't gotten her email yet because he was away, but he'd get it soon and then he'd definitely respond. Or he'd gotten her email and hadn't gotten the chance to respond to her yet because he was so busy, but he definitely intended to. Or he'd gotten her email and had no interest in responding, but she didn't like to dwell upon this possibility. He probably just hadn't gotten her note yet and would respond at any moment. He'd send her a charming note, his attention clearly piqued, and he'd tell her he'd been watching her work and wanted to see more. And they'd start exchanging intense emails about the nature of art, and he'd write so poetically and deeply and she'd sneak him into the cube and he'd look into her eyes....

But then she realized that there was a fourth possibility—maybe the email address on Rob's website was out of date. This could mean that she might never hear from him, but not because he wasn't interested in her. He might never actually get her note at all, and she would never know whether he didn't respond because he didn't get the note, or because he didn't consider her worth his time. How could she possibly tell the difference? She'd been checking his website daily for changes, but it always looked exactly the same. She held the hot end of the blowdryer close to her head and told herself to stop, that Rob was just a guy she didn't even know, and he was probably taken anyway, and she could never know anything for certain and here she was driving herself insane when she needed to focus on creating. She tossed her hair back and stared at herself auburn. She looked older and less innocent and oddly disconnected from her hair, as though it used to be a part of her but had now become an ornament.

She had told herself that she'd go outside and work immediately after she finished with the henna, but as she looked at herself in the mirror, she grew more and more unsettled. Her face and hair had harmonized before, but now there was something unbalanced and her face looked drab in comparison with the gleaming auburn of her hair. She decided to see what would happen if she painted her face—just a touch of makeup and she'd be presentable again. She'd never worn much makeup before—concealer over pimples and dark circles, and a bit of rosewater liptint and some eyeliner in a shade called khaki suede that didn't stand out too much. But if she could color her hair, why shouldn't she color her face as well? She placed an order with instantbeauty.com for a huge array of products—she had no idea what would look right with her new hair, so she ordered Milady's Makeover Collection in every colorway available. The advertising copy promised to transform her from blah into wow, which sounded tempting on this henna-scented day.

She checked her email again and again while waiting for her makeup. Twelve offers of pills to make her penis larger, a mass-mailed party invitation from somebody she'd fallen out of touch with years before, and an email from the grant people encouraging her to spend more time in the room outside the cube. The parcel finally arrived and she opened it greedily, stroking the shiny plastic casings of her powerful new playthings. She started with lipstick—applied a bold brick-red to her mouth and was amazed at the effect—all of a sudden she'd become so dramatic and glamorous. She blotted the excess on a tissue and blew kisses at the mirror and ran the tip of her tongue over her lips seductively. Next she selected a purple eyeshadow that was a beautiful eggplant color but made her look bruised. She moistened a tissue with eyemakeup remover and ran it over her lids until they were clear. Maybe blue would work better—she had a gorgeous peacock hue—but this one just looked tawdry so she took it off as well. She went through the entire color wheel of shadows getting more and more frustrated because all she needed to do was find the proper shadow to complete her glamorous new look and then she could go outside and work, but everything was somehow off—too muddy or too garish or clashing dreadfully with her hair. As she removed a problematic mauve she noticed that her eyelids were now rather reddened and puffy and made a mockery of her brick-red mouth. She couldn't possibly go out like this. But how else was she supposed to work? Here she'd spent all morning transforming her hair instead of working and she only wanted to go outside and have everybody see her and now it would be impossible until her eyes returned to normal and she wiped off the lipstick and hated the stain it left behind and glared at her hair in the mirror and lay down on the soft place on the henna-splattered floor and cried.

When she woke up several hours later she berated herself for breaking down like that. So silly, to let her appearance get in the way of her work. She figured that maybe part of the problem was that she'd been slightly sleep-deprived—she wore a black satin sleepmask to block out the perpetual light coming into the cube from the room outside, but she'd been having trouble falling asleep lately and she often woke up with the sleepmask off and found herself needing to nap during the day. So she'd needed a bit of rest after the henna. Not a problem. She looked around at all the little drops of henna paste and realized that she hadn't cleaned up anything. She took paper towels and soap and noticed that underneath every glob of green was left a little red spot. She scrubbed and scrubbed, to no avail. And the cube still smelled of rot. She told herself that she would never dye her hair again, and yet she couldn't stop looking at herself in the mirrors as she cleaned. Whose hair was this on her head? And why had she desired it? The proof would be in peoples' reactions to her hair—she'd gotten a constant stream of comments on her website about how fascinating her project was and some people went so far as to say that she was cute, but what would they say when they saw her with this new look? Could she consider her appearance part of the project too? This way, she could figure that she hadn't wasted any time coloring her hair—it would be sort of like performance art except that she had no intention of taking off her clothes.

Control top stockings, black paint-splattered skirt and t-shirt and she was ready to go outside the cube again. She looked at herself full-length in the mirrors and decided that she'd try again with the makeup—the brick-red lipstick would look so dramatic against all the black that she had on, and especially with her new hair, and she'd just avoid eyeshadow entirely this time and it would only take her a few minutes to put on a better face. She applied the lipstick again and then realized that she was famished, so she opened her little refrigerator and stood there for ten minutes eating buttered popcorn jellybeans and gummi frogs and malted milkballs until she got that queasy feeling in her stomach and her head began to spin. She'd done it again—eaten too many jelly beans and not enough chocolate—if she ate just one more malted milkball she'd set the balance in her stomach right. And crunch and oh! She loved the ancient dusty taste of malt and the buttery bittersweet chocolate overwhelming her mouth. And the way the malty filling stuck into her teeth and released itself into small malty pieces that she could roll over her tongue as the chocolate flavor faded and she craved another, just one more. And then another. And then if she had just one gummi peach, just a small one to clear her palate she'd be balanced, she knew it. So she nibbled on the flat orange sugar-coated gummi, marveling at the glimmering orange hue inside the matte exterior and the peach-flavored perfume filled her mouth and nose and scented everything with warm soft floral feelings and a citrus sharpness and a tropical sensation that stayed with her after the candy had been swallowed down. Enough! Her stomach was stinging and taut and her throat was coated with a sweetness. She drank a few handfuls of water and figured that she'd had enough to eat for the time being. Back to her makeup. The lipstick had worn off in the middle, so she reapplied it there but then thought it looked uneven—too moist in the middle and too dry around the edges, so she took it off entirely and applied it yet again. Not bad. Some dark brown pencil around her eyes and she was finished, finished! She would not let herself get carried away this time. She had important work to do.

Outside in the gray-canvassed room she noticed that she'd left a spot or two of pink behind. This would not do at all. She'd have to mix up some more gray paint to cover up the pink places so she'd have a uniform ground to start with. She squeezed some white into a bowl and delighted in its pristine cleanness. Then she went to work on her palette mixing up a bit of this and that until she had a neutral gray that she could use to tint the white. With a little flat brush in hand she went methodically over every corner of the room, reached up high to paint the ceiling and crouched down low to paint the floor. When she'd finished scrutinizing every inch of the room for lapses in the gray she stood back and noticed with horror that when the touch-up paint dried down it was slightly off in hue—maybe it was too purple, or too blue? In any case it was a cooler gray color than she'd used to paint the rest of the room, and she couldn't possibly start with a ground that wasn't even, so she sighed and went back to her palette and adjusted the balance with a touch of cadmium red and cadmium yellow until she was convinced that it was perfect. Mixed up another batch of white tinted with the new gray and chose a slightly larger brush to cover the areas she'd just painted. Started at a bottom corner and moved systematically up and over but then her eyes started crossing and her head started to hurt and she couldn't tell what she'd already painted, and she couldn't tell whether the newest tint was maybe slightly lighter than the one that was too cool, or maybe it just hadn't dried down properly, and had she painted that or was it just a shadow and the room started to spin gray around her and she put down the bowl and brush and cupped her paint-stained palms over her eyes. The lighting in the cube was playing tricks on her, she feared—she'd always had an unwavering sense of color but nothing looked quite right in here. She could certainly use some little robots now to help her mix the paint. Maybe Rob had emailed her while she'd been out here working? She went into her cube and opened her computer and still he hadn't sent her anything at all. She went onto her website and saw the final image of herself with her head bent forward and her eyes cupped in her hands and noticed that on screen the room looked perfect and her hair looked rather nice as well. What was this drama she'd just put on? A devotional dance of detail? A passionate quest for perfection? She checked the comments section of her website and was delighted to see that several people thought her latest work was brilliant, including one who thought that she was getting hotter every day.

April

THE ROOM DRIPPED WITH BUDS OF A SICK PALE GREEN. She had ordered them from a nursery and dipped them in shellac. And finally—oh finally!—Rob had written back. At first she thought she must have been hallucinating his response, because the fumes from the shellac were so heavy that they made her dizzy as she dipped each bud again and again until they were so thickly coated that they'd be preserved unbloomed forever. But no matter how many times she touched the screen of her computer, his email note remained. He told her that her work was cool, and that he was currently working on a project with his Rob-ots that brought him to Takoyaki for weeks at a time, and that he'd taken so long to get back to her because email access was spotty over there. He told her he was collaborating with some guys in a nanorobotics lab, and they'd created some tiny little Rob-ots that could move atop a canvas and squirt paint just like the larger Rob-ots, and she should drop by his next opening and say hi.

He'd invited her to an opening! But how was she supposed to attend? She went to his website and saw that he'd finally updated it, and that the opening of *NanoRob-ots* was in less than a week. Hadn't he read about her project on her website? Didn't he realize that the whole point was that she was living inside her art for an entire year? Perhaps he thought that she was just putting on some sort of show, maybe even that she was computer-generated or a robot herself. But he'd written her back, and this changed everything. A voice responding to her own. An invitation, even. She felt so confident and giddy that she stayed awake for days dipping those tiny green buds into shellac and hanging them on every surface of the room. As she worked she ruminated about Rob's note and whether he was interested in her, and how she could tell him that he'd misunderstood her project without hurting his feelings, and how she could tell him that she couldn't go to his opening without him thinking that she wasn't interested in him, and why he didn't have email access in Takoyaki, and why he wanted his robots to be so small. She dipped and dipped and composed a note inside her head, and when she had encrusted every surface of the room with lacquered buds she stood back and imagined that she was in a garden and delighted in the fact that she got to look at all this greenery without the risk of allergies or bugs. She'd carefully controlled the placement of the buds—some a darker green and some lighter—so that the overall effect was of a pointillist grid surrounding her. Satisfied with her latest creation, she staggered into the cube and collapsed onto the soft part of the floor, too exhausted to find her sleepmask or to rid her fingers of shellac.

She woke up screaming to a spider, her fingers too stiff to move. It had crawled onto her arm while she slept and she felt the tickling and flung it off across the room. It was fat and black and had thick legs, and her first instinct was to dash out of the cube, but she couldn't do that because she hadn't made herself presentable yet, and what if Rob saw her, and the spider was moving frenetic towards her and she looked for something to kill it with and grabbed her computer and brought it down hard upon the hideous moving thing. And she stood trembling in the corner and picked shellac off of her fingers and breathed shallow and fast and tried to decide what to do. A sudden isolation seized her. She'd broken her computer—she was certain of it—which meant that she had no way to communicate with anybody. She could die inside her cube from inhalation of shellac fumes and nobody would ever know. She picked her fingers miserable and thought of sneaking out the trap door, which would surely anger the grant people, or using the cameras to send a message, which would make her look like a fool. It would have to be the cameras, but how? Maybe she could go outside and hold an explanatory note up to a camera— somebody from the company that gave her the grant would notice before too long, and they'd send her a new computer soon. Or she could even write a note, a plea to anybody watching to contact the grant people and tell them about the problem. She'd look ridiculous, but it would be okay. At worst, she'd have to wait a few days without a computer; maybe it would actually be good for her to do without, to focus purely on her art. But what about Rob? Her next note to him was waiting fully formed inside her head, and she had to email him back soon or he might forget all about her. And she also had to check the comments on her website to see if people liked her latest work. And there was still a dead spider underneath her computer. And perhaps more live ones lurking all around, no doubt brought in among the buds. She tried to breathe deep. She got a tissue and lifted her computer while squinting her eyes slightly so she didn't have to confront the crushed spider in full detail, and she looked and she opened her eyes wide and looked again and didn't see the spider anywhere. And she realized that she'd brought down the computer upon the soft part of the floor, so the impact maybe wasn't that bad, but the spider seemed to have vanished despite the fact that she knew she'd put the computer down directly upon it. She imagined the soft floor-substance absorbing the spider somehow, sucking it in and eventually harboring hundreds of spiders, because surely there were more outside, just waiting to invade the cube. She grabbed a bar of darkest chocolate and ate the whole thing quickly while sitting in the corner of her cube and trying to clear her mind. Everything was fine. A nightmare, nothing more. The chocolate felt strong and soothing in her mouth. There might never have been a spider at all. Perhaps she'd simply been having a nightmare inspired by Rob's nanorobots. She opened the computer delicately and pushed a button and was greeted with a healthy chime. The screen looked fine, and the keyboard seemed to work, and everything looked intact, and she was so relieved that she stroked her computer and kissed it and told it she was sorry for what happened, but she'd had a terrible nightmare and she'd never use it to try to kill a spider ever again. She put on her sleep-mask and held the computer in her arms and fell asleep within seconds.

It would be a good day. She awoke to find that a new *Press* section had been added to her website, and somebody had written a glowing article about her. The article talked about her flowing auburn hair and full red lips and sexy legs and enigmatic artworks. It described how she was in a secret location with lots of cameras but no telephone or microphones or visitors or natural light. There was a long paragraph about how her corporate sponsor had recently begun to support the arts because they were fervent believers in freedom of creative expression even beyond the world of business, and they'd given her a lavish grant with an unlimited expense account that she could use for whatever she wanted. The article concluded by saying that it was anybody's guess what her next brilliant artwork would be, but it would sure be exciting to watch her and see.

She stared at the image of herself that accompanied the article and she stared at herself in the mirror and she stared at herself on her website staring at the grid of lacquered green. She was finally being seen. There were now hundreds of praising comments—people telling her that she'd made a brilliant statement about the modern disconnect from nature, people telling her that she'd made a brilliant statement about the puritanical fear of wildness, people telling her that she'd made a brilliant statement about the soullessness of contemporary architecture, and many many people telling her that she should take off her clothes. She was disturbed by all the people who wanted to see her naked—this project was about her mind, not her body—but she was also secretly flattered by all those people finding her physically appealing. She'd never in her life gotten this sort of attention—she was rather shy and had never felt particularly attractive and had always spent most of her time alone. Sure, she'd been obsessed with people before, but she had always acted too aloof for them to realize she was interested. And yet—here, inside the cube, something was changing. All these people watching her, but she was safe. She didn't actually have to talk to anybody face to face. No eye contact, no awkward conversation, just a purest line of contact with the outside world. Yes, today would be a lovely day. There were no spiders in her cube, and her computer was working fine, and she must've picked all the shellac from her fingers because they were free, and Rob had finally written back, and her work was going wonderfully. Her only concern was the large bar of chocolate she'd eaten during her nervous fright—she was really trying hard to lose a bit of weight, but it was impossible to keep from eating candy all the time. She decided that she'd take the advice of eslimming.com and write down the number of calories she was eating each day and try to keep it under 1,000 until she was skinny enough.

A little pad of paper and her favorite fountain pen and Chocolate Bar, 550, and she suddenly visualized an installation of a small round room with calorie lists spiraling down the walls. The handwriting would be girlish and bubbly and the lists would be affixed with pushpins like dead butterflies and the little pieces of paper would be in a neat line spiraling around and down, and the lists would get progressively shorter and the daily totals less and less until you had to crouch down to the floor to see the final series of notes, all blank. She thought about ending with a note that said *Embalming fluid, 3 gallons* in a careless male hand, but then decided that such a note would be too obvious—better to end with chillingly blank papers and then a bit of empty space on the wall.

Maybe she wouldn't write down her calories after all. Instead she'd just ignore her hunger calls. She was strong, and if she really needed to eat something, she'd just order a salad or some broth. She took off her clothes and stared at herself in the mirrors that lined most of the cube and resolved to become as skinny as those women on Rob's website. If they could do it, so could she. But her breasts still weren't very large. She searched online for breast enlargement products and read about pills and creams and electrical stimulators and strange plunger-like devices and settled upon the least threatening-looking option, a padded bra called the Abundacurve that claimed to add two cup sizes and create deep cleavage while maintaining a natural-looking silhouette. She imagined Rob looking at her wearing the Abundacurve and she wrote back to him telling him that she'd attend his opening in an instant, but that her corporate sponsor would retract her grant if she left the room, and maybe she could visit virtually instead—all he'd have to do would be to put a camera onto one of his robots and put the videostream onto the web, and then she could enjoy his opening too, at least through a robot's-eye-view. And she told him that she was just fascinated by nanotechnology and that his *NanoRob-ots* project made a brilliant utopian statement about the continuity of creativity from childhood to adulthood—such a beautiful vision, to have even the smallest creatures cavorting about and making art. She asked him how he'd gotten inspired to do this project, and told him that she'd created a new installation and that she'd love to know what he thought.

The Abundacurve was wonderful. She admired her new cleavage in a clingy black t-shirt with a deep v-neck and wondered how she'd gone so long without looking like this. It was just so easy, and such a transformation! She'd always seen images of women with breasts that went up and out and never quite understood why she looked so different from them, but here she was, looking so sexy all of a sudden, and she felt so powerful and bold that she wanted to step out of her cube at once and show everybody her new form. Concealer and brick-red lipstick and black eyeliner and a bit of Lash Lure mascara to make her lashes fat and black, and the control top stockings and the short black paint-splattered skirt, and she stuck out her chest at her reflection and ran her fingers through her snakes of reddened hair.

When she saw the green grid of lacquered buds surrounding her again, she startled and could only think of spiders. She stepped tentatively and looked among the buds for bits of black and kept fleeing from seeing her outfit reflected in shellac. Sideways and over and this corner and that corner and it was no use looking for spiders because there were so many black flashes to distract her. A bud fell from the ceiling and stuck inside her hair and she leapt when it landed on her and it felt sticky in her hand and she began to rip the buds from every surface of the room. A frenzied tearing and she gathered garlands in her arms and shoved clump after clump into the trap door until the room was bare and there was not a bud left anywhere.

Back inside her cube, she scrutinized every surface of every object and concluded that there was absolutely nowhere for a spider to hide. She was safe, and she had rid the room of all those nasty buds, and perhaps she had even made a brilliant statement about the destruction of nature that would capture Rob's attention along with her Abundacurves. She felt dizzy from hunger and sticky with shellac and began to run the water for a bath. As she unstrapped the Abundacurve she noticed how freeing it felt to let her breasts fall naturally. And she saw that there were deep red lines around her torso and her shoulders where the elastic had cut into her skin, and when she peeled off the control top stockings she saw another red line around her waist and she remembered something she'd read about bras causing cancer because they prevented lymph from circulating underneath the arms and she realized that she'd probably been wearing the Abundacurve for far too many hours because she felt so tired and there had been so many buds to pluck from the walls, and she climbed into the bathtub rather conflicted about it all. An entire installation destroyed because there might have been spiders, and a padded bra that made her look so beautiful, but she hated the way it constricted her, and what if it caused cancer, and she'd gone this long without wearing a bra most of the time, and why should she have to hide behind padding, but why shouldn't she look as sexy as those women on Rob's website, and why was she getting so fixated on him, and why had she suddenly torn the installation down? She shaved her legs and underneath her arms and up to her bikini line and tried to figure out what she was doing in this place. She remembered a garden where she'd gone when she was very young, with shallow ponds covered by enormous lily pads that were turned up at the edges and looked so solid that you could sit on them without sinking. She had always wanted to jump onto a leaf and feel herself floating on the soft sun-warmed surface, but her parents always held her back and by the time she was old enough to resist their grip, the garden had been destroyed to make room for a shopping arcade. There weren't any lily pads at the shopping arcade, but there was a fountain inside where people used to throw coins, and she would stare at the coins covering the bottom and wonder what happened to wishes. Maybe this installation had been a last farewell to nature, a way of controlling it and controlling it until it wasn't even possible anymore. Yes, she was done with nature, and from now on it was back to paint. Oh, she'd missed playing with color, smoothing brushes over canvas, making patterns with her hands. Those buds were entirely too much trouble, and they obscured her perfect gray ground, and she still didn't know exactly what had happened to the spider. She dried herself off and realized that she hadn't eaten anything since the candy bar and she looked at herself in the mirrors and felt terribly fat and vowed to eat nothing else until Rob emailed her back.

She must have fallen asleep without meaning to, because she realized that she was lying down on the soft place and she felt faint and there were little sleep-secretions in the corners of her eyes. She grabbed a box of crackers and determined that she'd eat one serving only, but then she'd eaten the entire serving and she was still famished, so she ate a broken one and then another broken one until she'd eaten another complete serving, but she had to keep going and the doughy taste of white flour enveloped her and she decided that she'd finish the box and then eat nothing for a long long time.

Her reflection in the mirrors told her that she needed to tweeze her eyebrows again—they seemed to be growing back in thicker than before. But she needed to check her email and her comments first—she felt embarrassed that she'd torn her installation down and she dreaded what people might say. An email from somebody at the grant company, and she was afraid to read it, but it turned out that they were congratulating her—it seemed that the popularity of her site had skyrocketed of late. And another note from Rob! His tone was warmer and he told her that he loved her idea of putting a camera on a Rob-ot, but actually he had a friend who was a cyborg who'd be recording the entire thing. All she had to do was go to his friend's website and she could watch the opening through the eyes of Panoptico. He told her that her idea about the little Rob-ots symbolizing creativity in childhood was really great, and he'd have to use that idea if anybody asked him what *NanoRob-ots* was all about. But mainly he'd made the robots so small because it seemed like a cool thing to do. He'd been tooling around Takoyaki and a friend took him on a tour of a nanorobotics lab and he just really liked the idea of making things so small. He had a cellular phone that was practically invisible, but you could still use it to surf the web. And he had a portable music player the size of a fly that could hold 1,001 days straight of music. And she shouldn't tell anybody about this, but he'd managed to get his hands on a prototype of a laptop computer so light that even a baby could lift it. Nanotechnology was where it was at, and since he wanted to get funding and all, he figured that his artwork should be at the cutting edge of technology. And he loved her latest installation—away with nature! He told her that it was awesome that she'd gotten such a lavish grant, but didn't it get lonely in that little room?

She couldn't abandon the Abundacurve now. After she read and reread Rob's note, especially the final line about loneliness, she checked her comments and saw that there were more than ever before. People were lauding her for her bravery, for taking destruction as far as it could possibly go, for teaching an important lesson about the fleetingness of life, for putting on an incredible show. Though she'd gotten the usual slew of crude remarks about her appearance, a few of the more personal comments were notable enough to set her thinking. One woman told her that she was playing a very dangerous game, tarting herself up to attract more viewers, and she ought to stop now and go back to her natural self before it was too late. But several other women told her that she looked so much more polished and sexy than when she'd begun, and that it was so inspiring to see someone who was artistically serious but not afraid to look like a woman.

Her eyebrows loomed huge and unkempt in the magnifying mirror as she plucked them carefully and thought about what it meant to look like a woman. She'd always felt so inadequate compared to all those images of women she'd seen on screens all her life—she'd assumed that other people had something she didn't, and that she would always be alone. But here she was all of a sudden with an image that commanded some attention, and she didn't see what was so inherently great about being natural. Evolutionary psychology even said that it was natural to try to make yourself look as sexy as possible in order to attract a mate, and it wasn't even like she was changing her appearance to please a man or anything—she was doing it for herself, because of her own aesthetic imperative to create beauty. And what was wrong with wanting to look beautiful? Maybe nobody had taught her these secrets as she was growing up, but she could certainly learn them now. She plucked a final hair and smoothed her perfect arches with a bit of tinted HighBrow gel and smiled at herself.

Panoptico's website was vast and deep and she twisted a curl of hair around her fingers as she tried to find Rob's opening. It seemed that Panoptico had lived most of his life through a camera. He wore special glasses with a tiny videocamera in front of one of his eyes and he wore a portable computer on his stomach that remembered everything the camera saw and heard. He even had a video display projected directly onto his glasses so that he could check his email or surf the web or program his computer no matter where he went. His website was full of articles about his defiant attitudes towards corporate surveillance, his fervent need to preserve everything he saw, his constant quest to create the smallest life-recorder possible. She looked at pictures from his archives and most were of his hands and little metal parts. One section of the website contained a progression of images of Panoptico in full cyberregalia over the past thirty years: the computers and cameras grew smaller and more stream-lined over time, and his hair grew thinner and his posture more slumped, but his facial expression remained stunningly consistent—mouth half-open and dumb and eyes staring blank into cyberspace. An interview described how useful it was to live through a camera—he could review his footage anytime if he forgot something, he could program his computer to remove unpleasant images like billboards from his visual field, and he could have his girlfriend tell him remotely which vegetables looked good if he was at the grocery store shopping for a meal. There was something endearing about Panoptico—he looked so vulnerable with all those wires and computer parts strapped to his awkward body, and his mouth gaped so bewildered wide, and she was glad that he had somebody to hold him and to soothe his fear of dying.

She felt terribly alone at that moment. She stopped reading Panoptico's site and went over to her favorite website, timetraveltrust.com, which allowed anybody to put money into a special trust fund so that when time travel finally became feasible, the money would have compounded into a sum large enough to cover the cost of being brought into the future. The site made no guarantees, but she had paid her money and received a certificate that declared her participation in the trust, and her name and address were in a database that would be preserved forever. The website was rarely updated, but she still loved to visit and reread the part that talked about how she could be brought into the future at any time during her life.

She suddenly realized that she still hadn't found Rob's opening, so she went back to Panoptico's site and looked and looked until she finally found the place where you could look through his eyes. The view through his camera showed the raw joists and pipes of an industrial loft ceiling, and she was jarred by the sound of snoring, and she realized that she had no idea what day or time it was, and that if she wanted to see Rob's opening she should figure out this sort of thing before she missed it. She went to Rob's website to see when exactly the opening was, and she spent a while staring at his images—oh, he was beautiful!—before she caught herself and established that his opening would be happening tomorrow at eight o'clock in the evening, and that it was now after midnight and she should really be trying to get some sleep.

There was something reassuring about hearing Panoptico

snoring out from her computer beside her, and she thought that maybe the repetitive human sound would help with her insomnia, which had gotten so bad that she could only fall asleep by staying awake until she collapsed—she seemed to alternate between long and futile attempts at sleep and hard involuntary naps. She'd often lie on her soft place for what felt like days, sleepmask on, ruminating about why she hadn't made more progress with her language of images and how glorious she'd look when she lost weight and what it would be like if Rob came and visited her and sometimes a memory from the past would bubble into her head and she'd have to push it away and try to relax by breathing deep and picturing soothing images, but her head was so stubborn these days and she'd find herself replaying things she didn't care to remember and no matter how many times she tried to calm herself and use the Zen technique of letting her thoughts flow into a river, the image of the river would soon dissolve and be replaced by ruminations again. She tried lying there and attempting to focus on Panoptico's gentle snoring, but she began to worry that she'd sleep so long that she'd miss the opening, so she set an alarm on her computer and tried to sleep again, but now she began to feel mocked by Panoptico and the fact that he slept so easily, even with that camera apparatus on his head, and she decided that she had to do something about her insomnia because she was getting terrible dark circles under her eyes that she couldn't cover up with even the most opaque concealer. She closed the window where Panoptico was still snoring and she read on the web about all sorts of drugs and techniques and con-cluded that a nightly dose of Lulliban would be the answer. It was supposed to put you to sleep softly and give you pleas-ant dreams and wake you up after eight solid hours with not even a hint of drowsiness the following day. She'd never liked taking drugs because she was so sensitive and often found herself with dreadful side effects, but Lulliban was supposed to be different from the older sleeping pills, and clinical studies showed no side effects at all. She found a website called drugs-r-us.com that would send her Lulliban without a prescription—all she had to do was answer a short questionnaire and check a few waiver boxes and a doctor would somehow approve her order and have it sent to her that very day. There were so many types of drugs available, and they were so easily acquired, and she decided to order Anorex as well—it was supposed to decrease hunger and increase fat metabolism, which was exactly what she needed. Some of the people who took Anorex seemed to experience nausea and depression, but she figured that she was always existentially nauseous anyway, and she could take an antidepressant if she got depressed—there were so many on the site to choose from. Questionnaire: no, she didn't have any allergies and she wasn't taking any drugs and she didn't have any heart problems or other medical problems that she knew of. Height and weight were easy to estimate, but what if they didn't think she weighed enough to qualify for Anorex? She added a hundred pounds to her weight just in case, and clicked the order off, and decided to buy a scale to track her progress on the Anorex. There were scales that told you your body fat and scales that spoke to you and scales that told you how dehydrated you were and scales that had a gypsy's face on top and prophesied your fortune for the day, and she was having trouble deciding when she noticed that she'd gotten a new email from the grant company. It was a short and friendly note, and it was just to say that maybe she didn't know about the full functionality of the cube, but if she stood with her feet aligned precisely on the footprints on the floor in front of the sink, a voice would announce her weight. She looked across the floor, and there were definitely some footprints that she hadn't seen before. They were rather subtle to see—matte, and the rest of the floor was glossy—but she didn't understand why she hadn't noticed them in all this time that she'd been living here. And she certainly didn't understand why she'd gotten this email at the exact time when she was searching for a scale. Were the grant people monitoring her websurfing? She considered emailing the person back and asking about the timing of the note, but she felt somehow nervous and got up to stand on the footprints and was so happy about the number announced by the booming robotic voice that she put the odd intrusion out of her mind and thought about how sylphlike she'd look during her next creative work.

She lay down with her sleepmask on and tried to relax, but she was so excited by the prospect of seeing Rob in person that she kept imagining what his voice would sound like and how he would move and how she would email him after the opening and tell him that it certainly did get lonely in her little room. Deep breathing and the river and fat spiders kept crawling in and making her shiver and she suddenly remembered an installation called *Seduction Couch* that she had seen years before. It was a black metal chaise in a black room with a sign that said *Touching This Couch Will Result In An Electric Shock* and she touched it and touched it and yes it hurt but she found herself unable to stop. Oh, where was her sweet Lulliban and why wouldn't her mind settle down without it? She reached out for a sketchbook and a pencil for each hand and found herself holding Milady's eyeliners in red and violet and the rhythmic patterns began to shape themselves into page after page of trembling arabesques and the pencils smoothed splendid and she felt herself rocking as she followed the swooping lines into sleep.

A chime from her computer and she woke at once. She went

to Panoptico's website and opened up his viewing window and heard his voice, a thin monotone, saying how he couldn't talk right now because he was at this art thing, and she saw a glowing urban streetscene and the sun was setting upon a river in the distance and she was so excited that she kept on reaching out to touch the screen. It seemed that Panoptico was talking to his mother on the phone and he was having trouble explaining what he was about to see, and eventually he told her that he loved her and that he'd call her back tomorrow morning.

As he stepped inside the gallery she heard voices all around her and she was struck by how immediate the experience felt. But she did not regret her choice to have no microphones—her work was purer if she wasn't heard. It was dark inside the gallery and people were crowded everywhere in clumps and she found herself moving quickly past everybody and staring at a platter of sugar cookies in the shape of robots and Panoptico's hand selected several and she began to hear him crunch. The cookies looked delicious and she realized she was famished but she didn't want to leave the screen even for a second, for fear that Rob would come. Plastic cups of wine, and then some gulping noises, and then a strained conversation with a short wiry guy about whether the robot cookies had neural networks inside, and maybe they should've had chocolate chips inside, or maybe they should've had bytes taken out of them, and the camera shook with choppy laughter and she noticed that Panoptico's apparatus didn't seem to allow eye contact at all—the wiry guy was looking puzzled and slightly uncomfortable—and she imagined that she wouldn't like staring into a camera lens either, and the awkwardness was palpable and she was glad that she was safe inside her little cube and not obliged to interact with anyone.

And then she saw him! There was a stage lit up and lots of little robots being set up by scruffy assistants and his voice was resonant and strong and he moved with such intensity and aplomb. He described the way his Rob-ots worked and how he was so glad that everybody could make it to see his latest group and how they'd learned to paint in really cool patterns and they were like insects because they could carry around bottles of paint hundreds of times their weight and she'd already read all about the theory behind his robots, so she mainly listened to the rich sound of his voice and watched his body move. There was a wild quality to him that was transfixing and she kissed his image on the screen.

Panoptico, unfortunately, seemed more interested in how the little robots moved. He made his way to the front of the crowd, just before the stage, and watched what felt like hours of the little machines skittering around to a loud soundtrack of techno music and leaving behind traces of paint on the canvasses below. Some of the robots looped wide and graceful and others crept linear and deliberate and others moved fast and random and swerved at the last moment to avoid collisions. She was amused to notice that one little robot barely seemed to move at all—just stayed in one spot and occasionally turned a bit and sat atop a slowly growing puddle of yellow paint.

She found herself getting restless and hoping that Panoptico would look at Rob, or even at the little wiry guy or at some cookies or some wine. But Panoptico was mesmerized by the robots, and so she stared at that one still robot and imagined that it was terrified by the crowds and the commotion and the pressure to perform, and she imagined that it must have been mortified sitting in that spot all alone. Rob entered the frame for a moment to pick the little robot up; she followed

Panoptico's gaze as Rob did something to the underside of the robot and put it down again upon the yellow spot, and still it barely moved and the crowd laughed and she felt so sorry for the little creature as the other robots swirled blithely around it. Her head was suddenly taken by a memory of an ice skating lesson long ago with a group of children who all seemed to know how to skate already and she had never skated before and she could barely stay upright and she kept on falling and she was wet and cold and hurt and the other children were skating smooth and confident and laughing at her as she clung to the wall and cried and the instructor kept telling her to push off, to glide, and she knew she'd fall and her nose was running but she needed her arms to balance and she fell again and hit her head and she stared at the little robot on that yellow spot and tried to forget.

The robots danced until their paint ran out and kept on dancing till their batteries all died. Rob reached in and took the robots off the canvasses one by one and lined them up at the front of the stage and as he hung each canvas up on panels at the back of the stage with great bravado she noticed that the lone robot was still moving ever gently, subtly turning and shifting as if taking in the situation and wondering how to escape.

The paintings looked abstract and rather random; the wheels had left behind and picked up so many traces of paint that the colors had muddied and blended gray-brown. She looked for the painting with the puddle of pure yellow and noticed that Rob had left it lying flat in the corner of the stage—she supposed that he didn't want the puddle dripping over the entire thing and onto the floor below. Rob was so poised and expressive as he apologized for the slight technical failure and thanked everyone for coming out, and everybody clapped and whistled and he extended his arm down towards the line of robots in a dramatic sweep with a mock-humble expression as if to say no no, it was all their doing, and the crowd laughed and clapped and whistled louder and she could hear Panoptico clapping maniacally as the scene shook and shook before her.

The platter of cookies was mostly empty, but Panoptico's hand went out to claim the last few broken ones, and then she startled at Rob's face and he was telling Panoptico that a special guest was looking through his camera lens and he'd better behave himself and not take too many of those cookies. She touched his cheek on the screen as Panoptico said how good the cookies were, and Rob told him to tell Debbie how good they were, since she's the one who made them, and maybe he said Devi or Nebbie because the room was so loud, and they started talking about the technics of the robots and her head was tense and confused and frustrated and she wanted to reach out to Rob and ask him who this cookie-maker was, but maybe it was just his sister or a friend, and yet he'd actually mentioned his special guest and sent her a message, and she didn't know what was happening and she was so overwhelmed and she was staring at Rob as he was discussing the merits of nanotechnology with Panoptico, who seemed to be opining that he liked the bigger robots better because they could hold more paint and make bolder designs, and she looked at Rob's lips and his eyes and she was so drawn to him and if only she could reach into the screen, and then a woman with a shrill voice screamed *Rob!* and said she was so happy to see him again and she lunged and hugged him and her nails were red and sharp and Panoptico sighed forlorn and walked back past the crowds and out into the glaring city dark.

She closed her computer as Panoptico began to snore. The opening was over. She sent Rob a briefest email telling him that his opening was wonderful and she couldn't stop thinking about that sad immobile robot and she did in fact get terribly lonely but the solitude allowed her to live a pure existence because her work was untainted by the chaos of the outside world, and then she noticed that her package of drugs had been delivered through the trap door while she'd been staring at the screen, and she tore the wrappings open and took an Anorex and a Lulliban immediately. Yes, she'd only woken up several hours before, but she figured that the best way to get stabilized would be to take the Lulliban while it was nighttime outside instead of waiting until she was tired. She lay down upon the soft place and felt her head sinking and her thoughts became blurred and she tried to fight the effects of the Lulliban just to see what would happen but it was so strong that it wouldn't even let her obsess and she fell asleep to visions of Persephone tumbling into the underworld.

When she woke up, her head was hurting and she felt dizzy and disjointed and sick. She crunched on some crackers as she tried to understand what she had seen inside her screen. Rob had spoken directly to her, and he was so compelling, and he had such an adoring audience, but who had made those cookies for him? She felt jealous and realized that no matter how bad she felt today, it was time to go outside the cube again and think about the progression of her work. She had been neglecting herself for Rob's opening, and she was in this room to be productive, not to focus on other people's art. She looked at herself in the mirror and saw that her eyes looked small and terrified without any liner or mascara, and so she began to paint her face again, starting with the concealer which she needed quite a bit of today because her skin seemed to have more pimples than usual, and the circles underneath her eyes were terribly dark, and she followed the concealer with a patting of powder all over like it said to do in *Milady's Book O' Tips* to help the concealer blend into the rest of the skin, and then a circling of blackest kohl eyeliner and several coatings of mascara on her top and bottom lashes, and a dramatically arching cupid's bow of burgundy lipliner to make sure her lips stayed sharp, and a layer of burgundy lipstick and then a blotting and then another layer for intensity, and a few brow hairs growing out that needed tweezing, and a few pulls and twinges and some gel to smooth them into place and she looked at her face and felt seductive and glazed.

On with the Abundacurve and a low-cut t-shirt pulled carefully over her perfect face and she'd begun to put on the control top stockings when she noticed that her bikini line was covered with red spots where she had shaved several days before. What if Rob were to come to her cube and see her skin like this? She sat down on the soft place and looked more carefully at the area and saw that there seemed to be a dark spot in the middle of each welt of red. She remembered why she rarely shaved that area—several times in her life she'd felt obliged to put a swimsuit on and she'd always gotten ingrown hairs every time she shaved her upper thighs. She sighed and found a pin and bent her head down and went from follicle to follicle, pinching the skin around each welt and sticking the pin underneath the black spot and flicking it out, freeing a little hair that had begun to grow into the skin. It was oddly satisfying to release the hairs from the sore spots, and some of them were more deeply embedded and she had to pick a bit with the pin to free them and her skin started to bleed and she swabbed at it with peroxide and went systematically over both her inner thighs until she'd liberated every ingrown hair. The area was now a mess of inflammation and her skin was stinging and she knew that the places where she had to go deep to get the hairs out would take a long long time to heal, and she thought of all the images of women she'd seen on screens with hairless bodies and the tiniest of bathing suits and she cursed her sensitive skin and dabbed peroxide on her mottled thighs and if Rob could see her now he'd probably be horrified. She searched on the web for a product to help her and ordered a bottle of Softly-U solution, which promised to soothe the redness away and prevent ingrown hairs from ever happening again and provide her nether regions with a lovely floral scent.

It had been a long time since she'd been outside the cube and she was horrified by what she saw. Grey walls splotched with pink where the paint came off. Gobs of glue. She'd never have a smooth surface again. She cursed herself for putting up the buds and cursed herself for pulling them down and grabbed a palette knife and began to pick the walls clean.

May

The room was a pure moist blue. She had printed out as many pictures of the sky as she could find online and pasted them over the mottled paint and glue. It had simply been too difficult to make the canvas surface perfect again, so she decided to take an archeological approach and allow the traces of her past displays to remain. Anyhow, this project was becoming a work of Process Art, and it wouldn't do to completely obliterate what had come before. She wasn't sure what she would do with all these squares of glossy blue—so far she'd found it deeply soothing to be surrounded by shades of sky and this was all that mattered. The blues were of wildly different hues, but she resisted the impulse to make another grid and tessellated the squares into a checkerboard instead. A game. What would the pieces be? What sort of game could she play upon the sky? She thought of game theory and the prisoner's dilemma and decided to let her mind mull a bit inside the cube—she'd been outside for quite a while now in a furious bout of cropping and pasting and she was beginning to feel rather dizzy and it occurred to her that she could use a bit of distance and sleep and food.

She stared at herself in the mirror as she undressed and stood on the footprints in front of the sink and scowled at the robotic voice that announced her weight. It was so difficult to keep from eating. She sat on the soft place with her little silver computer and chewed a rope of waxy red licorice as slowly as she could while she checked her email and oh! such a solid and delicious feeling to see another note from Rob. This time she'd been confident that he'd respond, so she didn't let herself get too anxious while she worked—she somehow knew that when she came inside from her checkered sky she'd find a note from him waiting folded in her inbox. But she could never know anything for certain until she saw it, and even her eyes were oddly unreliable since she'd begun to take the Lulliban and Anorex—sometimes she turned quickly and the world didn't follow quite as fast and she found herself dizzy when she stood or sat and little shimmers occasionally floated out of nowhere and danced around her visual field for a moment or two before dissolving. She touched the screen and caressed each letter of Rob's note, which was friendly and maybe even suggestive, and she was afraid that she was getting smitten with someone terribly inaccessible. She was living deliberately alone inside an installation, and he probably had a girlfriend anyhow, but his note was so touching that she felt like hugging him. He was frustrated because a critic had written a review that likened his Rob-ots to a robotic vacuum cleaner that had recently become extremely popular, and the review got very snide about how his robots would be much more impressive if they cleaned up messes instead of making them. He knew the woman who had written the review, and she was just jealous because her work—eight-foot-tall Venus of Willendorf sculptures wearing nothing but combat boots—had recently been panned in the press by a friend of his. NanoRob-ots had gotten good reviews in other places, but he was still upset about Venus-lady's comments. He talked about the Rob-ot that didn't move and said that he was so embarrassed that it just sat there—he'd examined its brain after the show and he couldn't tell what had gone wrong, because it always behaved just fine when he had it running around his loft. He said that he hoped it didn't ruin the show for her, and that it was awesome that she'd been able to come to the opening remotely, and that he was fascinated by her latest installation and loved how she got so obsessive about scraping away the glue and then decided to conceal it with pieces of sky. And then he said that he was impressed by her artistic purity and all, but that he found impurity to be useful too.

She emailed him back immediately and told him that he shouldn't be embarrassed about the little robot that didn't move—it was a beautiful and unexpected detail and she thought it humanized the group and added an element of mystery and pathos to the show. If the robots were supposed to have neural networks that learned on their own instead of being programmed with explicit algorithms, then he should be delighted that one of the robots developed such a quirky personality. Those puddles would dry, after all, and perhaps he could even sell the paintings with the puddles for more, since they were comparatively rare. She thanked him for his kind words about her installation and told him that she was trying to figure out what to do next—some sort of a game, perhaps. She told him that she'd really loved watching his robots dance, and she assured him that he should ignore reviews—it simply didn't matter what other people thought of his work, as long as he felt that he was being artistically true to himself. And she added that Panoptico was a fascinating guide, but he seemed to enjoy cookies more than people, and she asked who made those robot cookies anyway, because they were really cute.

She was not the type of person to describe things as cute, but she couldn't think of a more subtle way of finding out who this Debbie person was. He'd write back soon, she knew it. She reread his note and her note and she realized that she hadn't responded to his comment about impurity. Oh, why had she emailed him back so fast without thinking clearly about what she wanted to say? What if he felt rejected by her? This was all so difficult. If only he could join her inside the cube where nobody could see, and they'd hold each other and he'd tell her how much he loved her and how beautiful and brilliant she was and no no no she would not let her head keep fantasizing like this. She had to focus on herself.

Her room looked intriguing on her website—the checkered sky looked perfectly smooth, even though she had imagined that the photographs would end up looking bumpy because of the glue. There were cameras mounted everywhere on the outside of the cube, and she was able to spin the image of the room around and see the skysquares forming a gorgeous ground. What was it missing? She stared into the spinning blue and she became a dark blur and she realized that she had eaten all her licorice and her head was hurting hard behind her eyes and her stomach felt awry and she swallowed a Lulliban with a handful of water and spun into a dreamless sleep.

She woke up with a queasy feeling in her stomach and a thick fatigue behind her eyes. She sighed and opened a box of chocolate truffles and the smooth sweet filling soothed her and she took her computer onto her lap and her hands were trembling as she saw that Rob had written back. He talked a lot about how he'd gotten a slew of great reviews on *NanoRob-ots* and he'd been doing shows without the odd little Rob-ot and everything was working fine. He told her that he was really excited because he'd just won an online auction for one of the earliest talking dolls—he collected antique phonographs and these dolls were really rare. If she wanted, she could see a picture of the doll on the auction website, and he sent her the link to the auction and told her that she shouldn't think he's a weirdo or anything—he doesn't play with the dolls; he just collects them. He told her that she was so insightful and creative and he couldn't wait to see what sort of game she would unleash upon the room. And at the end of the note, almost as an afterthought, he told her that Nevi made those robot cookies; she was a food artist and they'd been dating for a few years now, but he wasn't really happy with how things were going and he planned to break up with her soon.

She was rather perplexed and overwhelmed by his note. She immediately began to search on the web for Nevi and found thousands of references to warts and moles, and she pictured this miserable girlfriend of his as a malignant mole, a flat brown slug of a thing crawling across his skin and leaving slime behind and why did he have to have a girlfriend, but why was he emailing her so much and why did he go out of his way to tell her they were breaking up? She did another search for Nevi and excluded any website that contained the word mole or wart or hairy or benign and finally found the site that she was searching for.

Nevi's website opened with an enormous image of herself— tall and blonde and buxom and emaciated—holding up what looked like a decorative pillow covered in icing. It seemed that she specialized in making cakes that looked like cushions—she claimed in a barely literate ramble that her work made a brilliant statement about what was food and what was decoration and how food was something that we all have in common, so everybody could relate to her art- work. She explained that she got into making food art because she was a model and she couldn't eat very much, but food smelled so yummy that she was always baking and she loved to decorate things because she was such a girly girl and liked everything to be pretty and somebody saw her cakes and said they looked so good that they could be art and she figured that maybe she'd actually been an artist all along without even realizing it. And the rest was history because her artworks were now in hot demand by galleries and celebrities and bakeries everywhere, and she'd heard that her cakes tasted really good too, but she wouldn't know because she had to keep her girlish figure. There were pictures of Nevi plastered all over the site, and she always seemed to be dressed head-to-toe in pink, with stiletto heels and tight revealing clothing and pink lipstick and long smooth perfect hair and tanned skin and long pink nails and lots of jewelry and the emptiest porcelain grin imaginable.

As she read through every article about Nevi on the website, she began to notice a pattern: all of them talked at length about her physical appearance, even if they purported to take her seriously as an artist. It seemed that pink was Nevi's signature color and fabulously sexy was her signature look and she never went anywhere without her signature pink stilettos and lipstick and golden bangle bracelets that jingled when she walked. One of the articles even raved about how subversive Nevi was to cultivate such a look when everybody else in the art world was pallid and wore black and decried traditional signifiers of gender.

She hated Nevi. She hated women who called themselves girls. She hated shallow untalented people who got rewarded because of their looks. She hated the entire concept of a signature look and the fact that people might actually care about something so superficial. But she began to think about what it meant to have a signature look and about her own trajectory and the article that mentioned her auburn hair and sexy legs and how maybe it could help her art career if she devoted some attention to constructing a personal look. It would have to be unique, of course—she was certainly not just another exhibitionistic bimbo claiming pink as her own. No, she would craft an image so extreme and magnetic that people would not be able to ignore her artwork. She would take herself beyond pretty and beyond beautiful into a place of searing hypnotic transcendence, a place of such demonic fascination that nobody would be able to resist her.

She would start with a new pair of shoes. She'd never bothered wearing shoes since she'd begun living in the cube, but she now realized that most of the powerful and alluring women depicted on the web wore high-heeled shoes. And so, she sifted through the web and looked at thousands of images of feet thrust forward in heels until she found an image that mesmerized her. Yes, here was a shoe so powerful and sexy that it could anchor her entire look. She had found the website of a cobbling shop that called itself Golden Lotus Design. Every pair of shoes was individually crafted using only the finest materials, and every pair of shoes was designed to make a woman's feet look half their size. The man who'd started Golden Lotus rhapsodized on his website about how Oriental women from centuries past were sexier than anything he'd ever seen, and that his goal was to bring back the lost sensual art of footbinding without the nasty odor of rotting flesh and the risk of toes falling off. His shoes were no more uncomfortable than a normal stiletto, which every woman today claims as an important part of her wardrobe and no woman feels fancy without, and yet his designs were so cleverly constructed that they made a woman look like she was floating above the ground on little jeweled hooves. Every pair of Golden Lotuses was personally constructed and bejeweled, and every pair was finished with a sparkling gold logo of a stylized lotus flower on the front of each shoe. Every woman who wore a pair of Golden Lotuses could be assured that all eyes would be drawn to her, that she would exude an aura of personal magnetism that no other contemporary shoe could hope to create. Ah yes, there was a wisdom to the ancient Oriental women who would bind their feet tighter and tighter each night until their feet were three-inch-long delectables that no man could resist—these women knew that their pain and determination would be rewarded with tender attentions and lavish gifts. Golden Lotuses were a marriage of ancient wisdom and modern technology—every pair represented a feat of engineering, a triumph of fifty-six patents and an ultrasecret recipe of micropolymers and reflective surfaces and tensile stabilizers, and every pair was handcrafted in a factory in the Orient as a show of deep respect to these fine people for giving the gift of footbinding to women for almost a thousand years.

She looked at all the different colors of the Golden Lotuses and settled on Burnt Poppy, a deep red color that mirrored her latest lipstick. From now on, she determined, everything she wore would be dark red or black, with golden accents and nothing ever deviating from this color scheme. She'd figure out the rest of her signature look as she went along, but she supposed that it was important to keep things consistent from the beginning—this was, after all, how corporations developed a brand, and she was sort of like a brand, except that she was an actual person. She measured her feet in eight different places and sent her order off with a note that urged them to hurry because she couldn't wait to wear her Golden Lotuses. Oh, she would be so devastatingly sexy in her Golden Lotuses that Rob would never be able to resist her. She reread Rob's latest note and went to the auction website and looked at his new talking doll. Its voicebox was broken and its eyes looked dead. She realized that her head was hurting terribly and she decided to take a Lulliban to make the Golden Lotuses come sooner and she fell asleep wondering why anyone would want a talking doll that couldn't talk at all.

She awoke to a red lacquered box embellished with gold lotuses. It looked too small to be a shoebox, and it seemed awfully quick for something that had to be shipped all the way from the Orient, but she knew that it had to be her Golden Lotuses and she untied the black velvet ribbons as quickly as she could. The box revealed a black velvet bag imprinted with a golden lotus, and the red lacquer was so deep and she'd never seen such elegant packaging before in her life. She lifted up the bag and found a handwritten thank-you note signed by the owner of Golden Lotus Design himself. The note was written in gold ink on thick black paper, and it thanked her personally and said that she should wear her Golden Lotuses as much as possible in order for the special materials to adjust to her feet, and that she was now a member of an elite cadre of women and she shouldn't be surprised if she started getting more attention than ever before. She opened the velvet bag and marveled at the little shoes—they shimmered with ruby-colored jewels all over and their heels were extremely high and made out of a material so clear that she didn't even see them at first, and the golden logos sparkled so boldly and the insides of the shoes looked so soft and silky and she felt so special and in the know and like a person of such discernment and taste. She slipped the Golden Lotuses onto her feet and was relieved that they fit just like normal stilettos, which admittedly she'd found uncomfortable the few times in her life she'd worn them, but she figured that if millions of women could get used to wearing stilettos, so could she. She was entitled to feel sexy too. And the shoes did indeed transform her—when she was barefoot, she'd always walked very quickly and directly and forcefully; the Golden Lotuses challenged her balance with every step, and she wobbled around the cube still wearing her sleepshirt but feeling like such a seductress; she watched herself in the mirrors as her hips swayed as she walked and her breasts jutted out and her entire body looked taller and slimmer and more curvaceous all at once. The shoes were so pointy and the invisible heels so high that she actually did look like she was floating on the tiniest feet imaginable. She was so delighted with the sparkling little things that she went onto the web and did a search for Golden Lotus Design because she wanted to see who else was in this elite cadre of women, and she was surprised to see that nothing had been written about the shoes except on their own website. She supposed that she'd discovered something very unusual, and she congratulated herself on her eye. And then she realized that she needed to keep working on her newest installation—she'd been so focused on her signature look that she'd been neglecting her work, which was the entire reason for her to be in the public eye in the first place. She briefly considered emailing Rob back, but decided that she'd wait until he saw her in the Golden Lotuses.

She contemplated her face as she went to work concealing her pimples and dark circles, and she realized that her skin must have been getting paler since she'd started in the cube, because her usual powder and concealer appeared too dark and too orange on her skin. She tried using a lighter shade, and it was slightly paler than her skin but she rather liked the effect. Yes, she'd make her face extra dramatic as part of her signature look. She'd take her skin lighter and her eyes fiercely kohl-wide and her lashes mascara'd out as far as they could go, and she'd use layers of liner and lipstick to make her burgundy lips precise with a plump pout and a cupid's bow. Abundacurve and clingy shirt and she dabbed some Softly-U on her bikini line and tried not to look too closely because she still had inflammations there from ingrown hairs and she knew she'd start picking if she started looking, and why wasn't the Softly-U working, and she decided to get out just the ingrown hairs that really needed help, and oh, the area was such a mess, and she took a pin and went into a trance examining every follicle, and a lot of hairs were growing back normally but there were still so many scabs with inflammations underneath, which meant that a hair was still trapped and needed to be freed, and sometimes she'd see a hair shadow beneath a translucent layer of skin and she picked and picked and so many places were bleeding and she hated herself for having such thick hair and sensitive skin, and she had to do something about this problem because what if Rob were to see her naked, but she had to go outside and work and stop getting distracted by her body, and she pulled her skin taut at every follicle and flicked out each hair with the pin and swabbed the entire stinging area with peroxide and another layer of Softly-U. She looked at her irritated and infected skin and tried not to cry. There had to be a way of getting rid of the hair without invoking ingrowns. The room with the checkered sky beckoned, but she had to solve this problem before she went outside again, so she looked around the web and ordered a depilatory cream called Koremlu, which guaranteed that it would remove her hair gently and safely for months at a time, and would even prevent ingrowns by keeping her follicles open with patented electrospheres. She pulled on her control top stockings and her skirt, and began to reapply her concealer and powder and lipstick and lipliner, which had gotten creased and smudged in her efforts to liberate every ingrown hair.

She held a paintbrush and a palette full of black paint and she shifted her weight from one Golden Lotus to the other as she drew a stylized eye over a square of pale blue sky. She stared at the eye for a moment and then stared at the rest of the room and moved on to another square of blue and painted yet another eye. She had been doing this for hours now, and her feet were in such terrible pain, but she didn't really care because it felt so good to be painting again. Some of the eyes were tiny and some were so huge that they spanned several squares, and some of them were only half an eye because they stopped at the edge where two squares met. She didn't know what sort of game she was playing, she only knew that the sky was filled with eyes and she had to paint each one where it belonged. As she painted, her head began to wonder about Rob, and whether he was actually interested in her, and why he would date somebody like Nevi, and why somebody so interested in technology would collect broken old dolls, and how beautiful he was and what it would feel like to touch him and what he would think of her new Golden Lotuses and how tight and painful they felt and she didn't know how much longer she could stand outside and paint without taking off her shoes and rubbing her feet and what was she getting herself into and whose eyes was she drawing and maybe there were enough by now, and she stood back from the walls and saw hundreds of eyes staring at her direct and fierce and unrelenting and she felt frightened and knew that she was finished and went back into the cube as quickly as she could without limping.

She sat down on the soft part of the floor and pulled off her Golden Lotuses and saw that her feet were red and creased and she massaged them as they yielded searing pain into her paint-black hands. That handwritten thank-you note may have recommended that she wear the Golden Lotuses all the time, but there was no way she could ever withstand such agony. She felt a dizziness and a nausea and a sense of terror, and she was so sleepy even without taking any Lulliban and she held the empty black velvet bag, which was so soft except for where the lotus was printed in stiff gold ink, and she curled up on the soft place and she felt her kohl-smudged eyelids close and she fell asleep to stylized black eyes floating all around her.

She tried to cry out, but she was having a nightmare and her mouth was paralyzed. There were eyes crawling all over her body, enormous dark eyes with fat black lashes and pupils menacing and sharp. She finally woke up with a cry that made her glad that there weren't any microphones around her. She was still clutching the empty velvet bag. Oh, why couldn't she just sleep like normal people? Her head was hurting and she didn't know if she'd been asleep for an hour or a day, or even what an hour or a day felt like anymore. So dizzy, dizzy, and her stomach was in terrible pain. She swallowed an Anorex and followed it with a fingerful of chocolate hazelnut spread and delighted in the toasted creaminess as she opened up her little silver computer and looked at herself on the screen wearing her Golden Lotuses. Such a strange effect, to see herself floating on tiny points of sparkling red jewels. The transparent heels were completely invisible on the screen, and she noticed that the backs of the shoes were encrusted with jewels that were almost non-reflective and the fronts were so electric shimmery that all attention was drawn to the pointy tips and her feet looked even tinier. She took another fingerful of chocolate and watched herself walking in the Golden Lotuses and didn't quite recognize herself—her posture and her gait had shifted so dramatically that she felt embarrassed to have gone this long without wearing any shoes at all. Yes, her signature look was proceeding rather nicely. Her face looked flawless and dramatic, and the Abundacurve cleavage was even more pronounced, and the Golden Lotuses definitely made her look slimmer, although she still needed to lose some weight.

Her latest comments were overwhelming. She massaged her temples as she read through hundreds of notes of approval—everybody seemed to love the effects of the floating eyes and the Golden Lotuses, everybody except two people. The first critic was an insistent man who said that he'd been hoping for an interactive game of chess, that she'd violated every rule of the game, and she didn't even have proper playing pieces, and he'd gotten his hopes up a couple of times when it looked like she was reenacting classic patterns, but she'd always broken them and could she please paint over some of the eyes and play a game of chess with him; she could even have the first move, as long as he could be white. The second critic was more challenging. It was the same woman who'd criticized her before, and she went on a long feminist rant that was difficult to ignore. She started off talking about how high heels cause foot, knee, and back problems and restrict mobility and that anybody who wears high heels is crippling herself for the sake of the male gaze. She continued on about how the heteronormative standards for female appearance destroy women's identities, that women may delude themselves into thinking that they're choosing their own personal appearances in this postmodern age, but the idea of choice is an illusion if everybody ends up conforming to the same rigid standards dictated by the capitalist media machine. She went into great detail about the tyranny of mirrors and the vanity of cameras, and she talked about how the ready availability of cheap pocket mirrors and photographic portraits in the early 20th century, along with the made-up images promulgated by magazines and the burgeoning film industry, brought about a drastic transformation in women's self-concepts, from a focus on developing one's internal qualities to an obsession with the external. She claimed that cosmetics were mainly the province of prostitutes until women began to see themselves fixed in photographs and didn't like how they looked compared to other images of women that they'd seen, and that even as women were making the first strides out of male bondage by claiming the vote and access to jobs and education, they were demeaning themselves by widening the appearance gap, by emphasizing their worth as ornaments. She declared that in order to have a truly egalitarian society, it was the duty of every woman to break free of the trap of normative femininity. And she ended with two pleas: Stop giving positive feedback to a push-up bra and a pair of heels. And stop tarting yourself up *now*, or you will be devoured by those eyes.

She pulled and twisted a lock of hair around her fingers as she thought. The feminist was certainly strident in her tone, but that didn't mean she was right. Evolutionary psychology said that it was natural for men to like women who were thin and busty and young and pretty and sexually available, and if clothes and makeup could help those qualities along, then it would practically be going against nature not to use them. Anyhow, she wasn't wearing makeup and push-up bras and heels for the sake of the male gaze, or because of evolution or culture or too many mirrors. She was doing it for herself, to meet her own aesthetic standards. She had free will to do anything she wanted with her appearance, and if she wanted to be beautiful, that was her own choice. She wasn't sure what the capitalist media machine was, but she searched on the web and discovered that it was a patented device that transformed pure water into an elixir so potent that it would give you visions of unlimited wealth and beauty and power, and so toxic that it would kill you in an instant.

Rob had sent her a curious email. It was very short and looked like a form letter and consisted of a link that seemed to be an invitation to chat with him. She had always eschewed the idea of online chattering—she didn't want her solitude broken by a constant presence of people on her computer who could talk to her whenever they wanted; she never understood how people could stand being barraged with conversational fragments while they were trying to concentrate. But here she was with an invitation from Rob, whom she craved so terribly that her concentration was occasionally broken anyway—she figured that it couldn't hurt to set up her computer so that Rob could chat with her whenever he wanted. She felt rather nervous as she set the proper programs and parameters for chattering, and she wondered what it would be like to talk to him without pausing. She assembled a list of conversational topics in her head: how did he get interested in robotics, how did he start collecting old talking dolls, why didn't he give that little immobile robot another chance, did he break up with Nevi yet, what exactly was he unhappy about in his relationship, did he want to come sneak into her cube and be with her, did he find her beautiful and brilliant and oh! she had to stop fantasizing and planning out everything in advance. Maybe Rob didn't really even want to talk to her—he might've sent that chat link to everybody in his address book and it might not even work. She took a fingerful of chocolate hazelnut spread into her mouth and tried to soothe her stomach, which felt sickeningly anxious about the prospect of such direct contact with Rob. Her heartbeat made her hands shake as she clicked on Rob's link and found herself inside a window typing hello. He was there. All too present and immediate, and it turned out that she hadn't needed to prepare anything at all, because the words came out of her fingers effortlessly in response to his. He told her that he was so excited because he'd just signed a life insurance policy to cover the cost of cryonically preserving his head, and she told him all about the Time Travel Trust, and they talked about transhumanism and posthumanism and she told him how she wanted to transcend time and culture and create a language of images that would transform the world, and he told her that he wanted to live forever and benefit from everything that technology would ever create. She told him how her mother or perhaps her grandmother used to reminisce about the nascent beatniks with such a feeling of energy, like there was something going on back then, deep cultural stirrings and people moving and changing and breaking away from staid lifepatterns into thoughts and feelings and actions that they couldn't even have imagined. She told him how she envied that unironic sense of movement and change in this postmodern age, and how she was always searching for the strange, always trying to create what she didn't exactly understand but one day hoped to. He told her that his uncle or perhaps his great-great uncle had invented the phonograph machine, and that all the old advertisements from that time told people that they never had to be lonely again. She asked him why he collected broken dolls, and he told her that his uncle had died quite bankrupt, but had left behind crates and crates of moldy old phonographs and ephemera, including a box of talking dolls, and he'd gotten fascinated by those dolls because they were the first phonographs sold for home entertainment—before people could buy machines to play music or record their own voices, they could buy these innovative dolls whose voiceboxes broke almost instantly because they were so fragile. And you had to turn a crank at a steady speed to play them, and their voices were so screechy that not even little children could stand listening to them, and the dolls turned out to be such a disaster that production was cut short and an enormous batch of dolls without voiceboxes was buried outside the studios where children had shouted nursery rhymes into large horns to record each ill-fated voicebox individually in an era before copying. Rob told her all about the history of early recording, how the talking doll fiasco soon gave way to home machines that allowed people to play two-minute wax cylinders of sound and to record themselves as well, and how home recording never took off because people didn't like the way their own voices sounded. She asked him why, and he told her that recorded voices sounded thinner and less powerful because people were used to hearing their own voices being conducted through bone as well as air, that the skull carried bass sounds better than air and added a bit of echo too. She told him that it sounded like what happened when people first saw their images fixed in photographs, how they didn't like the way they looked and tried to change themselves to look the way they imagined they should, except that it's not so easy to change the sound of your voice. He told her about the studios he'd seen in Takoyaki, where little girls could dress up in tight and shiny clothing and lots of makeup and then get their pictures taken, how every day at the same time he'd see thousands of uniformed girls swarming into these studios, giddy at the prospect of painting themselves into cartoons. She said that she hoped he didn't mind the image she put on for the sake of the webcams—it was only an attempt to market her artwork however she could. And he told her that he loved her look, that she was beautiful and reminded him of Theda Bara. She managed to stay composed enough to ask him how he knew who Theda Bara was, and he told her that he wasn't your typical transhumanist—he was obsessed with technology from the past as well as in the future, and he found it fascinating to watch old movies to see how far technology had come. And he turned the question around, and she told him about her uncle or perhaps her great-great uncle, who had made movies during the early days of cinema. He'd started out as a plucky young booking agent for a large studio, but soon decided that there was no reason why he shouldn't be able to make his own movies too, so he went out into the desert one day with some actors he knew, shot some footage for a trailer, sold the unmade film to his studio under a pseudonym, and shot the rest of the film in a week. Within a few years he was running his own movie studio, and within a few more, gossip columnists were describing him as the most eligible bachelor in Hollywood. He was the first person to create movie posters that used artwork from the covers of pulp novels, mostly voluptuous women in some sort of torment. Rob asked her what films her uncle made, because maybe he'd seen some of them, and she told him that there had been hundreds, but they all got burnt to nothing in a fire and her uncle never made another film. Rob asked her about the rest of her family, and she told him that she wanted to transcend her past, to create visions that she could never even have imagined. He pressed further for details about her past, and she told him that she grew up orphaned on the banks of the river Styx, or perhaps she was raised inside a Skinner box, or perhaps she spent her childhood trapped inside a suburb so soulless that even the houseflies fled to the city. It got lonely along the banks of the Styx, she told him, so she spent a lot of time making sculptures out of mud and stones and empty seedpods. She had stumbled into this room quite by accident, she told him, but she rather liked the view. She asked him how he found himself surrounded by scuttling robots, and he told her that he'd started out working with monkeys. He'd been a graduate student in a monkey lab, where every month another researcher would come in and want to test their human cognition theories on the monkeys. Can monkeys count, can monkeys tell one musical key from another, can monkeys tell ugly faces from pretty ones, do monkeys get scared of snakes, do monkeys get annoyed when caged and forced to look at things all day? A constant stream of studies and theories, and the answer was always yes or no or sort of, and he didn't feel like he was getting any closer to a useful understanding of the brain. He was a transhumanist after all, and he wanted to advance the human condition however he could, and he just didn't see a future in monkeys. So he moved into robotics, where you could skip DNA and evolution and still see patterns of behavior and even intelligence emerging. He fell into the art thing by accident, he told her—he was working in a lab where they were looking at robots moving around with neural network brains, and it was so cool to watch them because they acted human and all, and one day he was watching them and he noticed that they were leaving black smudges on the floor because somebody must've replaced their wheels with cheap ones made in the Orient, but the smudges made him think about putting paint inside the robots and letting them leave traces as they moved. He figured that people would pay anything for art these days, and since he wanted to be able to afford the best in cryonic preservation and smart drugs and brain implants, and since researchers don't make that much money, he decided to give the Rob-ots a try. He'd only been doing the Rob-ots thing for a few years, he told her, but he'd already gotten several awards and lots of media coverage and as long as he could keep coming up with new gimmicks, he might be able to afford to have his entire body cryonically suspended. She assured him that his work was brilliant and that she knew it would continue to attract attention. And then she asked him, fingers trembling, if he'd broken up with Nevi yet. He told her that he hadn't, but he was planning on it after her next opening, because he didn't want to upset her too much beforehand. She asked what their relationship was like, and he told her that Nevi was very affectionate, and she cooked and cleaned and did all sorts of chores for him, but she wasn't very intellectual or creative and he really wanted more. She asked him whether he loved Nevi, and he told her that he didn't believe in love. He started talking about the theory of eliminative materialism and the concept of folk psychology, and how concepts like love and hate and beliefs and desires were all just folk theories that people came up with based upon the shallowest introspections, and that one day when a completed neuroscience had come about, people would be able to understand themselves with an actual scientific basis, instead of just by intuition. Words like love would go the way of phlogiston, and people would be a lot better off. She told him that she knew a bit about eliminative materialism, and she didn't think that even a completed neuroscience would change the fundamental ways that people saw themselves and one another. We're not just robots, she told him, and our brain circuits run deep into our guts. He pointed out that people reconceptualized themselves when Freud discovered the subconscious, and she replied that she absolutely believed in change and growth, but she didn't think that neuroscience would provide the clues—it was simply too reductionistic, and expecting a deeper self-awareness from a completed neuroscience would be like expecting to explain away the qualitative experience of eating chocolate by describing its chemical composition. He asked her how she'd learned about this stuff, growing up along the Styx and all, and she told him that a book or two may have washed up on the banks from time to time. Then he surprised her by asking if she'd collaborate with him—he'd send over a couple of Rob-ots and she could let them run around the room. She told him that she didn't think her corporate sponsor would allow that sort of thing, but she'd check and let him know. He told her that he'd be really excited to see it happen, and that his friend had just come over with a new video game and he had to go play now, but he'd love to chat with her again. And she typed goodbye, but he'd already left.

She stared at the eyes on her computer screen and tried to understand where she'd just been. He found her beautiful. And he wanted to talk with her again. She began to worry that she'd offended him by not reacting more positively to his offer of Rob-ots in her room. She'd been so startled by his suggestion of collaboration that she hadn't thought to be polite, but she really didn't want his robots fettering her space—she just wanted him. And she hated Nevi more than ever. She went to Nevi's website and looked to see when the next opening would be, and it turned out that it was happening rather soon. She set her computer alarm to remind her of the time, and she wondered whether Panoptico would be there too. She'd lose her grant if she invited Rob into the cube, but she was craving him so terribly. Oh, why had she agreed to isolate herself like this? She found herself twisting her hair rather nervously and she noticed that a number of her hairs were splitting at the ends, and she began to pick the split bits apart while she thought about their conversation. It definitely seemed that he was interested in her, but she'd acted evasive and she didn't know why. She'd never even thought about the river Styx until today. She couldn't have told Rob that he was the first person who had ever asked about her past. She couldn't have told him that ever since she could remember, she would notice people who looked so sad and lost and she'd want to help them somehow, but all she could do was tell herself that she'd forget about them before too long. She couldn't have told him that once she was running so fast that she caught a child's arm in a revolving door. She couldn't have told him that all her life she'd screamed at night and nobody had ever come to soothe her.

The Koremlu had arrived. It came in a large pink jar, and the instructions told her to apply a thick layer of the cream to anywhere on her body where there was hair, excluding mucous membranes and her eyes. She was supposed to leave it on for fifteen minutes while the Koremlu worked its magic, and when she wiped it away, not only would her hair be gone for months, but the patented electrospheres would remain inside the follicles to prevent against ingrowns. She was so excited about the Koremlu—she hadn't shaved her bikini line since that first fateful time, and she'd managed to pick out all the ingrowns in the meanwhile, so she figured that after she applied the Koremlu she'd have a smooth bikini line and no ingrowns ever again. She covered her inner upper thighs with a thick layer of the stuff, which smelled strongly of sulfur and artificial flowers, and she looked at the time on her computer and began to search the web for information about monkey studies. She had vague memories of learning about a man who reared monkeys in isolation with artificial mothers made of wire, but she couldn't find anything online about his research except for a brief mention in a recent and well-publicized study that claimed that isolated monkeys actually turned out smarter and earned more food pellets in lever-pulling games, which the researchers felt had important implications for rearing children to be successful adults. She hadn't remembered this outcome, but the researcher claimed that the earlier monkey studies had been falsified to promote a liberal agenda. Just then, she felt an odd stinging on her upper thighs. It had only been seven minutes, but she was certain that the Koremlu wasn't supposed to feel like this. She looked at the instructions, and they didn't mention anything about a stinging. She waited, and the stinging became stronger and started to burn and there were five minutes left but she didn't think that she could stand the pain any longer, but she really wanted to give the Koremlu a chance to work, so she tried to breathe deep and she pictured her bikini line so smooth, and the burning finally overwhelmed her at thirteen minutes so she grabbed some napkins and wiped the acrid lotion off as quickly as she could. The entire area was red and swollen and the hairs were still there and the skin was blistered and the terrible burning wouldn't go away. She sat inside the little tub and ran cool water over her thighs and started to cry. She'd probably scarred herself for life, and the Koremlu didn't even work and the burning wouldn't stop. There'd been pages of testimonials on the Koremlu website about what a miracle product it was, so she didn't know what had gone wrong. She tried to stop crying and told herself to relax, that she'd never touch that nasty stuff again, that she'd figure out how to heal herself and she'd post an angry testimonial and she'd take the strongest painkillers she could find until the burning started to subside. She climbed out of the tub and draped wet towels on her inner thighs and quickly ordered some Numitol from drugs-r-us.com. She went over to the Koremlu website, quite prepared to complain at length, but she found that it was gone. Had she typed the address wrong? She checked again and found nothing but a *Page Not Found* message and an ominous white space where previously there had been an image of a glowing woman in a tiny white bikini against a background of hundreds of pink jars of Koremlu. She felt extremely unsettled. Maybe she could still contact them by email? She had gotten a confirmation letter when she placed her order, so she found the address and wrote a short but irate note and within seconds it bounced back into her inbox, recipient unknown. She stared at the large pink jar with the word Koremlu written in a girly cursive script and picked it up and tossed it down the trap door as hard as she could. She took a Lulliban because she couldn't stand the burning, but the pain was so intense that she couldn't even sleep, so she picked up two Milady's pencils and grabbed a sketchpad and drew through her delirium as the arabesques fell out more wrought and intricate and involuted than she'd ever seen.

The Numitol had come, and it gave her a blurred and floaty feeling as she looked online for what to do about chemical burns. The area was still red and blistered and hurt terribly whenever she moved her legs. Maybe she should call a doctor? And what about her stockings? She'd never be able to stand the chafing of the tight nylon against her thighs. But she had to wear the control top, or she wouldn't look toned and sleek. Could she even get the grant people to send her a doctor? She stared in fascination at the redness and blisters forming two wide bands at the tops of her thighs, perfectly delimited against her white skin where the Koremlu had been. It seemed that there was nothing to be done for chemical burns except to neutralize the chemicals involved, and she didn't have any idea what chemicals were inside the Koremlu and the jar was gone and the company had vanished. How could they betray her like that? She stared at Rob's name inside her chattering software and wondered what would happen if she clicked on it and started to type to him. She wondered why he cut her off so abruptly. She wondered if he would ever talk to her again if she didn't let his robots run around her room. Oh, these painkillers made everything feel so shimmery and insubstantial. Was there something gnawing at her legs? A curious itching, and the blisters glowed through with golden pus. Chemical burns, yes yes yes. She was supposed to go to a doctor if she got disoriented or fainted or if she saw little eyes inside the blisters on her thighs. A chime! It was time, then. Time for Panoptico to bring her to the place of cupcakes.

A loud crowd inside a darkened gallery, halogen spots dramatically illuminating pillows made of cake. Some of the pillows were sitting on simple wooden chairs festooned with signs that said *Do Not Sit*, and some of them were sitting atop pedestals next to placards that said *Do Not Eat*. Most of the pillows had a wedge cut out of them to show that there was really cake inside, and Panoptico seemed particularly drawn to the moist-looking interiors. She hadn't seen Rob or Nevi yet, but she got to see a lot of lengthy gazes at deep-frosted pieces of yellow cake. She grabbed a jar of chocolate hazelnut spread and ate it with her fingers as she tried to unravel voices from the cacophony around Panoptico. A snippet about being drunk, and a crushing swell of laughter, and she felt terrified for a moment until she remembered that she was safe away from all these raucous people. She imagined that if she had to attend, she would have spent most of her time hiding in the bathroom. Panoptico began to scan the room and she noticed Nevi smiling wide while listening to a bald man with a tattoo of a skull covering the back of his head. Nevi looked older and gaunter than in the photographs on her website, but she was still dressed completely in pink, and even carried a shiny pink purse designed to look like a little girl's head, with long blonde pigtails hanging down below the bottom of the bag. Panoptico walked over to Nevi, and the bald man quickly slipped away, and she found herself staring directly at Nevi and listening to Panoptico ask if he could eat the cake that was on the chairs, and Nevi giggled and said that he should read the signs more closely, and Panoptico replied that the chairs only said that he shouldn't sit, and he didn't much want to sit on the pedestals but he'd love to eat some of the cake that was on top of the chairs. And Nevi looked confused and giggled again and said that he probably couldn't read the signs with his whole cyborg thing on his head, but he couldn't eat the cake anyhow because she'd covered it all with bug spray. She explained that she'd been setting up for days, and bugs kept coming in and trying to eat her art, and she didn't know where they were coming from, so she got an exterminator to come in and spray the entire gallery space, including her cakes. She figured that cake was fattening anyhow, so it didn't matter if it was poisonous or not. Panoptico said that she might want to post more explicit warnings, and Nevi got exasperated and said that she'd spent a long time getting the perfect pink cursive font for the signs and she wasn't about to mess them up now. Panoptico asked her where Rob was, and she looked even more annoyed and said that he was supposed to be here an hour ago, and he was probably off playing video games. Nevi's face broke into a wide blank smile just then, and Panoptico turned to see a leering man approaching her, and he said goodbye and she greeted the leering man and turned away and Panoptico walked quickly through the crowds of people, stopping only to pull a toddler away from one of the cakes. He tried to warn the toddler's mother, who held a leash in one of her hands and a pink martini in the other, but she just laughed and laughed and yanked the child closer and said *Isn't Nevi so much fun!*

Rob was standing outside the gallery pushing buttons on his cellular phone. Panoptico touched his shoulder and Rob responded with a warm grin and said that he was playing an awesome new game on his phone and he really didn't want to go inside. He was wearing a stained white t-shirt and wrinkled tan shorts, and he looked deliciously rumpled and casual and utterly out of place among the gallery-goers in their artsy best. Panoptico told him that Nevi seemed to be getting pretty friendly with some guy in there, and Rob looked annoyed and said that Nevi was such a flirt, and he turned and went into the gallery too quickly to hear Panoptico say goodbye.

She watched the people on the sidewalk looking oddly at Panoptico as he walked. She imagined Nevi's pillows filled with maggots squirming out onto the floor, and she looked down at the lock of hair that she'd been twisting and saw a strand with six splits along its length, curling down into an end that was split so many times that it looked like a feather or a millipede. She picked off each little split until she was left with only a thin and fragile hair, and she began to search her ends for other strands that were so dramatically split. She found one startling strand with seventeen little splits branching off, and she fondled it for a while in disbelief and awe until she finally got up the courage to destroy it by taking it by the very end and drawing her fingers upwards, bending every little split up in the opposite direction until she finally pulled them apart from the main hair one by one. She doubted that she'd be able to find another hair quite that impressive, and she searched and searched until her stomach startled at a strand that had an irregular set of splits of different sizes and looked somehow menacing, like a tree that had been splintered apart by lightening. She played with the strand again and again, wetting it so that it looked normal and then watching the little splits pop out again into a splintery mess as it dried, and she finally picked the strand apart and continued to search and pick until she noticed a wispy blanketing of broken hair-bits covering her keyboard. How long had she been picking? She'd fallen into a trance, and she hated herself for destroying her hair. She had to stop herself somehow. How long had it been since she'd gotten a trim? She hadn't even thought about haircuts when she agreed to live inside this room, but now she began to panic as she realized that there was no way that she could get a hairdresser inside the cube. So many split ends, and she kept getting distracted by them and she'd look ridiculous if she tried to cut her own hair, but she had to get rid of the split ends or she'd go crazy. Another Numitol to soothe her pain, and a quick email to the grant people begging them to send in a hairdresser, and she sat and searched for fantastically split ends while she waited.

Her corporate sponsor was quick with a surprisingly positive response. They told her that they understood her predicament completely, and they wanted her to feel well groomed so that she could be free to focus on her artwork instead of worrying about her hair. And they directed her to a website where she could order a robot to perform any beauty-related services that she required. The robots were controlled remotely from Mumbalore, and the technicians who controlled the robots were highly trained and spoke perfect English. The grant people explained that it was cheaper to outsource haircutting to Mumbalore than to pay local people to do it, and she shouldn't worry about the skill level of the people in Mumbalore because they'd undergone rigorous training to create hundreds of different looks, and anybody who deviated even slightly from their training would be fired immediately. She was a bit skeptical, but she went over to the website and was immediately seduced by all the different services she could request. Hair and face and nails and body and she hardly even knew what to choose. All she'd wanted was a trim, but there were so many shapes to pick from, and when she'd selected a shape that looked okay she was offered a free hairdye at no extra charge. Her roots were beginning to show again, and she'd promised herself that she'd never dye her hair again because it was so difficult and such a mess, but she supposed that the robots would be able to handle the task, so she selected a dark rich black shade that would contrast beautifully with her pale face. She placed the order and took a Lulliban and fell asleep to the soothing sound of Panoptico's snores.

There was a robot in her cube. Four Shivaite arms jutting out from its metal sides, and three camera eyes staring unrelenting at her as she tried to rub away the terrible pain behind her forehead. The robot spoke to her in perfect English and said that she could call him Max and he was happy to be serving her today. She was so ecstatic for the company that she hugged the strange metal form, and she heard a voice saying that it was not within his duties to provide hugs, and whenever she was ready she should sit on the bench and he would begin. She didn't know what bench he was talking about, but then a metal shelf popped out from the robot, and she sat down and said that she was sorry about the hug, she hadn't meant to cross any boundaries and she was just so excited to finally see somebody after so many months in isolation. Max told her that it was not within his duties to provide emotional support, and he pulled out a smock from a compartment and gently draped it around her body. His hands were made of a soft rubbery material, and they felt warm against her neck. He began to paint her hair with dye with two of his arms while using the other two to keep her hair in order. As he worked he played a string of synthesized popular songs, interrupting the music occasionally to tell her to turn her head a little to the right or the left. She kept trying to talk to him, but no matter how many questions she asked him about what it was like to live in Mumbalore, and how he controlled four arms at once, and how many hours a week he worked, and what he liked to do when he wasn't working, he responded calmly that it was not within his duties to provide that sort of information. Eventually she gave up on trying to have a conversation, and she asked him if he could at least turn off the music, because it was cluttering her thoughts. He replied that he would be happy to turn off the music, and she sat in silence and luxuriated in the delirious feeling of his hands subtly touching her head. She watched herself in the mirror as her hair was gradually covered with a thick black paste, and she liked the way it contrasted with her pale face, but she felt terribly ugly without any makeup on. She had a number of pimples on her skin, and the circles under her eyes were darker than she'd ever seen, and the whites of her eyes were reddish even though she thought she'd been getting sleep recently, and her lips looked extremely pale without any lipstick covering them. Max told her to stand up and lean over the sink, and his hands made her shiver as he moved them underneath and around and rubbed her scalp again and again until the water all ran clear. He told her to sit back down on the bench, and he began to dab at her skin with a wet piece of cotton that seemed to take off all stray spots of dye. She was rather impressed with Max's efficiency, although she was still uncomfortable with his reticence to talk. He gently combed the tangles from her hair, and he snipped the ends with scissors so quickly that she was surprised when he pulled out a blowdryer and a round brush and began to dry her hair lock by lock, pulling it taut with the brush and holding the dryer up so close that her hair let out a bit of steam each time the drier passed. Max was somehow able to get her hair to look so smooth and silky—normally it was rather curly and tended to frizz if she didn't condition it enough, but now it was shiny and deep black and straight and controlled and more alluring than she'd ever seen it. She told Max that it looked beautiful and he did such a wonderful job, and he said that she could push the golden button on his shoulder if she wanted her credit card to be charged for a tip. She figured that the grant was paying anyhow, so she pushed the button, and Max told her thank you and asked her to move out of the way so he could tidy up. He used a vacuum attachment on the blowdryer to clean up every bit of hair from the floor, and he used the same cleaning fluid that he'd used on her face to clean up every spot of dye from the sink and the floor and even the mirrors. The red spots from the henna still remained, but everything else looked perfect. She told Max that he was amazing, and he told her that he was only doing his job and he hoped it was satisfactory. And the trap door opened and he wished her a good day as he waved to her with one of his hands and climbed down with two of them and used the fourth to gently close the door behind him.

She stared at her hair and swung her head and felt the glossy veil surround her. There were no more split ends for her to pick and her fingers felt jittery and the cube felt strangely empty. Those eyes outside were waiting, and she supposed that she should put on her Golden Lotuses and go outside and see what people thought of her new hair. Did a signature look have to be consistent? She hoped that people wouldn't be too confused by her hair transformation, and she told herself that she'd keep her hair this way forever. She began to wonder what Rob would think of her hair, and she stared at his name inside the chattering program on her computer and kept daring herself to click on it and start a conversation. It was almost like she had his presence with her inside the cube. He'd looked so beautiful in those rumpled shorts and that stained white t-shirt, and she tried to imagine what he was doing right this instant. All she had to do was click upon his name, and they'd connect so easily and maybe he'd tell her that he'd finally broken up with Nevi and he wanted to come and visit her inside the cube. And she'd tell him to dress up like a robot from Mumbalore and he'd climb up the trap door and she'd remove his metal shell and he'd be warm and rumpled and he'd reach out to her and no no no she had to stop this fantasizing. He hadn't even sent her any email or tried to talk to her since their last conversation, and she'd probably made him feel rejected about collaborating, and if he really wanted to break up with Nevi, then why did he seem so annoyed when Panoptico implied that she was flirting with somebody else? Nothing was clear at all, and she really had to put on all her makeup and go outside because the grant people had sent her another urging email, but she didn't want Rob to think that she was ignoring him, so she breathed deep and clicked on his name and trembled as she waited for him to respond. Nothing. She stared hard at her computer. Still nothing. Her head was hurting worse then ever and she took another Numitol. A movement on her screen! A word of greeting, finally, and so she typed and typed expressive and friendly about her strange robotic encounter, and she waited and waited and all she saw was silence. Wherever had he gone to? This was worse than waiting for email—she didn't want to leave the screen because what if he tried to talk to her and she wasn't there? Maybe she should tell him that she just wanted to say hi, and she'd try him again another time. But that would make her seem so desperate. And too formal. What was the etiquette about this sort of thing? She regretted not chattering throughout her youth; maybe if she had, she'd know how to handle a situation like this. If he wanted to talk to her, then why didn't he respond? And if he didn't want to talk to her, then why did he respond at all? She spent a few moments touching her new hair and eating several chocolate truffles, and then decided that she had to do something or she'd go insane, and so she typed a quick line about how she was going out into the eyes, and he responded almost instantly with a little winking smiley face and nothing more. She leaned into her magnifying mirror and startled because she seemed to have hundreds of blackheads clogging her pores. On closer inspection, she realized that her face was covered with tiny spots of dye. Oh, why did Rob reject her? Would he ever talk to her again? She scrubbed at her face with a washcloth and strong soap, but the spots wouldn't move. She found a bottle of cleanser that she used to remove acrylic paint stains from her hands, and she rubbed it on and rubbed and rubbed and finally the spots began to fade. Her skin was getting red from the rubbing, and she noticed that some of the spots were actually blackheads that must have been accumulating without her even realizing it. She leaned in very close and began to squeeze the blackheads out. Some of them came out little and white and others came out larger and slightly yellow with a darkness at the tip, and some of her pores simply wouldn't relinquish the blackheads no matter how hard she squeezed. She'd never looked at her skin this closely before—she'd only squeezed pimples or blackheads if they seemed extremely noticeable—but the closer she looked at her skin, the more clogged pores she saw. Almost every pore on her nose needed to be squeezed, and her cheeks were filled with tiny darkish dots, and there were cloggings between her eyes and underneath her mouth and even along her jawline. Some of the clogged pores were very subtle, but her magnifying mirror was double-sided and she turned it over to see her pores looming even larger than before. It was so satisfying being able to clean herself out so thoroughly, so satisfying to see a tiny darkened spot and intuit what was underneath and then squeeze and see a solid cylinder come out and leave behind an empty pore. She stretched her skin between her fingers so she could better feel the tiny bumps beneath, and she went systematically over every pore until her face was so red that she couldn't even tell where she'd squeezed before. She stepped back from the magnifying mirror and saw herself whole again, and she couldn't believe what she'd done. Her entire face was red and swollen and purple in places and more hideous than she'd ever seen. Her hair hung perfect all around her face as if to taunt her, and she took a cool washcloth and draped it on her face and hoped that it would calm down before too long. She lay down on the soft place with her shrouded face and tried to console herself by thinking about how beautiful she would look with her new hair and her Golden Lotuses. Next time she would ask Max to clean off her face more thoroughly, and she'd avoid looking in the magnifying mirror from now on. She wondered what was causing all the blackheads, and she told herself that she'd research the problem after she came inside from painting. She was feeling very agitated lying down without being able to see, so she got up and looked at herself and the redness had barely gone away. Was there something in Milady's kit that could cover the redness while she worked? Concealer on her entire face would look extremely artificial. *Milady's Book O' Tips* had an answer. She started with a layer of pale green cream, which neutralized the red as she might have expected from color theory. Her face was now a strange grey hue, so she found some liquid foundation that claimed to be full coverage, and she rubbed the beige paste all over her face until there was not a spot of grey remaining. A layer of powder on top of everything, and she was amazed to see that her skin looked flawless. She could still see that many areas were slightly swollen if she looked very closely, but she'd at least be presentable like this. She painted her eyes dramatic as usual, and as she lined her lips and colored them and blotted and lined them again, she visualized a sculpture of a clear glass head with the face covered by layers of makeup so thick that it would bulge out grossly, and she'd leave the eye sockets empty and she'd make sure that people could view the head from all sides so that they could see the empty space behind the mask, and she'd call the piece *365 Days of Makeup*. She pulled the control top stockings over her blistered thighs and delighted in the fact that she must be losing weight because her skirt fit a little looser around her waist, and she squeezed her feet into the Golden Lotuses and admired the contrast between her hair and skin and breathed deep and opened the door into her gallery of eyes.

She remembered her nightmare all of a sudden, but she tried to look poised and sexy as she felt the lashes crawling on her skin. She didn't have to be out here for long. All she had to do was paint more eyes and show off her hair for a bit, and then she could go back inside where she was safe. The Golden Lotuses were surprisingly comfortable today—must have been the Numitol—and her mind and fingers danced around the room. Eye in the sky, wandering eye, evil eye, Egyptian eye, and she painted and painted until every square of sky was broken.

The white washcloth turned stained and beige as she tried to scrub off every trace of makeup. Her skin was still red and bumpy, and she didn't want to make things worse by leaving makeup on her skin any longer than she had to. Some of the places where she'd squeezed had become painful and tender, and she feared that she'd given herself even more pimples by trying to get the blackheads out. She stared at her red and swollen face and felt grotesque. There had to be a way of fixing her skin. She sat down with her little silver computer and searched for products that would make her skin perfect and placed an order for a jar of vanishing cream that promised to make everything go away. Then she went over to her website and looked at herself surrounded by eyes. Her hair swung so gracefully as she moved, and her skin looked beautiful from the distance of the cameras, and she was definitely looking thinner than she ever had before. Her mood was buoyed even more by an article that said she looked like a model despite her dark artistic sensibilities—the article went on for paragraphs about her hair and her shoes and her dramatic look, and it even mentioned the Mumbalore robot, which she thought was rather odd, since a journalist wouldn't know what went on inside the cube. Just then, a movement on her computer screen and she saw that Rob was trying to talk to her again! She was very glad that he couldn't see her face right now as she typed exuberantly about her evil eyes. He told her that her eyes were beautiful, and that he was really excited because he'd just gotten to try out a prototype of a cool new product called the Innerself. It was a portable music player that could actually sense your mood and play whatever song it thought you wanted to hear. It was so tiny that it could be implanted in your ear canal, and all you had to do was subscribe to the Innerself network and the device inside your ear would wirelessly download all the songs you could possibly want. Rob opined that wires and visible devices were totally passé; pretty soon everybody would have an Innerself inside their ear and nobody would ever have to feel bored or lonely or confused about which song to play. She asked him how the Innerself could tell your mood, and he told her that you had to implant a few EEG sensors on your scalp, and they'd send data to the Innerself, and once you got the sensors implanted you'd be set, because every-thing was going to be all about the digital-cerebral interface in the future. She asked him what songs it chose to play for him, and he said that it was just a prototype, and for some reason it only played a techno version of *Mary Had a Little Lamb.* She asked him if it was possible to turn the Innerself off or request it to be silent, and he said he didn't know why anybody would want that, since nobody's life was really complete without a soundtrack these days. She asked him why he didn't have a weblog on his website, since he was all about a constant digital presence, and he told her that weblogs were as passé as wires—as far as he was concerned, a combination of extreme privacy and direct personal contact was the way of the future. Plus, he was too lazy to update things all the time. He asked her why she didn't have a weblog, and she told him that she wasn't allowed to. Her corporate sponsor controlled her site, but she didn't mind because she wanted to keep things pure. Rob told her that for an unlimited expense account, he'd sell out to anybody, and she asked him if he'd broken up with Nevi yet. He told her he was working on it, and she asked him if Nevi realized that her name meant an unsightly blob on the skin, and he responded with a smiley face and said that her real name was Genevieve, and she shortened it to Nevi because she thought that Genevieve sounded too serious. He quickly changed the subject and asked her if he thought they could collaborate. He could put a couple of Rob-ots in a box and have them sent to her immediately. She didn't know what to tell him, because she really didn't want the robots to be part of her work, but she definitely didn't want him to lose interest in her. She found herself typing that she'd like to give the immobile little robot a try, and he asked her why, and she told him that she liked exploring edges. There was once a deaf-mute, she told him, who made paintings out of sand. He filled up little bottles grain by grain, using tools he'd crafted himself and colored sands that he'd collected from mineral deposits so vivid that people thought he must have used some sort of dye. Most of his works were insipid commissions—somebody's new house, an American flag, George Washington on horseback with an eagle, a portrait of somebody's stern-looking wife encircled by a wreath of flowers. Even the borders of the images were rote and clichéd—grain-by-grain replicas of the sort of design that any proper Victorian room might display as a frieze pattern running below elaborate crown moldings. But beyond the friezes, something happened. He had already depicted his commission and framed it properly, but he found himself with extra spaces to complete the filling of the bottles. And in these spaces, he invented Abstract Expressionism without even realizing it. He created vibrant sandscapes of swirling shapes and undulating lines and galaxies of color, and these narrow spaces that he filled almost as an afterthought contained more energy than any of his startlingly realistic depictions of flags and flowers and dour faces. He was probably just playing when he filled those marginal areas with sand, and maybe if he'd been working on square canvasses rather than curved bottles he would never have let his liminal imaginings take form. We can never predict these sorts of things, she told him, and that was why she wanted to play with the little robot and see what emerged. Rob told her that he'd never thought of the robot in quite that way before, but he was willing to send it to her and see what happened. He asked her for her address, and he seemed impressed that they were living in the same city. He told her that he'd have a courier bring it over right away, and she told him that she was inside a strange warren of rooms inside a strange complex of buildings, and the courier only needed to bring the package to a certain point and the grant people would take care of all the rest. She asked him why he liked chattering so much, since he believed in extreme privacy and direct personal contact, and he responded with a silence that she didn't understand until she'd already started to miss him.

There was a strange email in her inbox. It was from a man who claimed to be the inventor of a new type of push-up bra called the Mammoglam, and the note intrigued her but also puzzled her a bit. It said that he knew she was a loyal Abundacurve customer, but he hoped that he could interest her in the Mammoglam because it was really a superior product. The Abundacurve provided lift and support, but the Mammoglam contained a patented electromagnetic suspension system that would actually cause her breasts to defy gravity and float up and outwards from her chest in a way that every man would find irresistible. He hoped that she would forgive him for taking the liberty of contacting her unbidden, but if she would provide him with a few simple measurements, he would be so honored to participate in her installation that he would send her a free lifetime supply of Mammoglams. She responded immediately and said that while she appreciated the offer and was interested in his product, she would like to know how he found out about her Abundacurve and how he knew her email address. She told him that she hadn't mentioned her bra to anybody, and she certainly hadn't worn it in public, and she purposely kept her email address off her website so that she wouldn't be distracted by a deluge of notes. She told him that she was rather baffled by his intimate knowledge of her undergarments, not to mention his knowledge of her private email address, and she didn't mean to sound harsh, but she didn't intend to send him any measurements unless he enlightened her about his sources of information.

It was feeling strangely warm inside the cube, so she took off her sleepshirt and fanned herself with a page of arabesques. The blisters from the Koremlu were beginning to weep. She stared at the golden pus and thought about beauty. This project was becoming more difficult than she'd imagined.

Where could she go from here, surrounded by those eyes? The vanishing cream arrived, and she rubbed it on her mottled face and hoped that it would make everything clear. Another package, this one with a tiny robot wrapped in plastic. She turned the robot on and placed it on the floor beside her. It moved gradually towards her, leaving a thin trail of yellow on the floor, and she held out her hand and it crept closer and she stroked it. She picked the robot up and put it near the door, which she opened up just wide enough for the tiny robot to enter the gallery of eyes. The robot turned around and sped into the corner of her cube furthest from the door. She smiled and closed the door and beckoned to the little robot, and it slowly approached her and she caressed it and told it that she'd never make it go out there again, and she took it in her arms and held it close to her and sang a lullaby that she remembered from a music box she had when she was young.

The Mammoglam man was deeply apologetic. He explained that he had gotten her email address from her corporate sponsor, and they provided it to him quite cheerfully after he told them about the wondrous properties of the Mammoglam. And as for how he knew about the Abundacurve, he was rather confused, because he imagined that everybody who visited her website had a very clear idea of the type of bra she wore and the brand of makeup she used and the name of the company that provided her with robotic haircuts—her entire website was surrounded by ads that flickered and beckoned to anybody who wanted to see her latest artwork. A brilliant marketing campaign, really, and some lovely artwork too. And if he could be so bold, he'd love to get those measurements so that perhaps his ad could soon be displayed instead of the one for those inferior Abundacurves.

She rocked the little robot in her arms and she told it a story in a singsong voice:

Once upon a time, when I was outside in the country, when I was very little like you are now, I remember I heard cicadas singing. They sang shrill and electric and overwhelmed the darkness with their sharp metallic whirrs. I don't think there are cicadas anymore, but ads are like cicada voices singing all together, singing shrill and unrelenting and announcing that yes, things are being made and the future will be faster and cleaner and we will come out of our worn and dusty shells reborn into a better world.

She held the little robot very close and yellow paint dripped slowly down onto her legs and she stared into the patterns that it made.

June

The room was blurred and stank of warm tan shorts. The Mammoglam man had sent her hundreds of bras in different colors, and their magnetic effect was so dramatic that she decided to use them in an installation with hundreds of pairs of shorts. Her pupils were extremely dilated from a product called Madame Velaro's Belladonna Drops that had been scientifically proven to make people more attractive, and she was having difficulty seeing what she was doing as she sat on the floor of the room and stitched magnetic padding into one pair of shorts after another. The Mammoglams did work extremely well to send her breasts into the air, but they ran on batteries and got entirely too hot to wear. There were many wires and magnets involved, and the magnetic padding was supposed to go underneath her breasts to make them levitate, but she'd found that she could also use it to make the shorts tremble away from the walls as if inhabited. Maybe it was just as well that she couldn't see clearly, because she was still rather terrified of all those eyes around her. She turned a Mammoglam inside out and pinned it to the wall and pinned the waistband of a rumpled pair of shorts in front of it and delighted in the way the shorts leapt from the wall. It had been surprisingly easy to acquire hundreds of pairs of used tan shorts—she went to the *Want It Now* section of the auction website where Rob bought broken dolls, and she put in a plea for rumpled unwashed shorts in any shade of beige, and within hours she'd received offers for more pairs of shorts than a person could pin in front of a lifetime supply of Mammoglams. It took her a while to figure out how much magnetic padding to use, because she didn't want the shorts to rise up so high that they revealed the eyes underneath, but once she'd developed her technique she was able to work rather quickly, even with her vision blurred by Belladonna Drops.

She stitched and pinned for hours or perhaps days until she'd covered every bit of eye and sky. She stood back and admired the fluttering mass of fabric and tried to figure out what she had done. She felt dizzy and nauseous and her head and feet were hurting terribly, but she had managed to created a glorious paean to the Mammoglam man. The shorts gave off a rather pungent smell from the heat of the electric magnets, which gave the installation an added sensory dimension, even though the people watching her on the web wouldn't be able to appreciate it.

She returned into the cube and immediately took off all her clothes. It had gotten warmer recently, and she felt very relieved to peel off everything constricting and sit down on the soft place and massage the pain out of her feet. The Numitol had made the Golden Lotuses bearable when she first started taking it, but lately it didn't seem to work very well at all. Her Mammoglam installation hadn't involved very much standing up, but her feet were still burning and cramped and they seemed to be developing large red swollen areas, and she told herself that she wouldn't go outside the cube again for quite some time. Anyhow, she had a lot to do inside. Rob had been talking to her often ever since he'd sent the little robot over, and she hated to come inside and find that he'd been trying to contact her and he'd given up and left. It felt so good to be wanted by him, but it was still rather maddening to be chattering with him—he'd rarely respond when she initiated contact, he'd often punctuate a conversation with long and unexplained silences, and he'd sometimes end a conversation so abruptly that she'd find herself typing and typing and in the middle of a sentence she'd see his presence suddenly vanish from the screen. It was maddening, yes, but also delicious. There was a certain resonance building between them. They played with leitmotifs of privacy and silences and hidden pasts and fictive futures. She'd never had this sort of rapport with anybody before, and she was becoming quite convinced that he actually liked her. But still, there was the Nevi problem. She suspected that Nevi's presence had something to do with Rob's sudden silences, and she seethed whenever he vanished without warning. He'd told her that he was trying to break up with Nevi gradually and gently—it wasn't easy because they'd been living together for a couple of years now and Nevi was so jealous and vindictive that she'd destroy him if he handled things wrong. It was horribly frustrating that Rob was breaking up with Nevi so slowly, but there didn't seem to be anything that she could do to hurry the process along, so she focused on being as magnetic as possible and hoped that Rob wasn't just leading her on.

Her feet were finally feeling slightly better, so she got up and stood carefully on the matte footprints in front of the sink. The booming robotic voice told her a higher number than she expected, so she stepped off and on and off and on again, but the number was still the same. She'd been eating almost nothing recently, so she didn't understand why the scale was taunting her like this. Perhaps it was time to take up a sport, she told herself wryly as she scrubbed the mask of makeup off her face. Yes, it would be quite alluring to start jogging around the room, getting sweaty and flushed and wearing unsightly white sneakers. She quickly slathered her face with vanishing cream before she could lean into the mirror and start squeezing things, and she sat down again and turned on the little robot and delighted in how it came right over to her and rubbed against her leg. She stroked the little robot and apologized for being outside for so long and warned it sadly that she was going to have to turn it off in a few minutes to conserve its batteries, but she'd try to get a charger soon. Rob had been acting strange about the charger. She'd been so excited when the robot first arrived, but she quickly realized that she had no idea how to charge or replace the robot's batteries, which were tiny and unlike anything she'd seen before. When she asked Rob if he could send her some power, he said that he'd only send her a charger if she could get the little Rob-ot to run around outside the cube. He only had a limited number of chargers for his nanoRob-ots, and he needed to use them before shows, and he wasn't going to waste a charger on a Rob-ot that wasn't even working properly. She told him that she was planning on training the robot to go outside and she knew that she could do it if she had enough time, and if he could just send over a charger for a few hours she'd send it right back again and he'd barely even know that it was gone. He told her that he'd given her the Rob-ot with a fully charged set of batteries, and if she couldn't get it working properly before the batteries ran out, then it was scrap metal as far as he was concerned. The effort required to implant and train another brain simply wouldn't be worth it—all the other Rob-ots were working just fine and he had better things to do with his time—she could use the Rob-ot as a paperweight or something if she still wanted to keep it. She confessed that she found the little Rob-ot kind of cute, and he told her not to anthropomorphize, and she told him that he should be glad that she was anthropomorphizing because it meant that his project was successful—nobody would want to watch his Rob-ots if they didn't seem to exhibit personalities and moods. He told her that she'd probably even anthropomorphize an old t-shirt, and she told him that everything had life to it, especially old t-shirts, and he told her that she was a hopeless luddite and she confessed that her anthropomorphism was more of a yearning than a belief—she was too far gone to be a good luddite, and he admitted that he wanted to upload his brain to a computer before he died, and he certainly hoped that the computer could somehow make him feel alive. She asked again if he could please send over a charger, and he repeated that he'd only send one if she could get the Rob-ot to run around outside, and so she found herself in the strange position of not wanting to force the robot to go outside, but not wanting it to die. She sighed and stroked the robot one last time and told it that she'd see it again soon, that she had to ration its batteries until she got a charger, and she turned off the tiny power switch and traced her fingers through the yellow paint that the little robot had left behind. She found herself forming yellow arabesques on the floor, and she luxuriated in the feeling of the soft cool paint below her fingers as she fell into a trance of patterns. A drip of warm clear liquid and then another and her tears blurred the paint in tiny circles as her fingers smoothed and moved vibrato on the floor.

Rob was extremely excited about a new machine called the Omniscope. She typed with yellow fingertips that she'd love to hear all about it, and he told her that it meant a complete revolution for anybody interested in the history of recorded sound. The Omniscope started out as a device meant to measure subatomic particles, but a particle physicist who also collected old phonographs realized one day that he could modify the device to capture old recordings from tin or wax cylinders that were entirely too delicate to play. Every time a phonograph stylus went over the grooves of a cylinder, it would damage the cylinder slightly, but the Omniscope could capture detailed images of the grooves of an old recording without even touching them, and special software could then convert the shapes of the grooves into sounds that could be played over and over again by anyone. The Omniscope could even be used to help save recordings that had been damaged by insects or rot—it collected such detailed information from the grooves that the software could use every nuance to reconstruct missing bits and eliminate scratches and static and other undesirable sounds. She asked Rob if the Omniscope could be used to find music in the bark of trees, in flowerstalks and fingerprints and strands of hair, and he told her that he didn't see why not, but he doubted that anybody would find anything worth listening to in there. She asked him what sorts of recordings people made on the delicate old cylinders, and he told her that it was mostly music, and that it was mostly big band stuff with brash instruments because early phonographs weren't very good at recording quieter sounds like the human voice or the violin. But there were still recordings in climate-controlled vaults somewhere of historical figures like Queen Victoria and Kaiser Wilhelm and perhaps even Abraham Lincoln, and the idea of preserving these recordings with the Omniscope was simply awesome. She asked him whether there were any old home recordings that still survived, recordings of people giving glimpses of their daily lives, and he reminded her that people didn't do much home recording because they didn't like the sound of their voices when they played them back, and he told her that he had no idea if there were any home recordings out there—he assumed that they existed somewhere, but he was really more interested in listening to Kaiser Wilhelm than to some anonymous dude who was just playing with his newly acquired phonograph machine. She told him that she'd rather listen to something spontaneous than to a formal declaration by a man obsessed by uniforms, and he sent a little smiley face and told her that he'd see what he could find for her. And then her told her that he loved her latest installation and he was completely baffled by how she'd gotten the shorts to float up from the wall like that. And she told him all about the Mammoglams and the magnets, and he told her that it was a brilliant idea to use the bras that way, and she thanked him and asked him if he could see the ads surrounding her website. He said of course he could, and she told him that she wasn't able to see them and she had no idea that they were even there until the Mammoglam man mentioned them to her, and her corporate sponsor hadn't told her that the ads would be there, and when she emailed them about the ads nobody even responded, and it made her nervous to be surrounded without having any control over what was surrounding her, and he told her to chill, that she should be grateful to have funding at all, that he had to do a show the other day for a group of zookeepers who wanted to start putting robots into cages because their animals kept going extinct, and they didn't even understand the first thing about neural networks or art, and if he had a grant like hers he'd order himself the most powerful computers he could possibly find, and she asked him how he knew she wasn't already buying herself the newest computer every week, and he said that he guessed he had no idea what went on inside her cube, and she asked him if he'd like to dress up like a Mumbalore robot and come and visit her one day and find out for himself, and her hands were trembling because she wasn't usually so forward, but she was feeling emboldened by Rob's friendliness today, and she waited and waited and realized that Rob had gone silent yet again and she hated this half-communication and she stared at the screen and wondered where Rob could possibly have gone. She moved her fingertips over the computer screen in an incantation of arabesques, and she traced invisible patterns over the warm electric trembling of her screen as she imagined her hands sculpting a layer of softest cotton and she stared at the dried yellow paint encrusting her flitting fingernails. And then! An email from Rob fell onto her screen, and she opened it as quickly as she could and it was very short but deeply encouraging. He had sent her a number of old cylinder recordings done by a guy who'd played the cylinders on a phonograph and recorded them digitally—the poor sound quality was typical, he told her, but the Omniscope would change everything soon enough. And as for the Mumbalore masquerade, he'd consider it only if he didn't have to handle any hairdye.

She was stunned. Did this mean that he actually might come and visit her? She knew that it would be useless to try chattering with Rob again right then, but she thanked him by e-mail and giddily tried to imagine what would happen if he visited her cube. So much to do! Her bikini line was finally healing, but she still had no way of getting rid of the hair without creating dreadful ingrowns. And her skin looked okay when it was covered with layers of foundation, but underneath the makeup she had so many ghastly spots! And the Belladonna made her vision blur, and she had dark circles underneath her eyes, and there was cellulite on the backs of her thighs, and her hair was looking frizzy again and she hadn't lost enough weight and her fingernails were still encrusted with yellow paint. She lay down on the soft place and held the empty velvet bag from the Golden Lotuses and she closed her eyes and tried to imagine what it would be like if she were holding Rob instead. Her mind was racing so frenetically that it took her hours to even think to take a Lulliban.

She listened through a blanketing of crackles to an ancient violin that played the most haunting interpretation she'd ever heard of Schubert's *Swansong Serenade*. Such a poignant sobbing inside the glissandos, such a plaintive sensitivity of tone, and the crackling muted quality of sound made her feel that she was listening to something very old and very special. She listened to the cries beneath the crackling and shivered and knew that the violinist who coaxed such tremulous notes out of his violin was as dead as the era when such a presence emanating from a cylinder of wax was surely felt as magic. She listened as the final vibrato tapered off into the cracking background, and she listened to the silence in her cube. She wanted to experience the *Serenade* again, but she wanted to keep it as evocative as possible, so she decided to ration it the way she rationed the batteries of her little robot. Perhaps there was a logic to the phonograph stylus destroying a recording a little bit with every listening. These recordings were a gift, created in the air by a violinist trying to play close enough to the recording cone so that his song would be heard, but not so close that his bow would bump against it. And when she listened she knew that she had opened something precious, something almost too powerful to be heard. She was listening to a life that was very much dead, and it was all too immediate and too unreachable at once, and she wondered if people should really have this sort of power. She began to listen to another of the cylinder recordings that Rob had sent, and she heard the singsong voices of little children playing, and the recording was so faint and crackly that she couldn't understand a word, but the energy and the cadence were unmistakably those of children's exuberant squeals. All of a sudden she remembered a recording that she had last heard many years ago, a recording that was probably locked up in a forgotten vault somewhere, a recording made when video was still a distant luxury and tape-recorders were the size of breadboxes. A little girl, not more than three or four. And her father's voice, serious, inquisitive:

And what would you like to be when you grow up?

An artist! And I would bring my fingerpaint over!

And if you weren't going to be an artist, what would you like to be when you grow up?

I told you already. I want to be an artist.

But if you weren't going to be an artist, what would you like to be?

I don't know ... I'm just a little girl....

Static and crackling and she knew that technology had gone too far. Some things were better left to the natural half-life of the human memory. She listened to the *Serenade* once more, listened to the mournful singing of the violin and tried so hard to wish away the burning behind her eyes because she knew that if she started crying she wouldn't be able to stop.

A company called Mesmereyes had created a contact lens that was completely black and oversized and was supposed to make you look hypnotically aroused and more alluring than Madame Velaro's Belladonna Drops could ever hope to achieve. She was still disturbed by all the ads around her, but she did like being contacted about these strange new products because it made her feel like someone cared about her. She told the Mesmereyes people to send over a pair, and she began to research concealers that would stay on her skin even through intimacies. Now that there was an actual possibility of Rob visiting her, she had an entirely new set of worries to contend with. The webcams were easy to fool—she could cover anything with makeup and clothing. But the idea of a real live person seeing her actual live body was rather overwhelming, and she hardly knew what to do first. The web told her a lot about what men liked and didn't like, and it seemed that she had to get herself skinny and fragrant and smooth and blemishless and hairless and wrapped up in expensive lingerie if she wanted him to find her at all attractive, which was a lot to accomplish all at once. She didn't know that he would definitely visit, of course, but his latest note had been so suggestive, and he was so capricious that she could imagine him just showing up inside her cube one day without warning, and she wanted to be ready.

Products seemed to be arriving in her cube almost faster than she could order them. It was proving rather difficult to find an appropriate concealer, so she found herself ordering so many little pots and tubes and bottles of flesh-colored goo that she could barely keep track of what she'd tried and what was still untested. She'd realized that there was no way her skin would be clear enough to show to Rob uncovered, so she had to find a product that would not only be undetectable, but would stay on even if he kissed her and their faces rubbed together. Oh, it would be so wonderful, and they'd hold each other ... but meanwhile her skin had pimples all over, and even though she'd been applying the vanishing cream diligently and trying not to squeeze, her skin was still entirely too broken out for Rob to see. There was no way of turning out the lights in the cube, so concealer was her only hope. It was so frustrating to try all these products with their grand claims and earnest promises—she must have ordered forty or fifty different types of concealer and all of them had a problem of one sort or another. Some of them were too oily and others too dry and still others somehow managed to be both oily and dry at once. A number of them were simply too orange, and some of them were so translucent that her pimples were clearly visible beneath, and some of them were so thick that they clumped into every pore, and some of them had artificial-looking sparkles in them because they were supposed to banish blemishes with special luminescent microbeads. She learned to not even bother ordering concealers that claimed to be age-defying, because they'd turn out terribly greasy and would slide off her face with the slightest touch, and she avoided anything that claimed to be long-lasting, because it would inevitably dry down into a pasty mess, half of which would wear off immediately and the other half of which would linger unevenly no matter how much she tried to scrub it off. She stared at her spotted skin and she stared at the array of concealers and she tried to figure out what to do. Why couldn't her skin just be clear like everybody else's? She decided to be systematic about this, so she separated the concealers into piles according to how problematic they were, and she realized that there were several that might be okay, and she might just have to lower her standards a bit and choose one that worked adequately enough. One of the best ones was a little too orange and too dry, so she mixed it together with one that was paler and slightly moister, and she mixed in a drop of one that had the perfect texture but was slightly too translucent, and she played with proportions and colors and textures until she finally arrived at a concealer that would do. She painted it carefully onto every blemish with a tiny brush and she dusted a thinnest layer of invisible powder all over her face, just to make sure that everything was set and blended properly, and she looked at her face very close to the mirror and decided that you couldn't tell that she was wearing makeup unless you looked very very carefully, and she began to mix up a large batch of the successful formula so she'd always be able to replicate her face, and she sighed at the thought of having to stay covered up all the time, even in her cube. She smeared a little bit of dark orange concealer onto a sketchpad in an impromptu arabesque, but she stopped after several seconds because she noticed that her nails and cuticles were a terrible mess. She had always been accustomed to having paint-stained nails and paint-encrusted cuticles, a smear of blue or green on the back of her hand, chapped areas and patches of glue that wouldn't quite peel off. She kind of liked the accumulation of stains that her hands acquired from one project to the next. But everything she read on the web seemed to indicate that having long polished nails and perfect cuticles was essential to being attractive, and she realized that most of the women she saw on screens did seem to have hands that looked more kempt than hers, so she went to the website for the Mumbalore robots and found that she could easily get a manicure. She selected a deep ruby polish that looked like it would resonate with her lips and her shoes, and she accepted the offer for an upgrade to a manicure-pedicure package, and she clicked the order off and wondered if they'd send Max to visit her again.

She ordered herself a cream that was supposed to make cellulite vanish and a cream that was supposed to fade the dark circles underneath her eyes and a cream that was supposed to make her hair less frizzy and a cream that was supposed to unclog her pores through the miracle properties of Chilean snail slime. A knock just then on her trap door, and what if it was Rob? Her creams hadn't even arrived, and she hadn't shaved in ages! She asked who it was, and a polite voice said that it was Max, and she pushed a button on the wall to open the trap door and let the robot in. It was definitely a standard Mumbalore robot and not Rob in disguise, because he spoke to her in perfect English with an unmistakable Mumbalore accent and told her that he was not authorized to perform the services she had requested unless she put on some clothing first. She was a bit surprised by this request, and she told the robot that it was kind of warm inside the cube, and she didn't really want to be wearing any clothing right then, and she was comfortable with her body and he was all the way in Mumbalore anyway, so she didn't see why it mattered what she wore. He told her that she was violating several different regulations by being unclothed, and if she didn't put her clothing on within a minute, she would be fined and he would have to leave. She grudgingly slipped on her sleepshirt, which fell to mid-thigh, and the robot's tone brightened slightly and he said that she could call him Max and he was happy to be serving her today. She told him that he'd already introduced himself to her last time, and he said that it was not within his duties to maintain continuity across visits. He told her to sit on the bench when she was ready, and a metal bench popped out that was slightly different than the bench from last time—this one had space for her to sit facing the robot and dangle her legs down below. A small shelf came out at the height of her hands, and Max asked her to put her hands onto the shelf as he reached around her with one of his arms and filled a small metal basin in the sink. He put the basin on the floor and told her to put her feet inside, and he squirted something soapy into the water and filled a small plastic bowl with more water and put it on the shelf and asked her to put her hands inside. She felt oddly immobilized with her hands and feet soaking in the water, but also rather cared for, like a baby or an invalid. She tried to ask Max questions about living in Mumbalore, but he kept repeating that it was not within his duties to provide that sort of information, so she asked him if he could please turn off the music and he obliged her and she focused on what he was doing to her hands and feet. He'd pulled out an array of creams and liquids and strange metal utensils, and she watched in awe as he snipped quickly at her cuticles with a tiny pair of clippers and the back of the clippers filled with a large clot of dirty bits of skin. He was using a similar utensil on her feet, and it was a strangely pleasant pain as the deliberate little nips traced all around her toenails and her fingertips. He began to sand the bottoms of her feet with a large purple file, and she found herself giggling because she was so ticklish, and the filing grew more forceful and she almost started to cry. Snipping and filing and clipping, and she felt that she was being gnawed at by determined little ants, and she began to wonder why she was putting herself through all this, but then Max put down the utensils and began to massage her hands and feet with cool thick cream and all of a sudden she found herself in a tingly blissful state. He rubbed between her fingers and between her toes, and sometimes he'd hold her entire hand in his and glide down past her wrist, and his fingers pressed deep and rhythmic into the soles of her feet and she felt the soreness from the Golden Lotuses melting warm into his hands, and she felt awash in the most splendidly sensual trance and she felt so loved and touched with such attention and detail and she hoped that he would keep massaging her for hours because she'd never felt this good in her entire life, but it was over all too quickly and he began to dab at her nails with cotton balls saturated with a liquid that smelled so noxious that she considered trying to send him away so she could lie down and luxuriate in the feeling of having been touched so transcendentally. Instead, she watched immobile as he began to paint her nails. The polish was a beautiful ruby color, deep and shimmery and quite a contrast with her pale skin. The robot's hands were quite precise about applying the polish in perfect ovals, and he put on several layers of red and then a layer of clear, and then he sprayed it with something that smelled even worse than the polish and he told her not to use her hands or put on shoes for at least a half an hour. She thanked him and he prompted her to push the golden button for a tip, and she pushed it and told him that she'd push the button twice if he'd massage her longer next time, and he told her that it was not within his duties to deviate from his script, and he bade her good evening and disappeared down the trap door with a cursory wave.

She sat and stared at her fingernails with delight. They were like little jewels at the ends of her fingers, sparkling and perfect and not a jot of ragged cuticle skin in sight. She was afraid to touch anything for fear she'd smear the polish, so she just sat there and tried to hold her breath because the chemical smell was still extremely intense. She held her fingers out like claws and felt extremely powerful and imagined drawing her ruby fingernails catlike across Rob's back. Just then, a flicker on her computer screen and she saw that it was Rob trying to chatter with her again, so she decided that it didn't matter if her polish got a little messed up—she could always call in another robot if necessary. Rob was extremely excited because he'd just gotten an award for his *NanoRob-ots* show—according to the organization that gave him the award, this was what the future of art was all about. She congratulated him and thanked him for the cylinder recordings, and he told her it was nothing and she should just wait until the Omniscope was working properly, because then she wouldn't have to hear any crackling noises. She told him that she actually liked the crackling, that she liked the patina of age that the popping and crackling and hissing noises gave. He told her she was crazy, and she told him that she'd been rather overwhelmed by the recordings and she was left with a strange feeling that maybe people shouldn't be recording things mechanically at all, that a perfect recording was too powerful a thing, that maybe the human brain wasn't even made to handle the illusion of being connected and the reality of being disconnected all at once, that she'd listened and she was brought too close but all too distant, that she'd listened to the home recording of the little children playing and all she could do was cry, because what else could you do when you got an all-too-living glimpse of somebody who had surely died? He told her that she was too sensitive for this world, and he hoped that she was prepared for the Time Travel Trust to bring her to a place where our brains would be so integrated with computers and so fine-tuned with drugs that we wouldn't even know what it meant to forget something or to have a patina of age or to die. He told her that he'd just tried out a sample of an amazing new neuroceutical from a friend of his, and it was absolutely incredible to get a glimpse of what the future would bring. He tested out the drug by playing a computer game where you shoot at monsters that come at you from all directions, and his reaction times were definitely faster than they were without the drug. His friend was working on all sorts of amazing things: drugs that could get your brain to work faster or slower, drugs that could increase your memory or wipe it out selectively, drugs that could give you such clarity and focus that you'd be able to solve any problem you wanted, drugs that could block out emotions like sadness or fear, drugs that could make you feel like everything was tremendous fun, and even drugs that could make you feel completely miserable, although his friend said that these would have to be kept strictly black market and slipped to people unawares. She told him that she'd like to see a drug that would eliminate all the side effects from the other drugs that she was taking, because it was rare that she didn't feel tired or dizzy or headachy or nauseous these days, and he assured her that his friend was working on that problem too, and all the drugs he'd be releasing would be perfectly safe. He asked her how things were going with the little Rob-ot, and she told him that it was getting closer and closer to the door every day, and she knew that she could lure it out if only she had more time. He told her that he'd given her a challenge, and then he started talking about how cool those cellular phones were, and she asked him what he was talking about and all she saw was empty space. Oh, how frustrating it was to communicate this way! She waited and waited and then typed that she was fascinated by his non sequitur about cellular phones, but she would have to be going now because she had an important meeting to attend along the banks of the Styx, and he responded immediately with a little blushing smiley face and said that he was so sorry, he was talking to his other friend about these cool new cellular phones for kids, and he must've gotten mixed up with all the windows on his screen. She told him that she understood, and he proceeded to tell her all about the cool new phones—they were shaped like cartoon characters from television shows, and they had neural networks inside that would figure out who a kid was trying to call, even if the kid pushed a button wrong, and they would even learn a kid's name and interests and reinforce the kid with messages like *Way to go, Jimmy! Rock stars use cellular phones!* every time a call went through successfully. She told Rob that she'd read somewhere that cellular phones can cause brain tumors if you use them over many years, and maybe it wasn't such a great idea to be encouraging this sort of thing. He told her not to worry, that those studies were faked by luddites who wanted to keep people from getting in touch with one another, and the phones were only fulfilling a consumer need because children wanted to be just like their parents. She asked him if he'd give a cellular phone to a child if he had one, and he told her that he'd never have children—he'd rather focus his efforts on uploading and cryonics because hemorrhaging his meager earnings into junk food and branded clothing and mass-market electronics for a kid who would most likely become a drug addict or a wage slave or a suicide or all three hardly seemed like the most efficient way to achieve immortality. She sent a little smiley face and asked him if everything he did was dedicated to achieving immortality as efficiently as possible, and he told her that seeing as how he spent most of his time playing video games and poking around the web, he'd have to say no. But he embodied the future of art in those little Rob-ots of his, and as long as he could afford to have his head cryonically suspended, he'd be okay. The Singularity would come one day, no matter what he did. She told him that if he'd like to take a break from his rousing daily activities, she'd let him sneak into her own virtual world—she couldn't promise it would get him any closer to immortality, but at least she wouldn't make him dye her hair. He told her that he might just take her up on the offer, but he would have to be going now because he had an important meeting to attend with a bunch of robots, and he'd ring her up on her cellular phone when he was ready to pay her a visit inside her Skinner box. And he vanished from the screen.

She stared at her nails, which were no longer perfect. The polish had gotten wrinkled from her typing, and she could see the white tips of her nails where the ruby red was chipped. But she had more important things to be concerned about. Rob could descend upon her cube at any moment, and she wasn't even close to being ready. Her hair was the biggest problem, so she ordered a Mumbalore robot to come and wax her everywhere. The website said that the wax they used had special growth inhibitors in it, and she could count on being hair-free for at least six weeks. She figured that Rob would certainly come over well before then, so even if the waxing caused some ingrowns, it wouldn't be a problem for a while and she could always put Rob off if things looked really bad. She tested out her new creams while she waited for the robot to arrive. She rubbed the cellulite cream into the backs of her thighs and dabbed the circle cream underneath her eyes and smoothed the frizz cream onto her hair and washed off her makeup and covered her entire face with a thick layer of the cream that was supposed to contain Chilean snail slime. Oh, he might actually be coming over soon! She went to Rob's website, but there was nothing new on it, so she contented herself by looking at pictures of him and imagining what he'd look like naked. She decided that she needed to be careful, because they'd probably end up having sex inside her cube, so she went to drugs-r-us.com and ordered herself a supply of Lunacede. The website warned that it could cause emotional numbness and blood clots and headaches and cancer, and she stopped reading about the side effects because she figured that millions of women took this stuff and nobody complained. She looked at the backs of her thighs in the mirror and the cellulite was still there. She would have to start eating less. She'd been rather good about only having a small amount of chocolate hazelnut spread every day, but the Anorex seemed to have stopped working and she knew there had to be a way of losing weight more rapidly, so she researched diet products on the web and ordered a drink called Dr. Tell's Great Remedy for Flesh that promised to eliminate any unsightly weight within a week. So many things to think about, and she reread their latest conversation on the screen and shivered when she got to the part where he said that he just might visit soon. She felt a stinging from the cream with the Chilean snail slime inside, so she wiped it off and slathered on more vanishing cream. Was Rob really serious about visiting? And what about Nevi? It definitely seemed like he wanted to break up with her, so everything would be okay. He'd visit her regularly in her cube, disguised as a robot so her corporate sponsor wouldn't find out, and once she was done in six months they would be able to be together all the time, and together they'd explore strange transformations of the human mind, and maybe she'd even consider cryogenic preservation, and.... A knock on the door, and it was Max again, and he told her that she was going to need to put on some clothing immediately. She asked him how he was planning on waxing her entire body if she was wearing clothes, and he told her that if she didn't put some clothing on, she would be fined and he would leave. She glared at him and put her sleepshirt on, and he told her that his name was Max and he was happy to be serving her today. He unrolled a wide sheet of paper from a dispenser somewhere within his metal body, and he spread it out on top of the soft place on the floor and asked her if she would please remove her clothing and lie down so that he could begin. She did as she was told, and she asked him why he made her put on her sleepshirt if she was only going to have to take it off again. He told her that it was not within his duties to deviate from his script, and he began to paint her legs with a warm thick yellow substance, and it was almost too hot to be comfortable, and then he pressed on a strip of stiff fabric and ripped the entire thing off and she screamed at the searing pain as hundreds of leg hairs were torn out of her legs all at once, and she asked Max to please be more gentle, and he said that he was performing his duties exactly as he should, and he worked his way up both of her legs using two arms to wax each leg, and it felt like torture as he made his way to her bikini line and he ripped and tore her hair and kept on going until he'd removed all of her pubic hair, and he waxed up to her belly button, where she'd never even thought she had a problem with hair, and he started to wax the front of her arms, which made her scream out in terrible pain, and she told him that her arms didn't have dark hair on them and could he please stop waxing those and could he please not wax anything else except her armpits and her legs, and he said that he was only performing his duties, and he continued up her arms into her armpits and even waxed around her nipples and between her breasts and she began to wonder if she should've been embarrassed all along because she had faint traces of hair there, and her entire body was stinging and he told her to roll over and she was feeling rather confused and powerless and she lay there feeling the pain of the hot wax and the burning ripping and he waxed her lower back and between her buttocks and down her legs all the way to her ankles which hurt the most of all. And he told her to stand up and he sprayed her front and back with something that smelled bitter and felt startlingly cold, and he asked her for a tip and she told him no, that he didn't listen to her requests, and he turned around and left without even cleaning up after himself. She noticed herself in the mirrors just then—her entire body was red and every hair follicle had a little red spot where a hair had been, and she was more hairless than she'd been since she was ten, and she felt unnaturally exposed, like a plucked chicken, and her entire body was still stinging and she felt terribly violated and she swore that she'd never get waxed again, and she pushed away the waxing detritus from the soft place and curled up and hugged her oddly smooth and clammy arms and cried herself to sleep without any need for Lulliban.

She awoke to a delivery of Dr. Tell's Great Remedy for Flesh, and she immediately opened up a little bottle and began to sip the liquid inside, which tasted sweet and medicinal and smelled of artificial cherries and gasoline. It was going to be difficult to drink this every day, but she was determined to lose weight. She sat down on her soft place and sipped from the little bottle and surveyed the mess around her. The robot had left behind hundreds of little strips of cloth, and she picked one up and examined it with fascination, examined the hairs embedded in the wax with their tiny bulbs sticking up at the end, examined the eerie way that the hairs were embedded in the exact pattern of growth that they had when they were on her body, and she petted the hairs by running her palm across the strip and she felt as though she'd killed a part of herself. She imagined an installation of hundreds of these strange pelts tacked to the floor like some sort of post-modern carpeting. *Walk All Over Me*, she'd call it, and she quickly put the installation out of her head and gathered up the hair-embedded strips and the wide sheet of paper and tossed them down the trap door and tried to console herself by reading hundreds of web pages where people wrote about how disgusting body hair was, how it wasn't feminine to have body hair anywhere and how it was definitely best to be bare. She hadn't expected to be completely plucked when she'd ordered a body wax—she'd imagined just her legs and underarms and bikini line—but the more she read the more she realized that men didn't like it if women had any hair on their bodies at all. She began to feel bad for Max, because he was only doing his job and she hadn't even tipped him and there was probably some poor guy in Mumbalore who'd been fired from his job because she'd misunderstood what a body wax was all about. She stared at the red spots covering her body and wondered how long it would take for them to fade.

The Abundacurve looked wonderful under clothing, but it had thick straps and gobs of padding and it was an unflattering putty color and it didn't have a jot of lace. Everything she'd read on the web said that men were turned on by sexy lingerie, which seemed to mean filmy and lacy and delicate, so she figured that she'd have to replace the Abundacurve with something more appropriate. Several websites said that men liked to be greeted at the door by a woman wearing only lingerie, so she figured that if he went to all the trouble of getting outfitted in a robot suit, it was the least she could do to greet him in a sexy way. She looked at hundreds of pictures of bras and panties and bustiers and garter belts and strange contortions of lace and shiny fabrics and felt jealous of all the women who were modeling them—emaciated and buxom and smooth-skinned and without a single imperfection. She finally found a website called realsexy.com that claimed to provide sexy lingerie for real women as opposed to airbrushed models. She looked at the models and didn't see any difference between realsexy.com and any other lingerie site, but she assumed that the realsexy.com stuff might fit a little better, so she entered her measurements and looked at the lingerie that the website suggested for her. Woman after woman wearing nothing but lace and straps and a vapid expression, and she tried to figure out what sort of outfit Rob might enjoy. She'd always worn underwear as infrequently as possible because her skin was sensitive and she didn't like the binding feeling of elastic—she always took off her bra and stockings the moment she returned into the cube. But Rob could appear at any moment now, and it would not do for him to see her naked when he arrived. Picture after picture of women in lingerie, and she felt like she was staring at chicken cutlets that had been gift-wrapped by a poodle groomer. She eventually settled on a simple bra and panty set in black lace, and she tried to imagine Rob looking at her in such an outfit. She looked at herself in the mirror and saw that her pimples had still not faded, even with all that vanishing cream. She picked up her concealer and brushes and powder and began to put on her face.

She noticed a small unopened box in the corner of her cube, and she realized that she had ordered so many products recently that she'd forgotten all about the Mesmereyes. There were two clear plastic vials inside, and she stared at the black circles floating in water like little dead fish. She'd never worn contact lenses before because her vision was perfect, and she wasn't certain how to insert them, so she read instructions on the web and realized that she would need some lens solution to wet them every night. A few quick clicks and the lens solution was on its way, and she also ordered some eye drops to take the redness out and some antifrizz serum for her hair and an exfoliating cleanser that was supposed to remove every bit of sebum from her pores. She checked to see whether Rob had tried to chatter with her or send her any e-mail, and she wondered what he was doing now and she clicked on his name and hoped that maybe he'd be there. At first she had a warm expectant feeling during the initial moments when he might possibly respond, but as the seconds went by she felt more and more hopeless. She waited and waited and saw nothing. Why was he never around when she tried to contact him? She opened a vial of Mesmereyes and put the slimy little thing on her fingertip and pulled her lower eyelid down with her other hand and tried to squish the lens into her eye. It dropped out and stuck to her cheek, and she peeled it off and saw that it was now covered with powder. She didn't have the lens solution yet, so she rinsed it off inside the vial that it came in and stuck her finger into her eye again and again until the lens finally stayed in. Her eye was red and stinging by this time, but the effect was so stunning that she immediately opened the other vial and squished her finger into her eye repeatedly until the lens slid into place. She stared at herself in the mirror in shock. Her pupils were huge and dramatically black and her gaze was more searingly hypnotic than she ever thought possible. She decided to test out the full effect, so she circled her eyes with kohl and extended her lashes with Lash Lure and added an Egyptianate flourish of kohl to the outer corners of her eyes and stared at herself until she felt so overwhelmed by her gaze that she had to look away. Rob would never be able to resist her Mesmereyes. She began to line her lips and she noticed a flicker on her screen. He had responded! He told her that he was in a virtual world right now, but he'd chatter with her soon. She told him to watch out for monsters, and he told her to watch out for robots, and she giggled triumphantly as she sent him a little smiley face and tried to imagine what it would feel like when they kissed.

She began to wonder what she ought to smell like. She always wore deodorant, of course, but all the web sites she was reading seemed to stress the importance of perfume. There were so many different scents available, each in a bottle more elaborate than the last. But what caught her eye was a nondescript-looking little tub of balm called Future Scent that was scientifically created to attract men with the smell of pheromones and pumpkin pie. It seemed that studies had been done to see what types of scents men found most arousing, and it turned out that food smells, specifically pumpkin pie and pizza, had the most powerful effects. Since pizza didn't smell very romantic, Future Scent focused on the pumpkin pie notes, with a base of molecularly distilled human pheromones taken from actual fertile women. Just a little dab of ultra-concentrated Future Scent was guaranteed to make even the most oblivious man instantly attracted to you and only you. She wondered what would happen if two different women in the same room were both wearing Future Scent, and she decided to give the balm a try because she liked the smell of pumpkin pie.

She pulled a lock of wet hair taut with a brush and held the hairdryer hot against it. She didn't understand why she wasn't able to get her hair as shiny and silky as Max had gotten it. No matter how hard she pulled or how close she held the dryer, she still ended up with hair that was frizzy and dull. She was hoping that her new antifrizz serum would help. Her Mesmereyes looked enormous in the mirror, especially now that she had eye drops to take the red away, and the Egyptianate flourishes had worn off in the tub but she intended to draw them on again every time she put on her face because they made her look seductive and exotic. Yes, she was definitely getting somewhere. She smoothed the serum on her hair and delighted in how shiny it looked. She noticed that the spots from the wax had almost vanished, and her thighs felt astonishingly smooth as she rubbed them with cellulite cream. She put her makeup on and opened up the box with her new lingerie. The lace was scratchy and the panties turned out to be a thong, which felt ridiculous, but she stared at herself in the mirror and was amazed at how much progress she'd made. She definitely looked sexy. She practiced posing lying down on the soft place and reclining on her elbow, and she noticed that her stomach wasn't very flat and her skin bulged out a bit at the bottom of the bra strap and she still had cellulite, so she resolved to consume nothing but Dr. Tell's Great Remedy for Flesh until she was thin.

Oh, where was Rob? How long could a person spend inside a virtual world? She began to read about the Singularity and Extropy and found herself staring at pages of photographs from transhumanist gatherings. All of the men had full and artificial-looking hair and all of the women were emaciated and buxom and everybody had faces so tightened and lifted and surgically resculpted that they all took on the look of aliens. She looked at all these smiling people wearing nametags and blazers and she saw beyond the tight smiles into a place of deepest terror. She imagined a row of these pinched and lifted heads suspended in a tank of liquid nitrogen and wondered whether their artificial hair would be suspended too. She turned on the little robot and held it on her lap and it dripped yellow paint onto her newly smooth legs and she stroked it and told it in a soothing voice that everything would be okay.

She woke up to a terrible stickiness inside her eyes and realized that she'd gone to sleep without taking out the Mesmereyes. These contact lenses were going to be a challenge to maintain. Her head was pounding terribly and the thought of drinking down a bottle of Dr. Tell's Great Remedy made her even queasier than she felt already. But her skin was still smooth and hairless, and Rob would surely get in touch with her today. She washed her face with her new exfoliating cleanser and looked at her skin with disgust. What if her concealer and powder wore off and Rob saw all the blemishes she had? She put on her face and lingerie and sat with her little silver computer on her lap and searched for a product that would help perfect her skin. She ordered a bottle of Famous Tula Water for the Complexion, which claimed that it would fade old blemishes and prevent new ones from ever occurring again. The skin below her eyes had been looking slightly dry ever since she'd been using the circle cream, so she also ordered a pot of Venetian Cream Amoretta, which claimed that it would take ten years off her eye region with patented lipospheres. She wasn't sure that she needed to look eleven again, but the website said that nobody was too young to start protecting their delicate eye region from wrinkles and creases and lines. She checked her email, but Rob still hadn't tried to get in touch with her. It was so frustrating to wait for him! She was sitting here all ready for him and he didn't even bother to get back to her and she didn't know what to do. She scrutinized her body and realized that the skin on her knees and elbows was feeling a little too dry, so she searched on the web a bit and ordered a body moisturizer called Princess Salome's Liquid Silk which contained a patented blend of pulverized silkworm cocoons and melted plastic. She had only been awake for several hours, but she was feeling so sleepy and so uneasy about Rob's absence that she decided to take a nap. She removed the Mesmereyes and took a Lulliban and curled up on her soft place and clutched her empty velvet bag to sleep.

She woke up to a delivery from instantbeauty.com and immediately checked her email. Nothing at all from Rob, but there was a polite note from the grant people telling her that she hadn't been outside the cube in quite a while, and it would be nice if she would make an appearance now and then. She ignored the note, because it was her project after all, and her corporate sponsor couldn't control what she did. She went to the mirror and washed her face and began to reapply everything, starting with her Mesmereyes. It was becoming monotonous to reapply her face every day, but she wanted to be sure that she did everything possible for Rob to find her beautiful. She finished up with two Egyptianate flourishes and sat with her computer and ordered more sets of the lacy black lingerie because she'd been wearing it continuously now and she wanted to smell fresh. She opened up the tub of Future Scent and dabbed a bit on her wrists and delighted in the smell of pumpkin pie. It smelled so delicious that she took a tiny fingerful of chocolate hazelnut spread and licked it slowly while she listened to the mournful singing of the *Swansong Serenade* and imagined Rob longing for her. She licked every bit of chocolate from her finger and noticed her wrinkled ruby polish and decided to call in another robot for a manicure.

She examined her body while she waited for the Mumbalore manicure to arrive. She wasn't getting any ingrown hairs, but she noticed that some new hairs had begun to poke their way up and they looked terribly dark against her white skin. She grabbed the tweezers and began to pluck the hairs out one by one. As she tweezed she thought about the Extropians and their grand hopes for an everlasting techno-happy future and she found herself wondering whether machines would ever be able to do anything more than what we tell them to do. Superficially, maybe. But most deeply she still held out hope for the creativity of the human brain. She plucked out hair after hair from her underarms and tried to ignore the pain and she thought about the Time Travel Trust and wondered what sort of fantastic place they would decide to take her to.

Her black lace thong was more of a joke than an actual garment of clothing, but it was still acceptable to Max, who introduced himself pleasantly this time and didn't ask her to get dressed. She sat on the metal bench and watched his robot arms remove her polish with noxious-smelling cotton balls. She stared at her computer as he clipped her cuticles and she stared at her computer as he massaged her hands. She still loved the deep tingling feeling of being touched, but she was distracted by the fact that Rob might try to contact her at any moment. Max began to polish her nails again with a fresh coating of the gorgeous ruby color he used before, and he'd gotten done with two coats and was beginning on the third, when she saw a movement on her screen and she leapt up from the bench and it was Rob! She told the robot that he could go now, and he said that it was not within his duties to deviate from his script, and could she please come back and sit down so that he could finish. Rob had just greeted her and she was so excited to talk, but she had to get the robot out so she could talk in privacy, and she pushed the golden button again and again, but the robot told her quite firmly that she needed to sit back on the bench right now. She typed hi carefully with her fingertips and told the robot to please go away, and he wouldn't listen so she took her thong off as carefully as she could and he told her that if she didn't get dressed she would get fined and he would leave. She told him to go right ahead and he warned her again and then he left. Her polish had already gotten wrinkled, but she was so happy that Rob was with her that she didn't care. He told her that he was sorry he took so long—he was about to get to the next level for the longest time, and finally he killed another player and stole his loot, so now he was much more powerful and there were so many awesome weapons he could use. She paused and tried to think of how to respond, and Rob continued and told her that he'd been playing the game so long that he hadn't even noticed when Nevi left. She felt ecstatic and told him that it was about time, and he told her that she hadn't exactly left for good—she'd gone away to her sister's wedding on some island. She felt rather let down and asked him what island she'd gone to, and he said that he couldn't remember which one, but it was nowhere unusual; just one of those places where they put the natives into slavery and build golf courses and jewelry stores where children used to run. He told her that Nevi wanted him to come along, but he didn't have time for that kind of crap, and he was planning on breaking up with her anyway. He couldn't stand her sister and her boyfriend—neither of them had ever had a thought inside their heads that wasn't placed there by a major PR conglomerate. Nevi's sister actually described her impending wedding as the best day of her life, which he thought was the most pathetic thing he'd ever heard—if you were living for a canned pageant thought up by barbarians and ad men, you might as well be dead. She told Rob that she agreed with him completely, that women in this culture were brainwashed into marriage myths from the time that they were old enough to watch movies that held up princesses as paragons to aspire towards. She was lucky to have avoided all that crap—the only myths that she grew up with were ancient Greek ones. Rob kept complaining about Nevi and how much money she was spending to go to the wedding and how she kept yelling at her sister for making her wear a bridesmaid's dress that wasn't pink and how she kept pleading with him to go along with her because she would be so embarrassed if he didn't show up also. Why was Rob confiding in her about Nevi's inanities? She told him that Nevi sounded really unpleasant, and he agreed and she told him that he was welcome to visit her inside the cube, and she promised not to bring up any myths, contemporary or ancient. He sent her a smiley face and told her that he'd ring her on her cellular phone when the time came. And he was abruptly silent yet again.

Her corporate sponsor was getting annoyed. They had just received a bill for a rather large fine for private nudity in the presence of a robot, and they didn't want to see any more such fines in the future. They also didn't know why she hadn't gone outside yet, but they strongly recommended that she do so as soon as possible. There was an ominous tone to the note, so she got dressed as quickly as she could, replacing the black lacy bra with an Abundacurve and trying unsuccessfully to pull up her control top stockings without further messing up her nails. What did it matter if those Mumbalore fascists charged a fine? Their rules were just ridiculous. Her corporate sponsor had said that her grant could cover anything she wanted, and she didn't see why it couldn't cover a fine that she'd incurred knowingly or otherwise. She stuffed her feet into the Golden Lotuses and dabbed a little extra lipstick on her pout and wiped off the smudges of Lash Lure from under her eyes and reapplied concealer over her circles and smoothed more antifrizz serum on her hair and steeled herself and went outside into the room. Several of the batteries must have died because some of the shorts were hanging down flat against the Mammoglams, but otherwise the installation was still intact. If she went inside again to order more batteries, her corporate sponsor might get annoyed, so she pantomimed elaborate arabesques over the shorts that had fallen and lost herself inside her silent gestures. The smell of the warm shorts blended reassuringly with the scent of pumpkin pie.

She returned inside the cube to find that somebody had sent her a little camera for her computer. She opened the instruction booklet and found a note. Bold black ink: *I want to see you*, and she knew it was from Rob and her stomach shuddered. If she plugged the camera in, she'd have to make eye contact with him. She had seen the intensity of his gaze while he was talking to Panoptico, and she didn't know if she was ready. She stared at herself in the mirror and wiped away smudges and reapplied concealer and powder and lipliner and lipstick and finished with the Egyptianate flourishes and gazed into her Mesmereyes and tried to imagine Rob staring at her as she stared at him. She attached the camera to her computer and turned it on and worried briefly about her corporate sponsor objecting, but they would have no way of finding out about the camera, and it didn't have a microphone anyhow, so she figured it would be okay. She looked at herself in the mirror one last time and tweezed several eyebrow hairs that did not belong and wiped a bit of lipstick from her teeth and parted her hair in the center and then the side and then the other side and settled on the first side and practiced smiling seductively at herself and put the computer on her lap and tried the camera in self-test mode and was horrified by how she looked from underneath. She stacked some boxes below her computer and sat cross-legged in front of it and adjusted the camera so that it was staring down at her a bit. Much more flattering. She looked at herself again in the mirror and breathed deep and clicked on Rob's name and she'd never felt so nervous in her life and she waited and waited and nothing. Oh, where had he gone? She knew quite well that he was sitting at his computer immersed in some virtual world or other, and here she was in person waiting for him, and she'd gotten her face all perfect and now she had to wait. What if he didn't want to look at her until she was asleep? This was becoming so tense, and she still didn't know if he would ever come and visit her in person, and she didn't know why Nevi was still in the picture, and she didn't know why her mind had gotten so obsessed with somebody so unpredictable and inaccessible. She consoled herself by covering herself with creams. She smeared cellulite cream on the backs of her thighs and dabbed a bit of Venetian Cream Amoretta underneath her eyes and rubbed some Future Scent behind her ears and anointed her entire body with Princess Salome's Liquid Silk. Oh, he would talk to her so soon now, she could feel it! She put on a new set of black lace lingerie and got dressed in a tight black low-cut top because she didn't want him to think that she was so forward that she'd talk to him in just a bra, and she put on a skirt because she figured she might move and he might be able to see more than just her torso and her face. She noticed that her eyes were extremely red and she put eyedrops in while feeling very relieved that he hadn't talked to her yet, because what if he had seen her eyes all red? She stared at herself in the mirror and realized that the black lace bra made little bumps under the smooth clingy fabric of her shirt, but she couldn't wear the Abundacurve because it wasn't sexy at all, and the camera may've been a ruse and he could still arrive inside her cube at any time. She checked her image on the screen and was relieved to see that the bumps weren't visible at all. She felt so giddy and sat and waited and waited and swooned into the *Swansong Serenade* and turned on the little robot and stroked it for a moment and told it that she was going to have to turn it off because Rob might see it in the camera and get suspicious, but she still loved it and she would see it again very soon. And she gave it a little kiss and turned it off and looked at herself in the mirror and wiped away some smudges of kohl from beneath her eyes and wondered if the Venetian Cream Amoretta was too moisturizing. She reapplied concealer and checked the camera angle again and waited. Oh, it would be any second now, she knew it! She decided to check her comments to distract herself and realized that she hadn't even looked at them in ages. It was so wonderful to feel all the praise upon her—hundreds and hundreds of people telling her that she was the most beautiful and brilliant creature ever, and then another comment from that feminist, and she grumbled as she read the note. The feminist told her that nailpolish and hairdye were very toxic, and beauticians were dying and getting terrible diseases and that's why all these services were being outsourced. She said that it was ridiculous that half the population should be forced to spend so much time and money so they could go out in drag, and didn't she know better than to follow these narrow cultural dictates? She didn't know why the feminist kept writing these strident comments, but she did know that evolutionary psychology said that only beautiful women got high-quality mates, so it was okay if she did everything possible to try to be beautiful. Anyway, she was above evolutionary constraints and cultural dictates. She was doing all this for herself, not because of a man, no no no, *I'm an independent thinking person and I'm doing this for me me me see you see me see you see me* and the screen became Rob's face and they were staring at each other and she could only type gibberish as she stared into his dark and searing eyes. *See you see me and I cannot see myself reflected in your eyes*, and he asked her what she meant because he could see her just fine, and she told him that she felt like she could look into his eyes but that she couldn't quite make eye contact, and he told her to adjust the camera so that it was staring right between her eyes. And it was closer, and she trembled as she gazed at him but something still wasn't exactly right, and she found herself telling him that she once did a painting called *The Pupil* of an array of eyes, each one with a little girl reflected inside. Sometimes the girl was smiling blandly and sometimes she looked terrified and sometimes she was lying on the ground and sometimes she wasn't there at all. She told him that *pupilla* was Latin for little doll and for the center of the eye, and that in Greek the word was *kore* and that in ancient times you rarely saw your full reflection unless you were looking into a still body of water, and that staring into someone's eyes was very powerful, almost too powerful, because it meant that they held you inside them, and she stared into his eyes and he told her that he'd never seen a more powerful gaze and he wondered if he would turn to stone. She stared at him with her Mesmereyes and he was hers. She could feel it. A rapt and carnal look.

See you see me and he stared deep into her Mesmereyes and he told her a story in a singsong voice:

Once upon a time I decided I was going to go out to the park without my cellular phone or my portable music player or anything electronic at all. They've got trees there—real trees, made of wood. And actual grass made of—I don't know—something organic. The problem is, I've got no attention span, no matter how much riddle-me-this they spike my smart drinks with. I get anxious if I'm not watching television and listening to music and playing a computer game and surfing the web and chattering with twelve people all at once. I wasn't raised along the banks of the river Styx like you were. I grew up staring at screens for every moment of my life, and by the time I learned enough to begin to look behind them, my brain had already become so dependent on mediated content that I simply couldn't be alone. I've tried, I really have. Anyway, once upon a time I decided I was going to go out to the park, and I went out past the traffic and onto the grass and I sat there and I found myself looking around frantically for screens. There wasn't a screen in the sky or on the grass or even hanging from the trees. And I thought to myself that people must be trying to call me on my cellular phone and my head started singing songs from commercials, songs that I didn't even want to hear, and I started to get anxious and I tried to put the commercials out of my head and fill it with a song about Shiva that I'd heard at a yoga class I'd taken once, and I thought about the computer game I'd been playing lately, which was a complex medieval world with knights and monsters and a currency all its own, and I tried to see eternity in a blade of grass and all that crap, but I couldn't even concentrate on the blade of grass for long enough to really look at it. I saw the blade of grass, but nobody was telling me what to think about the blade of grass or making witty comments about it or showing it animated and tessellated and dancing all over a screen. I ran out of the park and grabbed a cab and soothed myself by watching those commercials they run on little screens on the back of the seat. I'm a casualty of the postmodern age, I'm afraid, and my only hope is that technology will one day help my brain to heal itself. Once upon a time I was staring into your eyes as dead as any doll that I could ever buy, and I saw something behind them and I told myself I'd try, I'd come into your cube and....

And the screen went dead just then and she stared into the darkness and drew her wrinkled ruby fingernails across the warm vibrations of the screen. Her arabesques breathed.

Intermission

THEY HAD SOMEHOW CRAFTED AN ORNATE ANTEROOM OF ADOBE AND GOLD LEAF. Watch your step as you move through, please. The prickly pears are skittish and the wild rabbits sharp. If you're good, I'll let you take a fragment of gold leaf on your way out. Do you see the door? I'll give you a hint—it isn't where you think. And if you see yourself reflected in the mirrors, look away, and fast!

The door may still elude you, so please allow me to escort you back into the future theatre. You'll find the right way out of the anteroom later. Meanwhile, I suggest that you ignore the shadowy figures on the stage and admire the trappings of the theatre. It used to be quite beautiful, they say, and you can still see a certain fin de siècle elegance in the peeling frescos on the ceiling, in the tarnished gilded balustrades, in the long red velvet curtains that have faded down into a pale and dusty salmon hue. They say they plan to renovate the place all postmodern-like, with spiky metal seats and digitally projected frescos, but I'm not sure I believe them.

The stage is set with splatters of paint and a cube of glass with shadows inside. Somebody has painted elaborate arabesques on the back wall of the stage, and I suggest that you follow them. They may not lead you out of the future theatre, but if you pay attention they might whisper a clue.

Once upon a time I found myself in a labyrinthine medina with whitewashed walls and turquoise doors and minarets rising up beyond. It was hot and bright and I hid from the sun beneath a parasol and a large black hat. I walked through narrow passages and looked at every door and wondered what was behind the peeling paint. I walked past veiled women covered entirely in black and I walked past skinny kittens and I walked past children playing elaborate games with sticks. It was so hot beneath my hat, but I was terrified of sun and so I kept the hat on my head and the parasol above my hat and I kept on walking and I was soaked with sweat and the high white walls were closed and nobody spoke to me at all. Eventually I got so hot that I sat down in a shady spot and closed my parasol and took off my hat and began to run my fingers through my matted hair. And a funny thing began to happen. Two little girls came up to me and began to speak in broken French and they stared at me and I spoke back and then several more children approached me and suddenly I was surrounded by children all trying to sit close to me and chattering about their names and how old they were and asking me where I was from. I took out a notebook and wrote my name and the children all wrote their names in letters that looked like arabesques and the children giggled and I giggled and then I noticed a veiled woman staring at me and all I could see were her eyes and I was afraid that I had done something wrong, talking to all these children so openly in a city where women walked the streets in veils, and I got up to keep walking but the veiled woman asked me in broken French if I'd like to have tea with her, and I was surprised but I told her of course, and so I followed her through narrow passages and she pushed open a peeling turquoise door and I finally saw what was beyond: a large courtyard surrounded by more whitewashed walls and turquoise doors, and we went into another door and the room was tiny, with a thatched ceiling and a narrow bed and a low wooden table surrounded by faded floral cushions, and she gestured that I should sit down and she told me in broken French that she'd be back in a moment with her sisters and some tea. I stared up at the raw thatched ceiling and I stared across at the bare whitewashed walls and I was surprised to see the woman again wearing orange track pants with white stripes down the side and a matching hooded jacket and she looked so young without her veil and she put a cup of tea in front of me and I saw that her sisters were following right behind her, all dressed similarly and carrying plates of food. The low table sparkled with pomegranate seeds and amber dates and golden figs dripping with honey, and we all sat down on the soft cushions on the floor and the woman apologized to me in broken French and told me that she couldn't talk French very well and neither could her sisters because girls didn't go to school for very long. I told her that her French was very good and I thanked her for the wonderful meal and for inviting me inside, and I learned all her little sisters' names and ages and I told them mine and we all sat there eating figs and pomegranate seeds and her sisters were giggling and talking to one another and she told me that her sisters said that I was very pretty. I thanked them and told them that they were very pretty too, and the woman asked me if I'd like to try some special makeup and I told her of course I would, and she opened a little wooden box and gave me a piece of fibrous golden bark to chew on and it made my mouth numb and the little girls all giggled and she took a small glass vial with black powder inside and she dipped a narrow glass wand into the vial and the tip was black and she told me to lean forward and she moved the wand towards my face and gently glided the black powder around the inner edges of my eye and she dipped the wand into the powder again and glided it around my other eye and the little girls all giggled and my mouth was numb and the woman handed me a tiny smudged mirror with a cracked pink plastic frame and my eyes were enormous and searing and my lips and gums had a deep red stain. The woman told me that I looked beautiful now and I thanked her and the little girls all stared at me and I asked the woman how she spends her time during the day and she told me that she makes carpets, and I asked her if I could see her carpets and she seemed surprised that I would be interested in such a thing, but she gestured that I should follow her, and so we all went out into the courtyard and into another room behind a turquoise door which was filled with vertical looms and spinning wheels and skeins of yarn in deep soft colors. The little girls all wanted to show me the rugs that they had made and I was surrounded by pattern and I stared into the arabesques around me and I realized that I had forgotten my hat and parasol somewhere far away in the narrow passages of the medina, but it didn't matter because I could stare into these arabesques forever. I told the woman that I knew how to weave and I asked her if I could try a bit and she nodded and the little girls all giggled and the yarn was so soft and the woman asked me if I spent my days weaving when I was back at home and I shook my head sadly and told her that I was a scientist and I studied the brain and she told me that my weaving was beautiful and I thanked her and told her that her weaving was beautiful too.

The future theatre is crumbling. It may never be repaired. But the seats were once plush and red and posh with hat racks and parasol stands, and the carpeting was once so deep that you could lose your feet inside it. The shadows on the stage are growing larger and they will begin to beckon to you before too long, and I suggest that you try to leave the future theatre before you become a shadow too. The anteroom is filled with so many mirrors that you may never find your way out, but I'll save you a fragment of gold leaf, just in case. They say that if you cut a hole in a lemon and fill it with crystallized sugar and cover the hole with gold leaf and roast it in a fire, you'll end up with a cosmetic juice so potent that your skin will sing. But they also say that a gallon of cerebrospinal fluid boils down into a tablespoon of lost illusions, so I'm not sure I believe them.

July

THE ROOM WAS RED AND TASTED OF SWEAT. She wasn't sure if she was Persephone or Paciphae or even Pandora anymore, but she did know that she was living inside a box and a strange and marvelous creature had entered her trap door and she'd spent the past few weeks affixing pomegranate seeds to every surface of the room and she still had hope, much hope, that the creature would return. There was a nameless bottle of pills next to her Lulliban and Numitol and Anorex and Lunacede, and she'd been taking one every day, as instructed on the label, but she wasn't sure exactly how they'd gotten there or what they were supposed to do. Her skin stuck to the soft surface of her sleeping-place—it had been getting so hot in the room and she couldn't stop sweating and she was positive she'd told somebody to make it cooler in the room, but it was only getting hotter and she felt terribly dizzy and sticky and wet.

The walls glistened red outside, but the funny thing was that the shorts had all vanished and she didn't know how. One day she woke up and found that the shorts were gone and the Mammoglams had been pulled down and clung to one another tightly in a vast magnetic ball. She looked in the archives on her website, but all she saw were eyes. It was as though the shorts had never even happened. She pulled the Mammoglams apart and threw them down the trap door and noticed a half-eaten pomegranate in the corner of her cube. She stared at the deep red shimmering seeds and determined to encrust the walls with them. It had taken her a long time to glue the pomegranate seeds over the eyes because the seeds were just so tiny, and she also had to return into the cube quite frequently because her makeup melted quickly in the heat. But the entire room was shimmering beautifully now, and she rested on the soft place and felt her head spinning and tried to understand what had happened. She felt oddly numb and oddly languorous and she wondered if that marvelous creature would return and tell her what was going on.

Maybe it was time to stop taking all those pills. She didn't feel particularly sick, and she didn't know why she needed to be opening and closing all those orange bottles every day. What were her symptoms? She felt dizzy and nauseous and tired and numb, and her feet were hurting and her head was hurting too, and she was moving more slowly than usual and her fingers were definitely less nimble than they used to be and she seemed to have trouble remembering things. She looked online for a description of all the different drugs she had, and she concluded that she could certainly be thinner and she didn't want to get pregnant and she didn't want to be in any pain and she wanted to be able to sleep properly, but no matter how many times she looked at the nameless bottle with the stern label telling her to take one pill every day, she saw no sign of what exactly it contained. The pills were small and white and didn't even have any information printed on them, so she figured that it couldn't hurt to stop taking them—any pill that was worth anything these days was a nice bright color and had its name printed on it, just like those little candies she was so fond of. Oh, she was hungry! Why didn't anybody bring her any food? She looked around her cube and found a mostly empty jar of chocolate hazelnut spread and began to eat it greedily. No, that little white pill would not be necessary any longer. She was surrounded by pomegranate seeds now, so everything would be okay. She moved her fingers around the inside of the jar and got out every bit of chocolate that she could, and she threw the empty jar and the white pills down the trap door, and she licked every trace of chocolate off her fingers and looked at them with fascination. Wrinkled ruby polish chipped and growing out and dark orange stains everywhere, even on her fingertips. She suspected that the pomegranates may have had something to do with the orange stains, and she remembered that a robot named Max had painted her nails a ruby hue quite some time ago. She felt a wave of sleepiness just then, and it was so hot inside the cube and she lay down on the soft place and stretched out so she could be as cool as possible.

She woke up to a terrible headache and a deep hunger. She ordered herself a pizza, and as she waited for it to arrive she looked at the red room on the screen and admired how it glittered. She looked down at her fingernails and tried to figure out when she'd last gotten her nails done. They had definitely grown quite a bit since they'd been polished. She began to pick at the chipping polish and stopped when she noticed that she was peeling off the top layer of her fingernails as well. In the spots where she'd picked the polish off, her nails were now damaged-looking and matte, and she licked the matte spots to try to make them shiny again. She licked and licked and then she smelled something. A musky scent from underneath her fingernails. Something was shifting inside her brain. The smell was so familiar. She held her fingernails to her nose and breathed in deep.

The pizza was the most delicious thing that she had ever

eaten. She delighted in the crisp doughy crust and the thick soft cheese and the tangy salty sauce, and she ate the entire thing in minutes even though she'd planned to save some for the next few days. She felt flickers of guilt for eating so much food, but she figured that it tasted so wonderful that it didn't matter if she gained a bit of weight. None of her admirers outside the cube would care, because she had created such a wonderful installation of pomegranate seeds. She threw the pizza box down the trap door and began to sniff her finger-nails again. What had that strange creature done inside her cube? Were there any more pomegranate seeds to attach to the walls? Did she need another pizza? She felt so sleepy and her head was spinning and she decided that it must be time for her to sleep. Had night already come so soon?

She woke up screaming to a nightmare about being beaten by a robot and her blood was splattering all over the walls of the cube and it hurt so much that she didn't even know that she was dreaming. She lay sweating on the soft place and breathed deep and told herself that everything was okay. Robots were friendly, and those were only pomegranate seeds, and nobody was trying to hurt her. She reached over to the little robot and turned it on and it crept over to her and rubbed gently against her leg. She stroked it and told it that she was so happy to see it, and then she noticed the camera attached to her computer and wondered if Rob had been trying to talk to her while she'd been asleep. It seemed that she'd been asleep for quite a long time—it must've been very exhausting to fill the room with pomegranate seeds. Her head was in terrible pain and she still felt very sleepy, and she noticed her fingers shaking as she stroked the little robot. She kissed it and told it that she'd see it again soon, and she turned it off and stared at her face in the mirror and realized that if she was going to talk to Rob she would need to put some makeup on. She looked so timid and insignificant without red lips and kohl-rimmed eyes and a perfect white complexion. She tried to remember her last conversation with Rob as she began to put her makeup on, and she was having a lot of trouble reconstructing what they talked about or how it felt to look at him as he looked at her and they chattered. Maybe she'd been sick? Nothing was quite making sense, and she got so dizzy standing up and putting makeup on that she decided to lie down, just for a moment.

She woke up feeling ravenously hungry. She opened a bottle of Dr. Tell's Great Remedy for Flesh and recoiled from the scent as she sipped it. She stared at the pomegranate seeds on her screen and tried to figure out how she'd managed to encrust the entire room. Such a detailed project would take months. Had she been working on the seeds for that long? It felt like all she'd been doing lately was sleeping. She must have been recovering from a nasty virus that made her delirious. She certainly felt feverishly hot. She looked at herself in the mirror and saw that her face was a mess of smeared kohl and creased concealer. What if Rob decided to visit her and she looked like this? She washed her face and as she was rubbing exfoliating cleanser into her cheeks she noticed a strange musky aroma coming from underneath her fingernails. It was so familiar and she smelled her nails and inhaled deeply and then she realized that Rob must have been inside her cube and she must have drawn her fingernails across his back and yes it was definitely his scent she was smelling and she closed her eyes and saw a flicker of his head bent back and his mouth open round like a fish in mid-gulp and the image made her shudder but then her mind went blank. Why couldn't she remember anything else about his visit? She held her hands below her nose and closed her eyes and tried to summon memories from the smell of him beneath her fingernails but all that she could remember was that fish-flicker of an image. She must have been so feverish when he arrived that she was barely aware of what was happening. But still, he'd been to visit her inside her cube and they'd definitely had sex, because where else could that image and that smell have come from, and it was only a matter of time before he'd come to visit her again. She lay down on the soft place with a languorous warm feeling of triumph and giddy victory. She had done it. She had lured him away from Nevi, and now everything in her life would be wonderful. She fell asleep smiling.

She woke up with a feeling of urgency. She hadn't tried to contact Rob for so long now, and he probably thought she wasn't even interested anymore. She put on her lingerie and makeup as quickly as she could, and she tried to figure out what she was going to say to him. She'd obviously had an awful fever that reached into delirium, because she could barely remember a thing about his visit. But she didn't want to insult him by implying that he was so unmemorable that she'd forgotten everything. So she decided she'd act coy and elliptical and generically flattering and she'd be able to segue the conversation into another visit without him even knowing that she had no idea what had happened during his first. She drew on her Egyptianate eyes with a flourish and smiled at herself because she was so irresistible that she'd managed to attract someone as wonderful as Rob. She set up the computer and the camera at the most flattering angle and clicked on Rob's name inside the chattering box and waited. And waited. Oh, it was just like him to be so elusive yet again. But he'd certainly be back soon. She sat in front of the camera and stared at herself while fantasizing about what would happen when he visited again. They'd be so close, and he'd hold her and kiss her and tell her that he loved her and they would always be together. And when she finally finished with the room they'd live together and make art together and he was so intense and beautiful and oh! a movement on her screen, and she smiled into the camera and prepared to type verbal bouquets and she noticed with a sickening startle that it was not Rob at all who was chattering to her—it was a person who worked for her corporate sponsor who wanted to know if she was feeling okay. She turned off the camera immediately and typed politely that she thanked him for his concern, but she was just fine. The person suggested that she go outside and continue with her work, and she asked if he could please figure out how to make it cooler in the room because she was finding it difficult to work due to the heat. He said that he would see what he would do. And then he left the screen. What a terrible invasion! How had they figured out her chatting name? She felt so frustrated because she wanted to be available for Rob whenever he wanted to talk, but she did not want to be under constant surveillance from her corporate sponsor. She decided that from now on she would leave the camera off, and if she was talking to Rob she'd turn it on again, and if the grant people tried to chatter with her she would just ignore them. She decided to go outside, just to appease the grant people a bit, and she figured it might also make the time go by a little faster. She took off her black lace bra and thong and almost cried when she saw that her entire body was covered with stubble and dotted with red inflammations. She'd thought that the waxing had solved her problems, but it only seemed to have made things worse. If Rob saw her like this, he would never return again. She inspected her pores up close and saw that she had ingrowns in places where she'd never even had ingrowns before, and her frustration gave way to an odd feeling of exhilaration, as though she'd just been handed a shovel and a treasure map. She found a pin and began to pick, starting at the bottom of her legs and working her way up. The ingrowns were a lot deeper than the ones she'd gotten from shaving, but she was getting very skilled at releasing them without digging around too much. She would pinch the reddened bump between her fingers and poke the pin into her skin just next to the tiny black dot and she would flick the pin gently upwards at an angle and catch the hair underneath it and it would pop out suddenly in a moment of thrilling revelation. It was so satisfying to be able to release all these hidden hairs, and she fell into a trance of picking. Some of the hairs were more elusive, especially in places like her underarms and pubic area where the hairs were coarsest, but she was determined not to leave a single hair still buried, even if it meant digging in deep and bleeding and wiping away the blood so she could see the shadow of the hair to dig in deeper. She couldn't reach everywhere on her body, but luckily her lower back seemed to be growing in cleanly and as downy as before, and she tried to look between her buttocks in the mirror and she only saw a few minuscule red bumps that she decided she would have to live with. She surveyed her body and concluded that waxing was not going to be the solution she had hoped for. She was now covered with red dots that would take weeks to turn into scabs and fall off and fade completely, and her hair had grown back extremely quickly despite the special growth inhibitors in the wax. She thought about the problem and decided that she didn't need her hair removed from everywhere. She just wanted to look feminine. Her arms hadn't needed to be waxed, and neither had her thighs or her lower back. She inspected her torso carefully and decided that the hair around her nipples and between her breasts and around her belly button was slightly too dark to be feminine. She went online and researched hair removal and decided that she needed to get treated with a laser—it seemed that lasers were able to kill off the hairs at the root and permanently prevent regrowth. Yes, this would be the answer. She looked on the website for the Mumbalore robots and was frustrated to see that they didn't offer such a thing. She searched deeper and found another website that looked similar, but seemed to offer more expensive procedures, and she figured that her corporate sponsor would pay for anything she ordered, so it really didn't matter that laser hair removal cost so much. She didn't need her entire body done, anyhow, so she'd be saving her corporate sponsor a lot of money. She was very careful to indicate what body parts she did and didn't want lasered, because she didn't want a repeat of the body wax fiasco. She decided that she would continue to shave her legs and underarms because she'd been shaving those areas for so many years that she never got ingrowns there. She was a little bit afraid of the laser, and she wanted to see what it did to her before she got too many areas done—if it worked really well, she could always get her underarms and legs lasered later. Her main concern right now was her bikini line and her entire pubic area—she had learned from all those websites that it was very important to be completely bare down there. She also figured that she ought to get rid of all the downy but slightly darker hairs on her torso, because the websites said that it was crucial to remove any hair that suggested anything masculine or animal about the body. She went down the checklist of body parts and obsessed about each one and whether it was necessary to get it lasered. She still didn't see what was so bad about having hair on her arms, and she was surprised to see that people bothered with the tiny hairs on their fingers, and she'd never noticed any hair above her upper lip before, but she decided to check, just in case, and she looked into her magnifying mirror and noticed with horror that some of the hairs there were downy but a smidgen darker than the hairs on the rest of her face. She didn't know how she could've missed this problem for all these years; she thought that maybe it had to do with the fact that she'd gotten so pale inside the room, and she checked the box to get it lasered off, because it certainly wasn't feminine to have hair above her upper lip. What if Rob had noticed her hair and gotten disgusted and decided that he never wanted to see her again? She clicked the order off and stared at her face in the mirror and tried to figure out whether her hair was visible or not.

The lasering robot was also named Max, and two of his four arms were white and shiny and terminated in jewel-like points. He asked her to put on some clothing, so she put on the sleepshirt, and then he asked her to take her clothing off, so she obliged him, and he handed her a pair of goggles and told her to put them on and lie down. The world was dark orange, and she felt a cold sensation on her bikini line and then a sharp sizzling pain like somebody was trying to electrocute her skin one bit at a time, and the intense pain continued but she didn't want to move or complain because the operation seemed so delicate and she didn't want to distract the robot. The cube became filled with the smell of burning hair, and she clenched her fingernails against the palms of her hands and tried not to breathe through her nose and tried to think of calming things through the sharp searing pain and she wondered if the robot was doing something wrong because the pain and the smell were so intense, but she didn't dare move or say anything at all, and she wanted to scream and the lasers were moving so slowly, and she tried to imagine an Omniscope finding music in the contours of her skin, and she was in such excruciating pain that she thought she might faint and she felt one laser moving up her torso and the burning electrocution was driving her mad and she tried to focus on how soon the robot would be done and how she'd been so smart to avoid getting her legs done also, and she lay there and tried to pretend that she was outside naked in the rain and it was only raindrops falling down and feeling sharp and burning cold against her body, and she breathed and breathed and felt the robot leaning in to do her upper lip, and she felt as though she was getting electroshock treatments as the stinging sizzling pain moved closer to the center of her lip and she felt a sickening burning that was more intense than anything she'd felt so far, and her tears were fogging up the goggles and she needed it to be over now or she would scream and she clenched her jaw and dug her fingernails so deep into her palms and hated herself for having so much hair and breathed and breathed and it was over. The robot asked her for the goggles back and told her that her hairs were dead now and they would fall out during the next several days, and she looked down at her red and swollen skin and felt relieved that it wasn't black and blistered. The robot prompted her to press the golden button and she pushed it weakly and he picked up the piece of paper he'd used to cover the soft place and it dripped with her sweat and he wished her a good day and gave her a perfunctory little wave as he left. She lay down on the soft place and felt dizzy with the after-effects of the pain. Would her hairs really fall out in several days? She'd shaved everything before the robot came, as instructed on the website, and she was terrified that everything would return ingrown again. She tried to picture her hairs falling out as they grew and she imagined a little dying hair slipping resignedly out of a follicle and onto the floor and she thought about how she had finally triumphed over her bikini line and cleared up other areas too, and Rob would find her so beautiful now, and she felt so relaxed and she realized that she must have been tensing up her body the entire time and she felt herself melting into the soft place and her body still stung but it was such a soft stinging that she didn't even mind.

She woke up to a burning odor in the cube and it took her a moment to remember the traumatic treatment that she'd gone through the day before. She looked down and saw that her skin was still red and swollen and it was darker and blistered around her bikini line. She touched all the areas that had gotten done and everything still stung. She took all her pills, including an extra Numitol, and checked to see whether Rob had tried to talk to her and saw that her corporate sponsor had asked her again to please go outside. She hated the feeling of their presence in her cube, and she didn't know why Rob was ignoring her, and she was seized by an urgent need to go outside of the cube as soon as possible. She washed her face, being careful to avoid the area above her lip, and she put in her Mesmereyes and spent a while with green pigments trying to hide the redness on her lip, and she covered her skin and applied her eyes and her mouth and rubbed antifrizz into her hair and put on her Abundacurve and realized that her bikini area hurt so much that she'd never be able to stand her stockings rubbing against them. She had an extremely soft black paint-splattered skirt that wouldn't feel too bad against her skin, so she put it on without anything underneath and tried to put her Golden Lotuses on but they simply couldn't be squeezed onto her bare feet. It was so hot and sticky inside the cube that she needed the slipperiness of the stockings to get the shoes on, and she tried and tried but they simply wouldn't fit. She considered cutting up a pair of stockings and wearing only the feet, but that would look awful, and she remembered a movie she'd seen about a prostitute who'd worn stockings that went up to her thighs, so she cut a pair of stockings off at mid-thigh and tried them on and her feet slipped easily into the shoes but the stockings rolled down because there wasn't anything to hold them up. How could she ever go outside? She tried pulling an intact pair of stockings over her bikini line, but it felt so painful, and she wondered if the skin in that area had been more vulnerable to the laser because the burns from the Koremlu had never faded completely, and she ripped the stockings off and felt so injured and frustrated, but she figured that if she acted quickly she could order herself a pair of thigh stockings and still be outside by the end of the day. She searched the web and found a site called stalkingfeat.com that cheered her up considerably. They claimed to have the largest inventory of stockings in the world, and they had so many outrageous designs that everybody was sure to find something to express their personality. They prided themselves on their instantaneous shipping, because they believed that no stocking craving should go ungratified for long. She browsed the site with delight— so many beautiful options for stockings, so many patterns and designs she'd never even known existed. She considered stockings that were crawling with spiders and stockings that were printed like a jigsaw puzzle and even stockings that were printed to make her legs look like the bones of a skeleton, but she kept returning to the stockings with simple horizontal stripes; there was something timelessly evocative about them that attracted her more than all the others. There were so many different colors to choose from, and she was having some difficulty deciding what colors would be best. If she was going to make such a drastic change to her signature look, it had to be the right one and she had to be committed to it. The first stripe color was obvious: it would have to be black. But what color should it alternate with? She had decided months ago that everything else she wore would be deep red or gold, but red would compete with her shoes, and gold would look like yellow and make her look like a bumblebee. She liked the look of black and white stripes, but white would be extremely unflattering next to her pale skin. Orange looked dramatically alarming, but she didn't want to go off in such a different aesthetic direction. Brown was interesting in a more subtle way, but maybe a little bit too drab. But what about silver? She loved the way that black and silver looked together, and she held her arm up to the silver faucet on her sink and saw that it set off her skin quite nicely. There was something refreshingly futuristic about silver as well, and it would mean that she wasn't really introducing a new color into her look. In fact, all she had to do was expand her palette from just gold into simple metallics and she'd still be consistent. Yes, this would work beautifully. From now on, everything she wore would be either black or red or silver or gold. She was getting rather excited about how she would look in the stockings, and then she noticed that the site sold arm stockings as well. She considered the aesthetic possibilities. The models wearing the arm stockings looked incredibly sexy and exotic in a way that she couldn't quite identify. These would definitely help her to achieve the look of searing hypnotic transcendence and demonic fascination that she was striving for. And they would also help conceal the fact that her lower arms were still a bit unpleasant with stubble and spots from ingrown hairs. She sent the order off and tried to visualize herself striped. Her arms would look so mysterious, and the backs of her hands would be bare, and her fingers would terminate in long red nails that would fascinate any man who looked at them. She looked down at her nails and decided that she needed to get a manicure before she could go outside. Her fingertips were stained from the pomegranates and much of the polish had grown out and the polish that was left looked terribly wrinkled, and she ordered a robot and stared at her nails and suddenly remembered that she still had Rob's scent beneath them, and she inhaled the musky smell and pictured that moment of his mouth round above her and she felt somehow like maybe she shouldn't get a manicure because she'd be destroying all she had of him. What if he never came back? She sat down with her computer and tried to chatter with him, but of course he wasn't there. He hadn't sent her any email either, and she decided to send him a short note, just in case he was away and wasn't chattering lately. She kept the note spare and poetic and sensually graceful, and she massaged each word until it was perfect.

Max seemed to be female this time. She'd been flustered to hear a female voice coming from the robot, and for a second she was extremely worried because she thought it might be Rob joking around, and her skin was in no condition for him to see it, but it just turned out to be another Mumbalore Max with all the icy professionalism she had come to expect. She didn't bother asking the robot to turn off the music, because her mind seemed to be racing in a million directions and the music caught on her thoughts and prevented her from thinking so much. The massage was exactly the same as it had been the last two times she'd had a manicure, the precise orchestration of this move and that move and now the patting and now the wrist glide and now the squeezing of each finger individually, but she still loved the trancelike tingling of being touched so devotedly; a mechanical touch was better than nothing at all.

She sniffed beneath her fingernails when the robot had gone, but all she smelled were chemicals. She was determined to let them dry this time, and she stared at her long red talons until she simply couldn't wait any longer to open the box with her stockings. The silver color was gloriously shimmery—she'd been afraid that it would look too grey—and the arm stockings were so alluring the way they were open at the end, with a hole for her thumb so that the edges angled up her hand like an exotic sort of glove. The leg stockings stayed up nicely on her thighs with a ring of sticky elastic, and her Golden Lotuses slid right on and she dotted a bit of concealer on the tiny red spots on her thighs and applied a bit more lipstick and got the idea to color her lids with silver eyeshadow, just to carry the silver up into her face, and she had another flash of inspiration and dusted a bit of gold shadow onto the center of her bottom lip, and her skin was still stinging a little but she felt sexier than she'd ever felt in her entire life. Her look was really coming together now. She went outside and waved her hands in arabesques over the pomegranate seeds and tried to imagine Rob watching her.

She checked her email even before she pulled off her clothing and her shoes. She had sent Rob such a lovely note, and he must have responded by now. She looked in her inbox and looked in it again and saw nothing. What was he waiting for? She knew that he loved her, so why was he staying away? She got undressed and thought of all the wonderful conversations that they'd had. Rob was so much more exciting than anyone else she'd ever met. They resonated so wonderfully, and she loved his deep cynicism and he was so beautiful and intense and he had to get back to her soon—he just had to. Maybe he'd gone to Takoyaki again and he just wasn't checking his email right now. There had to be an explanation like that. He would email her soon enough, and his note would be intense and loving and poetic and he would tell her all sorts of evocative things about the time that they'd shared inside her cube, and he would tell her that he couldn't wait to see her again soon. She figured that it would take probably a week for her bikini area to be minimally presentable, and she supposed that she could even pluck the little hairs and cover everything with concealer if he wanted to come by even sooner. But this time she'd try to get him to tell her exactly when he planned to visit, because she really didn't want to be taken by surprise. She couldn't guarantee that her makeup would always be perfect if he arrived so unpredictably, and she didn't want to wear the lingerie all the time because it chafed her lasered skin, and she tried to remember how she had looked when he arrived last time and she was so frustrated because she simply could not recall. She must have been extremely sick. She'd have to ask Rob about that too, next time she saw him. She'd ask him if she seemed off or out of it when he was there, because she was having trouble remembering everything that happened, and while she certainly had plenty of wonderful memories of his visit, she also had a vague feeling that she hadn't been entirely present. Just a nasty flu, no doubt, and she'd use that ruse to prompt him for details of what actually happened in the cube.

She looked at footage of herself in her new striped stockings. The effect was stunning. Her look was definitely being honed in an interesting direction. She couldn't even see the concealer that she'd applied to her thighs, and the metallic accents on her face were rather subtle on the screen but still visible as alluring flickers. There was one problem, though—she'd gotten accustomed to the waist-slimming effect of the control top pantyhose, and even though she was definitely losing weight, her waist didn't look quite as narrow as it had before. She couldn't go back to the plain black stockings now that she'd introduced the striped ones, and she loved the sexy effect of the thigh-highs anyhow, and she didn't want to have to obscure her upper thighs again. She tried to envision something that would narrow her waist a bit, and a web search revealed that her problem could be solved with an archaic-looking garment called a waist cincher. It covered the waist and extended down to the hips and up the torso a bit, and it was made of powerful elastic, with a row of little hooks down the back and plastic boning all around to keep it stable. She ordered herself one in the smallest waist size that they sold, and she put on her tightest shirt and tried to imagine how she would look if her waist was even smaller. She worried briefly about the waist cincher irritating her skin, which was still a bit red and sensitive from the laser, but she figured that it wouldn't chafe her skin like the stockings did—it would just hug her waist snugly and stay put. She checked her email again and there was nothing from Rob, but her corporate sponsor seemed very pleased about her new look and said that she was doing excellent work lately, and they encouraged her to spend as much time outside the cube as she could. She felt relieved by the email, and she sent them back a note asking them to please make the room a little cooler. She looked at her makeup in the mirror and tried to figure out what to do. Her lipstick had bled into little lines around her mouth that she didn't even know she had, and her mascara and eyeliner had smudged dark below her eyes, and her silver eyeshadow was creased and her concealer and foundation and powder had become shiny with oil and sweat and coagulated into an odd cracked pattern, like the varnish on an old master. Her makeup would simply not last in this stifling heat and humidity. She nibbled on some crackers while she looked online for products that would help her makeup withstand the heat. It seemed that there was a huge world of products designed for just these sorts of problems, and she felt exhilarated as she ordered product after product that claimed to keep lipstick from bleeding and eyeshadow from creasing and oil and sweat from ruining a carefully constructed complexion. Yes, she would be able to solve all her problems and Rob would write her back and everything would work out perfectly. Meanwhile, she would make herself as beautiful as possible in anticipation of another visit. She felt a bit of sleepiness and a lot of agitation and she took a Lulliban and lay down in the heat and tried to picture how she'd look wearing the waist cincher.

She woke up and immediately opened her computer. He had to have sent her something by now. She opened her inbox and held her breath and there it was! He said that he'd had fun too and he'd been really busy lately and they'd catch up later, and he'd gotten another award for *NanoRob-ots*, so that was really cool. She reread his note again and again and tried to understand what he was saying. He wanted to catch up later, so that was the main thing, and he'd had fun with her, which felt so wonderful to hear. She wondered what was keeping him so busy, and she hated the fact that his note was so short and he didn't say anything about chattering or anything to match the poetic flourishes of her own note. But they'd catch up later, he said. And that would give her time to perfect her makeup and let her bikini area heal. Oh, it felt so good to finally hear back from him. He was still in her life, and it was only a matter of time before he'd come and visit her again. She responded immediately and said that her cellular phone was always on, but if he didn't act quickly she might be whisked away by the Time Travel Trust. She stared at herself in the mirror and determined to figure out how to get him to want her all the time. The more time she spent outside the cube, the more likely it would be that Rob would see her and be captivated by her new look, so she began to get ready to go outside again, starting with her new waist cincher. She hadn't expected it to be so tight—she had to suck in her stomach as hard as she could to get the hooks to close around her. And then she had to figure out how to turn the thing around so that the hooks would be in the back— her skin was still a bit sore from the laser and it burned when she tried to drag the rough fabric and elastic over her skin. She turned it gradually and tried to ignore the soreness and eventually it was on properly and she was amazed by how thin her waist looked all of a sudden. She put on the Abundacurve and a tight low-cut t-shirt and marveled at how incredible she looked. Why hadn't anybody ever told her how easy it was to create such beautiful curves? She smoothed antifrizz serum into her hair and smoothed on a bit more because her hair had been so frizzy lately, and she washed her face and put in her Mesmereyes and unwrapped her new products and began to apply them to her skin. A mattifying lotion to prevent shine and an eye primer to prevent creasing and smudging and a lip sealer to provide a smooth and impervious surface to glide her lipstick onto. And then a few eyebrow hairs to tweeze and the special green concealer for redness and the regular concealer and foundation and powder and eye shadow and eyeliner and mascara and brow gel and the Egyptianate strokes of kohl and a careful cupid's bow of lipliner and a layer of lipstick and a blotting and another layer of lipstick and a dab of gold in the middle of her lip and the soft black skirt and the arm stockings and the leg stockings and the Golden Lotuses and she stood back from the mirror and stared at herself and felt so dangerous and powerful and mysterious and demonically alluring.

She moved her ruby fingernails in wild arabesques over the pomegranate seeds and loved the look of her arm stockings and white hands and long white fingers with perfect glittering talons as the end. Yes, she was very powerful today. She danced and twirled as much as she could manage in her Golden Lotuses, and she sculpted the air with arabesques so fervent that she lost herself inside them. She moved her hands through the heat and the stinging of her lasered skin and the pain of the Golden Lotuses and the tightness of the waist cincher and the last vestiges of fatigue from her strange illness, and she moved her hands wide and intricate and unpredictable and she threw her head back and danced and moved against the sparkling red seeds until her arms began to undulate more slowly and her movements became more languorous and she thought of Rob and wondered if he was looking at her and she stared into one of the cameras with a mesmeric gaze that came from a place that she hadn't even known existed within her.

She checked her email and he hadn't sent her anything yet, so she pulled off her Golden Lotuses and peeled off her sweaty clothing and struggled to release herself from the waist cincher hook by hook until she could breathe again. She began to massage her feet with Princess Salome's Liquid Silk while she watched a replay of her latest spate of arabesques. She was getting rather graceful in her Golden Lotuses, and the waist cincher was much more effective than the control top stockings had ever been. She couldn't quite believe that she was looking at herself dancing on the screen. She looked almost like a stylized cartoon, a black sprite against a glittering red background, a perfect femme fatale in black and silver stripes. There was no way that Rob would be able to ignore her. She read through her comments and felt so loved because people were absolutely smitten with her latest installation. There were so many comments that it took her a long time to read through them, and she amused herself by seeing how quickly she could categorize each comment before she'd barely even read it. There were the Aficionados, who offered detailed interpretations of her works, evoking symbolic possibilities that she'd hardly even considered. There were the Boosters, who weren't sure what her works meant, but they really enjoyed watching her. There were the Gentleman Callers, who wanted to know if she was single, the Provocateurs, who wanted her to take off her clothes, the Zealots, who considered her their hero, and then there were the people who simply couldn't be categorized. The feminist definitely fit into this final group. Yes, the feminist was back again, this time with a critical analysis of her new look. She claimed that vamps and prostitutes and strippers were hardly powerful women to be emulated. The image of the vamp was merely a sadomasochistic construct of the male imagination. Vamps were not deeply threatening and had no real power; by identifying as dangerous and somehow evil, the vamp actually licensed her opponents to commit gynecide. It was no surprise that the classic dominatrix image was not of an actual powerful woman but a Victorian prostitute—if you freed her from her stays and wiped off the makeup and gave her a pair of running shoes and a hundred years of progress, she might just look a little too threatening to be attractive to the common man. And strippers and prostitutes were mainly drug-addicted and desperate women with a history of sexual abuse—the myth of the stripper as an empowered businesswoman was just a sick joke promulgated by guilty men and naïve self-hating women who had been brainwashed by the dehumanizing mindset of capitalism and the destructive imagery of heteronormative femininity. The entire lingerie industry was based on an image of women as delicate and immature and ornamental and frivolous and weak—men wouldn't be caught dead wearing filmy lace garments unless they were fetishists; the psychology behind lingerie was all about maintaining the illusion of female fragility and vulnerability and keeping the existing power structures in place. Power, the feminist opined, had nothing to do with whether a guy wanted to pay you or have sex with you or both. Power was something much deeper than that, something that came from being enlightened enough to see beyond money and sex, and from being fortunate enough to live the life you truly wanted to live and have the world support you. By making your body a commodity, the feminist concluded, you dehumanized yourself in the most basic of ways.

She read the feminist's comments with a scowl on her face. Here she was, trying to create an aesthetically wonderful look, and the feminist had to be a killjoy by bringing up history again. Sure, there were women who were marginalized in the past, but the women of today had choices. If she wanted to dress in sexy lingerie and stylized makeup and a waist cincher, she had every right to do so. Evolutionary psychology even said that only women with a certain waist to hip ratio and facial symmetry got men, so there was nothing wrong with trying to change those around. Not that she was altering her body to attract a mate—she was doing this strictly because she found herself so aesthetically pleasing when she looked this way. She was an artist, after all, and she was allowed to do anything in the name of aesthetics. Anyway, she was a strong and sexy and powerful women, and she wasn't going to let one comment out of so many make her miserable. She looked at herself in the mirror and thought about symmetry. Her makeup was definitely much less smeared today, but her features weren't necessarily as perfect as they should be. She went online and read about beauty and found a template called the Golden Mask, which was a set of coordinates based upon the Golden Ratio. If you overlaid the Golden Mask onto your face, you could figure out where you deviated and make changes accordingly. She went to work printing out an image of her face and printing out a properly scaled Golden Mask on tracing paper, and she compared her face to the ideal and felt rather sad and helpless because her nose was too wide and her lips too thin and her eyes too close-set and her chin was not quite small enough to be attractive. She found the section in *Milady's Book O' Tips* about fixing imperfections, and she went to work at making her face perfect. She graded her eyeliner so that there was more on the outsides of her eyes than on the inside, and she put a bit of white shadow below the outer edges of her eyebrows, and she sculpted her nose and chin with three different shades of concealer until they looked as small as they should, and she put concealer on her lips until they vanished, and she drew on an entirely new set of lips. She may not have been born with perfect features, but at least she had learned to draw them. She looked at herself in the camera and printed out another image and compared it to the ideal, and she was excited to see that she was getting closer. She checked her email and took a Lulliban, congratulating herself on getting so much done that day.

She woke up covered with sweat. Something had to be done. She checked her email and found nothing from Rob, and then sent an urgent note to her corporate sponsor, telling them that she'd asked them to make the room cooler several times now and she'd really appreciate it if they would listen. She checked her email again and again and still she hadn't heard from Rob. Before he visited, it seemed like they were talking almost every day. How could he possibly be so busy? She went to his website and nothing had changed, and she went to Nevi's website and nothing had changed there either, and she even went to Panoptico's website and saw that he seemed to be sleeping. She reassured herself by rereading Rob's latest email and telling herself that he had fun and he'd be in touch soon, and she knew that he loved her and everything would happen soon enough. She only needed to be patient. And meanwhile, it would be the perfect time to work on her signature look. Her hair had been getting frizzier and frizzier lately—no matter how much she tugged at it with the brush and blasted it with the hairdryer and lacquered it with antifrizz serum, it still frizzed up and resembled less and less that smooth black masterpiece that the first Max had created. She did a bit of research and discovered that she could have a robot come to her cube and administer what was called a blowout—her roots were showing a bit, anyway, so she could have a robot do a touch-up to her dye and then make her hair silky and beautiful afterwards.

She searched online for useful products while she waited for the robot to arrive. She found a serum to make her lips plump and some pills to make her breath fresh from the inside and a gel to make her breasts as firm as an eighteen-year-old's. She was already twenty-one and maybe even twenty-two by now, and she looked at her breasts in the mirror and wondered if she was already past her prime. She ordered another product for her pores, because the Famous Tula Water for the Complexion had made her face sting, and she ordered an earwax removal kit, because what if Rob decided to lick inside her ears? She began to read about the pore-cleansing benefits of alpha hydroxy acid versus salicylic acid versus benzoyl peroxide, but the robot arrived before she could figure out which would be best.

She put on the sleepshirt without any complaint and told Max that last time she got her hair dyed, it had splattered all over her face and she didn't have the proper solvent to get it off, and could he please clean her face off thoroughly this time. He said that it was within his duties to be clean and thorough, and she listened to the floaty music as he went to work brushing cold dye onto the roots of her hair. Oh, her hair would look so beautiful when he was done. And all she had to do was call him back in for a blowout every time she washed her hair and she would never have to worry about frizz ever again. She felt his hands against her scalp as he rinsed her hair clean, and she did love that feeling and then he told her to sit up and she watched him as he magically transformed her frizzy hair so that it looked as sleek as a wig. He cleaned her face meticulously with his special solvent, which felt wonderfully cool against her skin, and he asked her to push the golden button and she admired herself as he scrubbed every black spot from the floor of her cube.

She was extremely excited to go outside again and show off her new hair and her Golden Masked face, so she made her way through layers of creams and pigments and she put on her clothing that made her feel so powerful no matter what that feminist said, and she went outside and created arabesques in the air until her feet began to hurt so much that she simply couldn't keep the Golden Lotuses on a moment longer.

Oh, where was Rob and why wouldn't he send her any email? She rubbed her feet and told herself that it would happen any moment now—all she had to do was wait. And the longer he took, the better her bikini line would look when he arrived. She inspected her skin and saw that the redness was almost all gone from everywhere except her bikini line, which was still red and slightly crusty and discolored darker in places. The little hairs were starting to make their way out of her skin—she tugged at a few and they slipped right out. She would heal, and her hair would never grow back again. She saw that there were still some ingrowns on her legs from the waxing, so she got out a pin and picked at her legs until there was nothing lurking inside. She looked under her arms and was amazed to see a red bump bigger than any she'd seen before, and she looked at it closely and squeezed it and yellow pus came out and she picked at the lump with her pin and her skin was torn and bleeding but she wouldn't give up, and suddenly a hair popped out that must have been half an inch long. It was so fascinating to see what happened when things got terribly ingrown. She imagined hairs several feet long coiled around and around inside enormous pus-filled cysts, and she imagined what it would be like to pick out such a hair and see its length emerge from such an unlikely place, and she felt uneasy and turned on the little robot and stroked it and told it that she didn't know where Rob had gone to, and she needed to turn it off now but she'd try so hard to get a charger. She kissed it and turned it off and took a Lulliban and tried not to cry.

He still hadn't sent her any email. And it was definitely getting hotter every day inside her cube. She splashed cold water on her face and washed the makeup off and felt miserable about her complexion. She hadn't picked her skin for a while, because she was wearing makeup all the time these days just in case Rob decided to drop by, but she had noticed from these brief uncovered moments that her skin definitely seemed to be getting worse. She was seized with a terrible urge to squeeze, and she clenched her fists and tried to restrain herself. The last time she had squeezed her pores, her face had exploded into so many pimples that she still hadn't recovered. She figured that there had to be something she could do to fix her skin. She sat down with her computer and checked her email and searched through all the Mumbalore services and decided to get an acne-blasting facial. The website claimed that a facialist would remove every impurity from her skin and treat it with a special ultrasonic device that would penetrate deep beneath her skin to eradicate any lurking blemishes before they even started. She ordered a robotic facialist to come as soon as possible, and she tried to imagine all her blemishes being destroyed deep within her skin.

She drank a bottle of Dr. Tell's Great Remedy for Flesh because she still had cellulite on the backs of her thighs despite her diligent application of cream. She was still sickened by the taste and smell of Dr. Tell's, so she smeared herself with Future Scent when she was finished and inhaled the warm sweet spicy pumpkin pie aroma from the backs of her hands, and she was so enticed by the scent that she licked her hand ever so slightly and was surprised to find that it tasted incredibly bitter. What if Rob had licked her and tasted Future Scent? She realized all of a sudden that she was anointing herself with so many creams to make her skin look and feel and even smell good, but she'd completely forgotten about the taste. She began to taste a bit of every cream that she'd been smearing on herself, and she was horrified to learn that they were all bitter.

Max was female this time, and didn't seem bothered by nudity. She unrolled a sheet of paper and draped it over the soft place and asked her to lie down and then proceeded to go through an elaborate process of washing and steaming and smoothing on some sort of masque and washing and steaming again. Those soft robotic fingers were rather zealous about squeezing every pore, but she figured that the robot was experienced enough and wouldn't make anything worse. After the squeezing she felt another masque and then a smooth metal wand that vibrated pleasantly over her entire face. And then the robot rubbed cool lotion into her face and down onto her neck and shoulders and the robot's hands glided beneath her back and cradled her shoulders so tenderly and began to rub her upper back and she felt the robot's fingers kneading deeper and there were tense and painful places underneath her skin but the robot was exquisitely gentle and penetrating all at once and seemed to know exactly how deep to go and she felt her muscles burning into calm and she was overwhelmed with a warm melting feeling that filled her with sadness and she tried hard not to cry and she was very surprised when Max's voice broke the silence and told her that she looked so sad and asked if she was okay. And she found herself opening up to Max and told her all about Rob and how beautiful he was and how he must've come into her cube but she'd forgotten it all, and now he'd barely even talk to her, and she thought she loved him and that he loved her and she couldn't even smell him underneath her fingernails anymore, and he used to talk to her for hours and now he wouldn't even answer her emails, and she felt so powerless and she didn't know what to do.

The robot nodded sympathetically and told her to close her eyes and massaged the center of her forehead in gentle little circles and told her a story in a singsong voice:

Once upon a time, I was living in a village far from Mumbalore. I helped my parents on their farm and I went to school and I played with fallen blossoms underneath my favorite mango tree. One day my parents told me that it was time for me to marry. They were very poor and they could not afford much of a dowry, but they finally found a man whose family was willing to accept a television set. He was nasty and ill-tempered, but there was nothing I could do. After I moved in with him and his family, he began to beat me every day, and his mother made me do chores all day even though I wanted to keep going to school, and his father would hit me and tell me that my parents had promised him a bigger television set, and if he didn't get one soon, he'd throw acid in my face. I pled with my parents, but they simply could not afford it, and the beatings became so bad that I could hardly stand up to do chores. One night my father-in-law came home with a container of kerosene that he claimed was for a heater he was going to buy, but I had heard of dowry deaths before and I knew I had to flee. I crept out of bed in the middle of the night and I moved more silently than I ever had in all my life and I took all the grocery money from the box on the kitchen counter and I opened the door just wide enough to fit through but not so wide that it would squeak and I closed the door behind me and I ran. I ran and ran with every bit of energy I had, past the next village and the next and my chest and legs were burning but I didn't stop until I came to a train station. I sat on a dark bench and the sun began to rise and I was so terrified that somebody would find me, but the train came and it was crowded and I was safe. I found my way into a women's shelter in Mumbalore, where they helped me find a job and an apartment and they even helped me change my name.

Now I work eighteen hours a day squeezing impurities out of the faces of women who I'll never even meet. I live in a tiny apartment with two roommates who I never see because they work all through the night. On my two days off each month, I spend most of my time buying food and cooking and doing laundry for the days ahead, and when I'm finally finished I'm so tired that all I can do is sit at home and watch television and look at commercials for things that I could never afford to buy and watch movies about lives that I could never live and my apartment is dark and I miss the smell of wild vetiver and mango trees. I miss my family too, but I'd be killed if I went anywhere near home. They'll probably fire me for talking to you like this, but it doesn't matter. I had to tell somebody. I went back to the women's shelter several months ago and they told me that there was nothing else they could do to help me— I was lucky that I had a job and that nobody was beating me every day. I told them that I wake up screaming every night and I can't fall back asleep, and they told me I was normal and they gave me a bottle of pills to take. The pills made me sleepy during the day and I almost lost my job, so I stopped taking them and I've been carrying them around with me everywhere, because if I left them in my apartment my roommates might steal them. I intend to swallow every pill tonight. I'm told it hurts much less than kerosene.

The robot's three camera eyes did not blink. She stared up at the robot and saw herself reflected in the lenses and said that she was so sorry and she wanted to help, and Max laughed and said that she'd been planning this for months now and there was nothing anyone could do. The robot's arms embraced her and she hugged the robot back and she heard Max whispering that they were coming over right now to fire her and the robot's arms went limp and it turned and left the cube so abruptly that she didn't even have a chance to push the golden button.

She got out her collection of concealers that weren't quite right and she found a large pad of thick paper and she emptied every pot and tube and bottle into a huge agglutination on a palette. She stuck her fingers into the warm soft mass and began to paint. She made arabesques so vivid and intense with all ten fingers caressing the paper in a trembling frenzy, and she dipped her fingers into the concealer again and again and ignored the way her nails dragged against the paper and she filled page after page with a rhapsody of shapes and she loved the smeary oily texture of the warm concealer as it fell into forms from her fingertips and she felt herself rocking back and forth as her fingers moved and drips of sweat fell onto the paper below and she got bolder and bolder, making swoops that surprised her and daring herself to go further, and she moved her fingers ecstatically until she'd cleaned the palette of every last bit of concealer. The floor of her cube was now entirely covered with paintings, and she hung them up on the walls and sat down on the soft place and stared at the shapes all around her. She wondered if the concealer would ever dry.

August

The room had become smaller and flies got in. She didn't know where the flies came from, but they must have been attracted by the rotting pomegranate seeds, which were becoming shriveled and brown in the sweltering heat and no longer shimmered. Her corporate sponsor claimed that the room had not become smaller, but she knew otherwise. Somebody had moved the walls closer together while she was asleep. She had been working inside this room for a long time now, and she knew exactly how large it was, and she wasn't going to be fooled by a cruel joke. She didn't know why her corporate sponsor would do such a thing—she had been going outside at regular intervals and keeping her costs relatively low, and her comments and press had been impeccable. Maybe it had something to do with the air conditioner problem. She'd asked her corporate sponsor a million times to adjust the temperature, and they'd either ignored her or claimed that there was no evidence that it was getting warmer in the room. So she'd decided to take matters into her own hands and order herself an air conditioner. A window air conditioner would obviously have been impossible, but she did some research and found that free-standing air conditioners worked just as well as window-mounted ones. And so she ordered one. A small one, even. Not too expensive; after all, she only had a little space to cool. She ordered it from a place that understood the urgency of cooling and claimed that they would deliver instantly. But the air conditioner never arrived. So she ordered another. And another. Still nothing. She spent several days ordering air conditioners from every store that she could possibly find, and none of them arrived. She asked her corporate sponsor what was going on, but they told her they had no idea what she was talking about. So she turned to fans instead. She figured that even though a fan wouldn't provide that icy freon bite, it would at least be better than nothing. So she ordered herself a simple little fan, and it never arrived. She tried again. And again, And still nothing. She even went onto that auction website and bought some beautiful antique fans with blades like flower petals inside metal cages, but none of them ever came. She suspected that her corporate sponsor had something to do with this, but she really had no way of knowing what was happening, so she made it a point of ordering every single cooling device that she could find on the web, which turned out to be a lot of cooling devices. And she had been doing this every single day. She hoped that one of the fans or air conditioners would somehow slip through, but she figured that if it didn't, her corporate sponsor deserved to pay for all of them anyway. When the room became smaller she wasn't even entirely surprised, but it made her a little nervous that her corporate sponsor could do something so dramatic, so she decided to stop ordering air conditioners and see if the room would get larger again. So far it hadn't, but she was still hopeful. The only problem now was that she wasn't ordering cooling devices constantly anymore, which left her mind entirely too free to obsess about why Rob still hadn't gotten back to her. It had been weeks now since he'd last emailed her, and she was feeling extremely agitated about his absence. If he hadn't wanted to talk to her again, he would have simply ignored her email and gone back to his video game. But he took the time to write her back, and said that he'd had fun and was very specific about wanting to talk to her again. He'd even gone so far as to share the news of his most recent award with her, which meant that he still considered her his confidant. Why, then, the dreadful silence? She'd been very good about not trying to chat with him or email him recently, because she didn't want to seem like she was too eager, but she was considering sending him anther e-mail note if she didn't hear back from him soon. Maybe she didn't know the etiquette of chattering, but she did know email etiquette, and she knew that double emailing was something to be done only in the most desperate of circumstances. If you emailed a person twice before giving them a chance to get back to you, you put far too much pressure on the other person and risked them feeling crowded and backing away. The only way to handle double emails gracefully would be to come up with another reason to email the person again, some sort of timely matter that you couldn't possibly have known about when you wrote the first note, and optimally something that suggested that you were doing a favor of some sort for them, couched in terms so casual that the issue of the first unresponded email could be entirely glossed over. She couldn't very well ask him what was taking him so long, but she could ask him something about the little robot, because he was the one who'd wanted to collaborate in the first place. Yes, it would be completely reasonable to email him about the little robot. And so, she decided that it was time to send Rob a second email. She tried very hard to make it sound casual and lighthearted, and ended up saying that she had great news about the little robot—it had actually made it outside the door of the cube, but then its batteries finally died. If he could please send her a charger, she was convinced that they'd have a great collaboration on their hands. She would definitely send the charger right back to him, but she really did need it as soon as possible, because she couldn't exactly feed the robot dead flies. She reread the note a number of times and changed a few words back and forth and briefly considered signing the note *love* but decided against it because she didn't want to seem too forward and so she sent it off ultra-casual with no closing words or signature at all. He'd know who it was from and how she felt about him.

She looked over at the little robot and realized that she'd just done a very bad thing. She had lied to Rob about the little robot being out of batteries, and if he decided to dress up like a robot and bring the charger by in person, he'd find out that the robot still had power left and that she'd lied to him and manipulated him and maybe he'd get angry and never return again. He was so unpredictable and he'd acted so proprietary about the charger—she could imagine him making a point of stopping by, just to try to catch her in a lie. She imagined him showing up suddenly, and she looked at the little robot sitting vulnerable on a dribble of dried yellow paint and she tried to decide what to do. If she turned it on and let it run until the batteries died, she'd be ensuring that Rob wouldn't get angry at her, but she'd be losing her only companion. But if she kept on rationing the batteries in tiny moments, Rob could come by at any time and discover that she'd lied to him, and then she'd lose the only man she ever loved. She put her hand on the little robot and couldn't bring herself to turn it on. Rob might never come by again, and she would have spent the robot's batteries for no good reason whatsoever. But he had to come by again. She could tell by the way he had looked at her through the camera and talked to her so warm and open and expressive that he loved her. He had never been predictable, and he was probably off in Takoyaki creating another breed of Rob-ot and he'd be back so soon and he'd come into her cube and they'd hold each other so tight and she'd never be lonely again. She turned on the little robot and it rubbed against her leg so trusting and innocent, and she stroked it and told it that everything would be okay, and she loved it so so much, and she was going to need to let its batteries run down now, but that was only because she was going to recharge it soon and they'd be able to play together all the time, and she'd tell it stories and she'd stroke it and it could drip yellow paint wherever it wanted and she'd never make it go outside the cube. And she picked it up and felt it vibrating softly in the palm of her hand and she caressed it gently with her other hand and it was so tiny and helpless and she told it that she'd see it soon and she'd take good care of it in the meantime and she wouldn't let any of the Mumbalore robots step on it, and she could feel the vibrations getting weaker and yellow paint pooled into her hand and she was seized with a need to turn it off, just to preserve a moment more, but she resisted and her tears fell onto its metal body and she murmured soothing words to it and told it that she'd see it again so soon and she loved it and it was the sweetest little creature she'd ever known and she meant well, she really did, and she found herself singing the *Swansong Serenade* so quietly, lingering on the long vibratos and holding her face so close to the little robot, and the vibrations grew weaker and she knew it was the end and she couldn't believe what she was doing, and she pictured the little robot sitting terrified under the spotlights with all the other robots flitting blithely around, and her voice broke into sobs and the soft vibrations stopped and she turned the robot off and on and off and on again and she felt an emptiness inside her cube and she had done something so cruel and she wrapped the little metal body in one of the stocking legs that she had cut off and she put it safely in the corner of the soft place where her head rested at night, and she began to use the yellow paint that was still wet in her hand to create a layer of arabesques over one of her concealer paintings and the rhythmic moving soothed her as she cried and tried to reassure herself that Rob would come at any moment now.

It was so hot inside the cube that she'd given up completely on wearing lingerie. Her skin had mostly recovered from the waxing by now, but even though the painful chafing was gone, the last thing she wanted against her body was scratchy lace and tight elastic. If Rob showed up unannounced and found her naked, hopefully he would still find her sexy. He'd already seen her in lingerie anyhow—she didn't exactly remember what she'd been wearing when he arrived, but she'd worn the black lacy stuff continuously before he came, so she couldn't see how he could have missed it unless he'd arrived while she was bathing. And she hadn't even been bathing all that often in those days; it was only recently that she'd been spending so much time soaking in cool water to avoid the stifling heat. Yes, it was swelteringly hot inside the cube, but at least she could be slightly comfortable because she had plenty of cold water and she didn't have to wear any clothing. Outside the cube, however, she felt like she was drowning. She'd committed to this signature look that involved stockings on all her limbs and a waist cincher and tight clothing, and she loved the way it made her look, but every time she stepped outside she felt like she was about to faint from the heat. Plus, she was positive that she sweated a lot more than most people. She'd conquered her makeup problems with the liberal application of mattifiers, but her t-shirts became drenched almost immediately, and she felt horribly embarrassed to have everybody see that she had so little control over her bodily fluids. She hated having to go outside and confront the heat and the rotting pomegranate seeds and flies, but she did need to go outside occasionally because she wanted Rob to be able to see her in her searing splendor. And so, she looked online for a solution to her sweating problem. She had already tried a number of different antiperspirants, but she needed to find something even stronger. She poked around the web and discovered that there was a new procedure being done that actually involved paralyzing the nerves that stimulated sweat glands, which would stop all sweating completely. It involved the injection of a harmless little bacterium called anthrax into the nerve site, and it sounded painless enough except for the pinch of the injection, which she figured she could handle easily—compared to that hair laser, a little shot would feel like nothing. She went to the website where she'd found the lasering robot, and she was thrilled to see that they offered the procedure. She read in detail about what she could expect and was interested to see that this harmless little bacterium was also good for banishing wrinkles from the face. She read through a checklist of all the places where a person might get wrinkles, and she looked in the mirror and scrutinized her face. She certainly didn't have smile lines, but she did have small vertical furrows above the inner edges of her eyebrows, which the website blamed on worrying and scowling. Yes, she'd been a bit anxious lately, but Rob would definitely come soon and there was nothing to worry about, but she figured that in the meantime she would get her worry lines smoothed out with anthrax because the website said that a negative facial expression could cause others to judge you negatively, and she didn't want to be judged negatively by anyone. She checked off the proper boxes and sent the order off and picked out ingrown hairs from her legs with a pin while she waited for the robot to arrive.

Max was clad in a white lab coat with four sleeves for his arms and an official-looking insignia on the breast pocket that said *Dorian Gray Clinic of Mumbalore*. He asked her to put some clothing on and then asked her to take her clothing off so that he could perform the injections. He pulled out a metal shelf and began to fill four syringes from a little vial of fluid, and he told her that she should stay vertical for six hours after the injections, and that she should see results within several days. She was nervous about the shots, but she closed her eyes and clenched her fingernails into her hands and felt a cascade of stinging pinches under her arms and on the center of her forehead and then it was over. The shots had been so tolerable that she told the robot that he'd done a great job, and she asked him how she could go about tipping him because she didn't see a golden button. He told her that he was a medical professional, which meant that he got to wear a white coat but was not supposed to receive tips, and he turned around and left without even a wave.

Six hours vertical. This was not going to be easy. She fell asleep often these days, and sometimes so unexpectedly that she woke up with her Mesmereyes sticking to her eyeballs, and she also spent a lot of time bending over so that she could get a good view of her ingrown hairs. She sat down on the soft place and put her computer on a stack of boxes so that she didn't have to bend to use it, and she set the clock on her computer to play the Westminster Chimes when six hours was complete, and to chime once every ten minutes just to make sure she was awake. She realized that she hadn't checked her email since before the anthrax robot came, and she hoped so much that something from Rob would have fallen into her inbox while she'd been away. She held her breath and looked inside and there was nothing. It just didn't make any sense. He'd been so nice to her before, and he asked her about her past, and he sent her a camera because he wanted to be closer to her, and he even visited her inside her cube and he told her he had fun and they must've had sex and his skin had smelled so warm and musky underneath her fingernails. She reread some of Rob's old emails to her, and she found herself reliving the excitement and indeterminacy and the undercurrent of powerful attraction between them, and she told herself that he would be emailing her back so soon. She stroked the little robot inside the wrapped-up stocking and told it that everything was still okay, and they'd be back together before too long and she knew that it was somehow still alive inside there. And she turned back to her computer and began to read about the anthrax treatment she just received—it was a medical procedure, after all, and she wanted to educate herself about what she could expect. She searched for *anthrax* and *side effects* and it didn't seem like she could expect any serious problems, but then she noticed a page that looked intriguing and saw that it contained thousands of individual complaints. The problems ranged from numbness to constant pain and even death, and it seemed that the safety statistics about anthrax had been highly exaggerated by unscrupulous dermatologists who knew that they could make huge amounts of money for a two-second jab. She twisted a lock of hair around her fingers and read page after page of complaints and got more and more worried. Were her arms going to end up so weak that she'd never be able to paint again? Would she start feeling a burning sensation that would get so bad that it felt like her flesh was being ripped off her bones? Would she die suddenly without anyone even knowing? She began to get furious with herself for doing something so risky, and then a curious thing happened. She tried to load the next page of comments and got a *Page Not Found* message, so she tried to load it again and got the same message and then she tried to go back to the page she was reading before, and she got a *Page Not Found* message instead of the page she'd just read, and she tried to go back and back but nothing could be found. She searched again for *anthrax* and *side effects* and the list of websites did not include the one that she'd been reading for so long. Could a website vanish just like that? She didn't know how the web worked exactly, but she imagined a cavernous building full of women sitting prim in front of switchboards with flashing lights and copper wires, and she supposed that there were certain times when a wire snapped and nobody even noticed. Maybe it was best that she didn't read too much about anthrax anyhow—she was feeling perfectly fine right now, except for the headache and nausea and dizziness and fatigue and lethargy that she'd come to accept as normal these days, and maybe all those people who were complaining about anthrax were just trying to get money for medical malpractice. It was so hard to know what to believe, but she'd be okay and the anthrax would start kicking in and she wouldn't sweat ever again and her face would look perfectly happy and calm no matter how miserable she felt. She checked her email again, and still nothing from Rob. She looked at his website and there was nothing new, so she looked at all the pictures and text that she had read a million times before, and then she looked at Nevi's page and Panoptico's ceiling and got a terrible urge to tweeze some of the tiny hairs that were beginning to grow back around her pubic area, but she resisted and kept her head up and did a search for Rob's name and found nothing that she hadn't seen before—shows and robots and publicity spots and the occasional fawning article. She began to reread his emails again, starting at the beginning, and she realized that he had sent her a link to that doll he won months ago, and she could maybe still follow the link and figure out what else he'd bought. She knew that the auction website only saved transaction pages for several months, but she was hopeful. She clicked on the link and was so excited to see that the page about the doll was still there and she clicked on Rob's username, which was *robotdood4evr*, and she was thrilled to find a long list of completed auctions that he had bid on. It was as though she had just discovered a part of Rob himself, and she clicked hungrily through link after link to see what sorts of things he had bought. She clicked and clicked and was becoming rather disappointed because she'd hoped to be getting secret insights into Rob's character, but nothing that she found was particularly revealing. It was mostly phonographs and robots and broken talking dolls, with the occasional foray into antique computers and vintage cellular phones. She found herself frustrated because the website only let her see information about items from the past six months, but it was obvious from Rob's feedback comments that he had bought thousands of items during the past few decades, and she wished so much that the website had saved a record of what these items were, because she was convinced that the interesting stuff was just out of sight. She read through page after page of his comments, listening to the chimes go by and twirling her hair between her fingers while she looked in vain for something more revealing than *Smooth transaction!* or *Great buyer A+++++++*. She felt especially dejected when she checked the date and realized that Rob's most recent transaction—an early cellular phone with a rotary dial—had happened only yesterday. He was definitely around a computer and checking his email, which meant that he might actually be ignoring her. Or maybe he was still away, and he'd just set up a bot to place his bids for him. That must be it. She read through every single one of Rob's comments and found nothing of remotest interest and checked her email and checked the time and looked at her worry lines in the mirror and decided to work on her signature look. She was very happy with her striped stockings and her hair and makeup and of course her Golden Lotuses, but she'd been getting dressed from the same collection of black skirts and t-shirts for a while now, and she thought that maybe it was time to make her clothing more alluring. A lot of Provocateurs had been telling her to get naked lately, sometimes even mentioning her sweaty shirt and saying that she'd be a lot more comfortable if she took her clothes completely off. She was no harlot, so she wasn't about to go outside naked, but she figured that she could probably make her signature look even sexier if she wore some clothing that showed a bit more skin. She began by looking for a shirt, and decided that a low-cut tank top would be just what she needed. The only problem would be hiding the Abundacurve underneath, so she ordered a number of styles, just to make sure. As for a skirt, she wanted something as short as possible, to make the thigh-high stockings look that much more dramatic. She looked through hundreds of pictures of miniskirts and finally found one that seemed especially striking—it was made of black patent leather and it had a silver zipper going all the way down the back. It would continue the silver motif, and the shiny leather would add an interesting textural counterpoint, and she could even unzip the zipper just a tiny bit if she wanted to look even sexier. The only problem she could see was that the skirt was extremely tight, and she couldn't imagine that a skin-tight leather skirt would be especially comfortable in this extreme heat. She looked at other skirts and vacillated and then ordered the leather skirt anyway—she'd killed her sweat glands off, after all, and if she could stand wearing the Golden Lotuses, she could stand wearing a tight leather skirt in the heat. She checked the clock and it was still a while before the Westminster Chimes, so she checked her email again and sent a letter to the creator of the Golden Lotuses telling him that she loved the shoes, but they were sending shooting pains up her calves whenever she wore them and the balls of her feet hurt so much that she couldn't even stand up in the shoes for very long, and she'd been wearing them as often as she could but she thought that they were getting more uncomfortable than ever, and she would very much appreciate it if there was anything that he could do to help. Perhaps a different size or a different style would be more appropriate, or perhaps there was some sort of adjustment that he could make to the mechanics of the shoe. She reassured him again that she adored the Golden Lotuses, and he definitely had her as a customer for life; it was just that she wanted to be able to wear them for more than a short period of time. She checked the clock and checked her email again and looked at Rob's list of auctions, just to see if he had bought anything during the past few hours, and she looked at her worry lines in the mirror and felt underneath her arms for sweat and almost looked down at her armpit because she felt a bump that she was certain was an ingrown hair, but she remembered just in time that she needed to keep her head completely vertical, so she resumed surfing the web with one hand and twisting her hair with the other, and she set about to look for products that would make her look beautiful but not taste bitter. She ordered herself a vanilla milkshake body lotion and a lemon sugar scrub and a white tea serum for underneath her eyes and a buttercream hair conditioner and a caramel lip gloss and a coconut body wash and a crème bruleé perfume and a chocolate ganache neck gel and an angel food cake hand lotion and a carrot cake foot lotion and a gingerbread cellulite cream and a honey body glosser and a white chocolate macadamia nut facial masque that claimed it would revive even the most blemished of complexions. Which she was rather certain that she had at the moment— she'd tried almost every cream available on the web, and still the pimples came. She knew that it had something to do with her picking and perhaps with the fact that she was wearing makeup nearly all the time these days, but she'd found it impossible to stop picking lately, and she certainly wasn't going to chance going without makeup and having Rob stop by. She doubted that the white chocolate masque would do much good, but at least it was worth a try. She realized all of a sudden that she was famished, and she was really trying to stick to Dr. Tell's and not much else, but she was feeling so nervous about the anthrax injections that she decided to soothe herself with some chocolate hazelnut spread. She grabbed a jar without even looking down, and proceeded to stick her finger in again and again while she used her other hand to check her email. Nothing from Rob, but the Golden Lotus man had already gotten back to her, and he assured her that the Golden Lotuses would grow more comfortable over time, and he told her that they'd recently received an endorsement from the prestigious International Podiatry Guild, which claimed that the Golden Lotuses were actually therapeutic to the feet because they provided a challenge to the wearer and exercised new muscles and tendons and even promoted personal growth because they taught the wearer how to transcend pain. He added that some clients found it useful to remove a toe or two or at least have their toes shortened a bit or have extra collagen injected into the balls of their feet—another wonderful thing about the Golden Lotuses was that they encouraged self-expression through creative foot transformations. Tattoos were really so superficial and passé—the newest way to express your inner self fully was to declare your transcendence of generic bodily configurations and show the world that you were empowered enough to alter yourself into a new superbeing. He'd seen hundreds of women with four and three and even no toes at all, and there was nothing more beautiful than a smooth-ended foot surgically sculpted into the exact shape of a tiny Golden Lotus, no toes at all to encumber the graceful form, just a fragrant tapering hoof of velvety flesh, so delectable to fondle and suckle and play with in any number of ways. She began to wonder if she'd been locked up inside her room for so long that she'd fallen out of touch with the current zeitgeist, and then she began to wonder if she'd ever been in touch with the current zeitgeist, and she tried to imagine how her feet would look without toes and then *mi-do-re-SOL sol-re-mi-DO mi-do-re-SOL sol-RE-mi-DO* and finally the chimes and she lay down on her soft place and kissed the little robot inside the stocking and took a Lulliban and fell asleep to visions of toeless feet.

She woke up to find that Rob had finally written back. Her double emailing technique must have worked, because it hadn't taken him too long to respond to her last note, and he was very apologetic about the fact that he'd been so uncommunicative lately—he'd been really busy working on a project that she'd actually inspired. He said that he was sorry about the little Rob-ot, but they'd made a deal, and anyway he'd moved on to a new project now and maybe he'd revive the nanoRob-ots if he ever had to do a retrospective, but he was totally focused on the next big thing at this point and he couldn't wait for her to see it. She was so excited to be in touch again that she emailed Rob back immediately and told him that she would love to know what his next show was about, and it was completely okay about the little robot and she understood about moving on and whenever he wanted to chatter about his new show or stop by she'd be around. And she sent the note off and then reread it and felt like an idiot for being so enthusiastic and hasty in her response. If he was done with the nanorobots he could easily send her a charger so she could revive the little robot, but she couldn't very well email him back at this point and ask him for a charger because it would be clear that she wasn't really interested in collaboration, and she looked at the little robot wrapped up in the black stocking and told herself that his next generation of robots would likely be even more exciting if she'd inspired it, and he'd definitely send her one and she'd let it run around the room and he'd be so grateful for her grand idea, whatever it was, that he'd kiss her and hold her and tell her that he wanted to live with her forever. Yes, everything would work out wonderfully. She began to apply her makeup and it took a while to get everything perfect because flies kept landing on her face and she'd smudge her makeup every time she brushed them away. She opened up her new skirt and put it on, and it was shorter than any skirt she'd worn before, but it showed an alluring expanse of thigh above the top of her stockings, and she played with the silver zipper and unzipped it just a smidgen, and she tested out every tank top until she found one that covered her Abundacurve completely, and she realized that everybody would be able to see her underarms and she inspected them and got a pin and began to extricate ingrowns, and she loved that feeling when the little hairs popped out and revealed themselves, but her armpits were now all red so she smeared them with her driest concealer and noticed that they actually felt drier than usual already, and she inspected her worry lines and saw that those too were fading, and everything was all of a sudden going so well and she slipped on her Golden Lotuses and wondered if foot surgery would make them more comfortable, and she gazed at herself in the mirror and dotted concealer on some of the red marks on her arms and her thighs and she gazed at herself again and felt overwhelmingly sexy, and Rob had just been busy but he would definitely be looking at her newest look to see if the room would be appropriate for his newest robots, and she opened the door and strode out confidently into a morass of flies and rotting pomegranate seeds.

The flies kept landing on her and interfered with her grace-ful and precise gesticulations, and the smell of rotting fruit was rather pungent when she stood close to the walls, which was difficult not to do because the room had definitely got-ten smaller, but she persevered and told herself that the longer she stayed outside, the more likely it was that Rob would see her. The leather skirt was incredibly tight and much hotter than the cotton ones she'd worn before, but it was certainly more comfortable than the waist cincher and the Golden Lotuses, so she kept going and going until her feet were in too much pain to continue, and she returned into the cube by opening the door just wide enough to get inside but not so wide that flies would swarm in with her.

She pulled off all her clothing and breathed deep and mas-saged her feet and checked her email to see what Rob had to say about the new show that she'd inspired. He hadn't said anything. She checked the auction website to see if it con-tained any clues, and he hadn't bought anything new, and she went to his website and Nevi's website and checked her email again and felt slightly agitated and tried to figure out what to do. She watched herself on the screen for a while, and she was pleased to see that the new skirt and tank top were working beautifully, and the flies actually added an atmosphere of decadent drama to the installation, and even though her feet had been hurting almost the entire time, she was getting quite good at disguising her limping by moving her arms in an arrhythmic way to correspond to each limp; nobody would ever have guessed that she was in any pain at all. She checked her press and comments, and she was thrilled to see that everybody had wonderful things to say about her, and the feminist was nowhere to be seen, and there was a sudden preponderance of young girls among the Zealots who said that they read about her in *Teen Preen* magazine and wanted to look just like her. She felt so powerful and she checked her email again, and still nothing from Rob, and it was so sweltering inside the cube that she climbed into the bathtub and ran the cool water and was surprised to find that the water was only coming out hot. She climbed out of the tub and emailed her corporate sponsor and even ordered several extremely expensive air conditioners just to make a point, and she washed her makeup off and leaned close to the magnifying mirror and began to scrutinize her skin. Such a bounty today! There was a cluster of enormous blackheads on her jawline, so she squeezed them one by one and delighted in how they were dark at the end and almost orange inside and so fat and round. She kept squeezing out more and more blackheads and she lined them up on a tissue as she squeezed them out and she stared at them all and then crushed them with her finger and marveled at the thick dark smudge that her facial oils made. She proceeded on to the whiteheads—the easy little shallow ones that emptied with no trouble at all and the deeper ones that took a harder squeeze but shot out onto the mirror with such a satisfying click and the even deeper ones that she probably shouldn't even have tried to squeeze quite yet because they usually just turned redder and more swollen and oozed a bit of blood and clear pus. If she was lucky, there would be deep reservoirs of white or yellow pus inside that would reveal themselves tomorrow when she squeezed. She'd been developing a ritual of removing her makeup and enjoying the release of all the impurities she had lurking inside and then challenging herself by reapplying her makeup to her newly mottled skin until everything looked as perfect as she could possibly paint it. The only problem was the weeping, but she had even developed a great technique of blotting with tissues and then encrusting the oozing places with powder again and again until the powder had coagulated together and she could then use concealer and special micro-reflective bump disguisers to hide the fact that there was even anything wrong at all. She'd gotten a delightful new product called Poudre Ophelia that was ultra-pale and milled so finely that a thick dusting of it on top of everything made the surface of her face so porcelain perfect that nobody would have ever guessed that only a short time ago she had been staring at a face so mottled and distressed that she looked like a burn victim. And she'd look forward to her next unveiling because she never knew what sorts of ripe delights she would find behind her perfect white façade.

Another Lulliban, another awakening with a terrible throbbing behind her eyes, and another fruitless email check. She had been heartened by Rob's last email, but he still hadn't tried to chatter with her for so long now, and she couldn't help but feel neglected. They had been chatting almost every day before he came into her cube, and she didn't care how busy he was with his new show—he wasn't too busy to be bidding on antique electronics, and it just didn't make any sense that he'd be so busy that he couldn't even come by again, or at least chatter with her for a while and explain his absence. She'd been so friendly to him, and she'd agreed to take his little robot in, and she'd even had sex with him quite willingly, she imagined, and he couldn't even be bothered to tell her what his new show was about. She clicked on his name in the chattering program and waited and waited and then clicked again and again and still nothing. She was determined to get through to him somehow. She took her tweezers and began to pluck her pubic area clean. The laser treatment had caused a lot of her hairs to fall out afterwards, but a number of them seemed to be sprouting back and she was never going to subject herself to such agony again, so she'd taken to tweezing out every hair that she found. There was something relaxing about using the tweezers to pluck the little hairs out one by one; she would pluck quickly and marvel at the fat dark bulb at the end of every hair before moving on to the next. She had made it into a game to try to pluck the hairs as soon as she saw them peek out through the surface of her skin, and sometimes it meant that she'd have to dig a bit with the sharp edge of her tweezers, but she'd always persevere until every hair came out. It took her a long time to tweeze everything out, since she had decided that she had unsightly hair on her upper lip and her nipples and between her breasts and on her stomach and her pubic area and of course her bikini line, but it was such a satisfying feeling to pluck each hair and see the little root and know that she had conquered it. She was still shaving her legs and underarms, but she was considering beginning to tweeze those areas as well, because she did love the process of hunting for hairs, and even though it definitely caused more ingrowns than shaving, she had begun to relish finding little red bumps with hairs inside and picking them out. It was so exiting to pick and pick and finally free the hair, and she always put concealer on her skin after she picked, so if Rob came by he wouldn't even know that anything was awry. She always fell into a wonderful trance when she picked—she relaxed and got so focused on the process that her mind wasn't even able to concentrate on anything else. She scrutinized her skin for every last ingrown hair and applied concealer to the reddest areas and checked her email again and he still hadn't sent her anything at all. She tried to chatter and that didn't work either so she took a Lulliban and fell asleep and woke and checked her email again and still nothing. She saw that more hairs were sprouting again and she felt tired already but she couldn't go to sleep again because she'd just woken up. She looked around the cube and realized that she'd completely forgotten about the boxes with her new delicious products, so she opened them and sniffed them and tasted them one by one and found that all of them smelled absolutely scrumptious but tasted as bitter as the Future Scent. The products left her craving chocolate, so she made her way through an entire jar of chocolate hazelnut spread and felt sick and miserable when she had finished. Her new black skirt was already extremely tight, and if she gained even a tiny bit of weight it wouldn't fit and there would be hideous bulges at the top where it cut into her skin, and she had no place to hide the bulges because the tank top was skin-tight as well, and Rob would think that she was fat and everything would be ruined. She suddenly remembered a weight-loss tip that she had read on the web, so she leaned over the toilet and stuck her finger down her throat and tried to vomit. They made it sound so easy on the web, but she practically had to tug at her glottis to get anything to come up. She finally spat up a bit of sour chocolate several times and then stopped because her throat was hurting too much to continue. She washed her hands and saw that she had cried her eyemakeup into smudges, so she washed her face and was all set to start squeezing when she noticed tiny red spots all around her eyes and her forehead and her upper cheeks. Where had those come from? They weren't raised and they didn't look like a rash, and she definitely hadn't seen anything like them before. Her entire face was actually a bit red in a general way, especially around her eyes, and she thought that maybe the vomiting had something to do with it. She hadn't thrown up since she was very young, and she never even noticed her skin in those days, so she didn't really know what the effects of vomiting were. She went online and discovered that the red dots were broken capillaries that would fade in several days. She felt extremely reassured, because she could cover anything with her arsenal of products, but she was also feeling even sicker and extremely agitated, and she ate several crackers to calm her stomach and she looked over at the little robot all wrapped up in black and she checked her email and Rob's website and that auction site and he had bought another broken record player and she didn't know what to do. She was feeling so tired and she didn't feel like going outside because the seeds were rotting and there were too many flies, but she didn't feel like taking the seeds down because the eyes would be behind them, and her head felt like it was filled with warm glue, and the room had gotten smaller and she didn't have any more cold water and she hadn't changed the installation in so long now and people would start leaving nasty comments and telling her that she was just a sham, and her stomach was hurting terribly and her head was throbbing and she held the little robot all wrapped up and told it that she didn't even know if she'd ever get a charger and she was so sorry for letting its batteries run out and she looked at all the little yellow traces of paint on the floor and she felt so lonely and she was painfully tired but she didn't know why and she saw that hairs were sprouting everywhere but she didn't even feel like tweezing them out and she looked at her concealer paintings and realized that something had to change. She went online and began to search for an antidepressant that would make her happy again. Maybe her problem was that she had a chemical imbalance of some sort, and if she could find the right pill it would cheer her up. She had never taken antidepressants before—she had always hidden them inside her napkin when her teachers handed them out to everybody at lunch because she was worried that they'd make her into a different person. But now she didn't even know quite who she was anymore, so she figured that the pills couldn't make things any worse. She searched through all the different antidepressants on drugs-r-us.com, and it was very difficult to decide which one she wanted, so she looked at all of them and eventually settled on Happyam because the pill was dark scarlet with golden lettering.

She woke up and noticed that she wasn't lying in a puddle of sweat. It was still ghastly hot inside the cube, but the anthrax must have finally started to take effect. She looked at her worry lines and those too were gone. She tried to make a miserable expression, but she couldn't do it, no matter how hard she tried. She opened the package with the Happyam inside and marveled at the beautiful little pills and she swallowed one down with all her other pills and tried to look miserable again but she still couldn't do it and she felt a flicker of optimism that things would be okay. She began to start cleaning up her cube, which was filled with empty boxes and jars and wrappers and piles of tissues spotted with dried blood and pus, and she imagined that she was wearing a little apron and high heels and she was straightening up her sleek modern house with all the latest electrical appliances, and Daddy would be home from work any day now and she'd baked him such a yummy-smelling pumpkin pie, and Junior had tracked yellow paint all over the floor again, but she didn't need to clean that up because this was a modern home and Junior had created modern art, and Daddy would have a lovely present for Junior when he got home from work, just the thing to give Junior lots of pep, and Daddy would be so glad to see Mommy and they would kiss each other and maybe soon there would be another little tyke for Junior to scamper around with, and everything would turn out so lovely in their tiny little house, and she spun herself giddy with her fantasy and threw piles of detritus down the trap door. She folded up her clothes and put them neatly on a shelf and lined up all her products in front of the mirror as she applied a beautiful new face of makeup without squeezing first, and she even put all the half-opened jars of chocolate spread into the refrigerator because they seemed to be attracting a lot of flies. She rarely put anything into the little refrigerator, but she noticed an ice cube tray and a tiny freezer compartment, so she filled the tray with hot water and imagined filling the bathtub with ice and relaxing inside.

She sat down on the soft place with her computer and surveyed the cube. It definitely looked much neater now—she had let it get entirely too messy and she would never let it get this bad ever again. She checked her email, thinking that maybe something had shifted in the universe and things would start going well again, but there was still no word from Rob. She spent a few moments watching Panoptico eating dinner with his girlfriend and having a conversation about some jerk with a metal detector and two guns who almost wouldn't let him into a building where he was supposed to give a lecture, and Panoptico's girlfriend told him he was very brave and she leaned over to kiss him and the screen went black and a message appeared that said *Private* and she was glad to see that even Panoptico still respected certain boundaries. She went over to the auction website and looked to see whether *robotdood4evr* had bought anything else, and there was a new item and she clicked on it and she was horrified to see that Rob had just bought a ring. It was extremely inexpensive—only a fraction of what he routinely paid for old phonographs—but it was gold-plated and had a big fake diamond in the middle and it looked like the kind of thing that people used as an engagement ring. She felt furious and confused and didn't know what to think, and she tried to calm herself down by telling herself that it was probably just for a project that Rob was working on, maybe something to do with his latest robots, and she knew how Rob felt about marriage and about Nevi, and somebody as materialistic as Nevi would never agree to wear a fake diamond anyway, and she told herself not to worry and went over to Nevi's website, just to see if she could get any clues, and the page came up with big pink letters that screamed *Im getting married!!!!* and all the text about food and art had vanished and been replaced by a self-congratulatory ramble about how she was going to be a princess and she would wear the prettiest dress in the world and she was going to be the center of attention and it would be the best day of her life and she was going to buy the most expensive dress and everybody would look at her and she would have such a fancy party and her sisters and her friends would all be jealous because she would look so beautiful and she was going shopping right now for a dress because her wedding was in less than a month so nobody better expect any cupcakes from her anytime soon!

This had to be a joke. But Nevi had no sense of irony that she'd been able to discern, so she had no idea what to think. Rob had told her repeatedly that he couldn't stand her. And he'd talked so scathingly about her sister's wedding. This simply had to be a joke. Or else they'd broken up already and Nevi had found somebody else to marry her, which was entirely possible, since there wasn't any mention of Rob in Nevi's breathless paragraph. But what about the ring, then? Rob had just bought it a few minutes ago, so there would be no way he could've given it to her already, and somebody like Nevi would probably not consider herself engaged unless she had a ring on her finger, and none of this made any sense and she tried to click on Rob's name and chatter with him because she was just so furious, but of course he wasn't there, and she looked online for information about his phone number or address and everything was unlisted. She had to reach him. This was absolutely wrong and she had to reach him fast. She was sure that there was an innocent explanation for all this, but she wouldn't be able to rest until he talked to her. She went to one of those websites where you pay for information about a person, and she paid for the most information possible but still his number was unlisted. She tried to chatter again and again and her hands were shaking and how could he do this to her, after everything they'd talked about and done together, and she felt so sick and angry and she screamed as loudly as she could and was very glad that the cube didn't have any microphones, and she tried and tried to chatter and finally got an idea of another way to reach him. There was an online game that he talked about a lot, and she suspected that he spent most of his time in there. But how would she be able to find him? Everybody who played that game pretended to be somebody else. She went to the website for the game and she paid to start playing and she found herself on a screen that let her choose what sort of character she could be. She had no idea how she was going to find Rob or even approach him if she found him, but she figured that she should try to look as unrecognizable and innocuous as possible, so she chose an avatar of a fat little man dressed in a toga, and she outfitted herself with a slingshot and a bag of gumdrops and went off to look for Rob. She found herself in an open green field with mountains in the distance, and she saw that there was a way that you could search to see if a particular character was online. She tried Rob's full name, and that didn't work, and she tried every combination of his first and last names that she could think of, and still nothing. But then she got the idea of trying *robotdood4evr* and she found him! They were finally inside the same world! According to the game, his character was a 253rd level Magnum Potentate, and the game even gave her a map to go and find him. She walked through the field and into a forest and all of a sudden an enormous cyclops lunged out at her and she watched her character get pummeled and her hit points were going down, and the cyclops ate her slingshot so she started throwing gumdrops at it and a gumdrop lodged inside its eye and she ran away as quickly as she could. This was not going to be easy. She tried going around the forest, but she soon came to a river that she needed to cross, and every time she tried jumping into it, the game told her that she didn't have a bathing suit. She tried and tried to cross the river, and the game just wouldn't let her, and she had to get to Rob somehow but her character was just a fat little man with a toga and a mostly empty bag of gumdrops, and Rob's character was a Magnum Potentate with a list of possessions so long that she probably wouldn't even be able to get close to him. But she knew exactly what she could do to find him—she had read an article a while ago that described how somebody paid an insane amount of actual money for a private island in one of these online games, and she figured that people must put characters up for sale on the auction site all the time. She went to the site and did a search and was thrilled to see a long list of powerful but discarded characters. She found one that looked especially advanced—the man who was selling it said that he'd played the game so much that his wife and kids had abandoned him, and he'd lost his job, and his landlord was going to evict him if he couldn't pay his rent, and he'd put years of his life into this character and it was all he had left, but he had to sell it because otherwise he'd be out on the street and somebody might steal his computer and then he wouldn't be able to play games anymore. She paid the man a huge sum of money for the character, and she got his username and password and stepped into the game as a 389th level Grand Sovereign Orc of All Eternity. Her avatar was tall and extremely muscular, with orange skin and an enormous codpiece that jutted out proudly, and she strode confidently through the land until she found the castle that Rob seemed to be residing in. She bribed the guard to let her enter, and she walked through huge rooms lined with mirrors until she came to another door, where a guard told her that she didn't have permission to enter His Majesty's harem because she was a man. She told the guard that she was a friend of His Majesty, but he wouldn't let her enter, and she offered him money and possessions but he was still quite firm. She told the guard that she really needed to talk to His Majesty and what could she do, and the guard told her that His Majesty wasn't actually inside the harem—he was inside his game room off to the right trying to win enough money to advance to the next level. She asked the guard if she could enter the game room, and the guard said he didn't see why not, since she was obviously a person of much prestige and dignity, and so she walked to the right and opened the door and saw a large metallic man feeding gold coins into a slot machine. She greeted Rob's avatar and he greeted her and asked her what brought her to his chambers, and she said that she was on her way to a very important meeting along the banks of the Styx and she figured she'd stop by, and Rob's avatar went completely silent and motionless, and she said that the slot machines could wait, and she really needed to talk to him about Nevi, and could he please respond to a chattering request, and he nodded and she finally saw a movement inside her chattering window and she told him that she'd been looking on Nevi's website because she wanted to find a recipe for cupcakes, and she was very surprised to see that Nevi seemed to be highly excited about a canned pageant thought up by barbarians and ad men, and she would appreciate it if he could please tell her what was going on. And he confessed that yes, they were getting married, and he urged her not to get mad—he would explain everything. She sat there numb while he told her that Nevi had been nagging him about this for years now, and he had always ignored her, but one day she started yelling and telling him that all her sisters and her friends were married already, and she'd dreamed of being a princess all her life, and every girl had the right to a wedding, and if he wouldn't marry her then she'd leave him and find another man who would. He thought about breaking up with her, but the more he thought about it the more he realized that it would have a major impact on his life if he wasn't living with her anymore. He said that robot technology had only come so far, and Nevi cooked and cleaned and did his laundry and all the shopping and bill-paying and telephone calls and grungy stuff, and she even managed his shows, which gave him so much extra time to think and work. He told her that we can't all be so lucky as to have grants that'll take care of everything, and his goal was to become rich and famous so he could afford all the latest in transhuman developments—a full-body cryonic suspension was so expensive, and they hadn't developed the technology for a total mind upload yet, but he wanted to be the first in line when it was ready. He really wanted to break up with Nevi because he couldn't stand her, but the more he thought about the situation the more he realized that that the marriage thing would work out pretty well for both of them—he would get a servant to take care of all the crap in his life, and she'd get to bask in his glories and lose herself in premodern myths. She'd been so brainwashed all her life that she really didn't want anything more. So he agreed to buy her a ring and have a wedding, but only if the wedding could be a publicity stunt involving lots of robots. Nevi was so stupid that she wouldn't even be able to tell that the ring was a cheap fake, and she had agreed to having as many robots as he wanted at the wedding as long as she got to have hundreds of pictures taken of her inside a big white dress. Like a schoolgirl in Takoyaki, yes, but at least it would make for interesting publicity. Nevi wanted babies of course, but he'd had a secret vasectomy years before, so he wouldn't have to worry about any babies fucking up his life. He told her that he had only agreed to marry Nevi so he could keep on living his life the way he wanted, and then he startled her by telling her that he would come to see her again after all the wedding crap and his next opening were over, because he'd really had fun talking to her and visiting her, and he urged her not to judge him for getting married—he still thought the whole idea was ridiculous, but he was just being a pragmatist and it was really the best thing for him to do.

She had listened numb throughout his entire explanation, and she still didn't know what she was feeling, but she found herself asking him whether he would tell Nevi about what had happened between them. He told her that he could never tell Nevi about anything like that—she was very jealous and closed-minded and would absolutely destroy his life if she found out. She asked him about honesty, and he said that honesty was irrelevant with Nevi, since she already had nothing inside her head but cultural lies. She found herself telling him that he shouldn't get married now because it was only a few months until she got out of the room and then they could be together without subterfuge so soon. And he reassured her that he'd love to see her again before too long, and he'd definitely want to see her frequently in the future, but they were going to have to stop talking like this—Nevi often snuck up behind him just to try to catch him at something devious at the computer, and it was a wonder that she hadn't suspected something about them already, and it was just too risky to be chattering together all the time. But they could still communicate by email, and he'd definitely come and visit her again. She pleaded with him and asked him if he could please reconsider this marriage thing, since it would make it really difficult for them to spend any significant time together if he was living with Nevi, and she'd never met any-one like him before, and she really wanted to see what would happen between them when she was done inside the cube. He told her that it would never work as more than an inti-mate friendship, that if they lived together she'd be off in a trance chasing down hallucinatory visions in the air, and he'd be chasing little robots around and nobody would do the laundry or pay the bills or take the garbage out. They'd drown in dust and neither the Cryonics Corporation nor the Time Travel Trust would ever discover their bodies. She tried to think of how to respond, but he had already vanished from the screen.

She pulled on her clothing so quickly that she burned her skin turning the waist cincher around, and she ran outside and began to rip every pomegranate seed down. She scraped the walls with her nails until they all broke off and then she scraped the walls some more with her jagged nail stumps and bare fingertips, and she scraped and scraped and tore at the seeds with a frenzy so intense that her fingers bled and flies were swarming everywhere around her but she didn't even care, and she scraped the rotting seeds away until the eyes were exposed again behind a lumpy mottled surface of glue and bits of seed pulp that she couldn't scrape off no matter how much she tried, and she didn't even notice the heat or the stench or the pain of the Golden Lotuses and she screamed as she scraped the walls and clawed at them and used every bit of shredded fingernail she still had left to scrape the seed flesh from the walls, and she scraped every-where she could and flies were getting in her nose and in her eyes and even going up her skirt, but she could only focus on scraping and scraping the walls until she had destroyed every single pomegranate seed. She gathered the brown mush into a mound and the eyes were staring at her and she found a plastic bag inside her cube and scooped everything inside and screamed at the eyes and at the flies and gave a look of utter fury to the cameras and slammed the door behind her with a crash so loud that people would have been rather startled if they'd actually been able to hear her.

She threw the seeds down the trap door and washed her hands and looked with horror at her fingers. She used to have perfect ruby talons and now she had bloody jagged nothings. She would have to get a manicure with artificial nails immediately. She ordered a robot and paid extra for super rush service and lay down on her soft place and clenched her entire body and screamed until the robot arrived. She hadn't even thought to take off her clothing, so the robot was extra polite, and he obliged her when she asked if he could turn up the music to the loudest volume he could possibly produce. The music screamed inside her head as the robot took a set of perfect ruby talons out of his body and glued them to her fingertips, and the music stopped only long enough for the robot to tell her that the glue was so powerful that she could go right back to work without waiting. She pushed the golden button and stared at the nails that had been restored to perfection so easily, and she washed off her makeup which was miraculously unsmeared during this whole ordeal, although her lipstick had worn off a bit in the middle. She looked at all the blemishes that needed to explode out of her face and she leaned into the magnifying mirror to start squeezing and she realized that the artificial nails were so thick that they didn't allow her to squeeze properly. She tried and tried and the nails were so clumsy that they kept on slipping, and she couldn't get a good grip, and she grabbed a pin and experimented by sticking it into a pimple, and now she was able to pop it just by pinching it between her fingers, and she had discovered a new tool for her face, so she went over every blemish and stuck the pin inside and sometimes stuck it in even deeper and moved it around a bit, and it was amazing how deep she could stick it into her face without feeling any pain, and she got the blackheads out by using the pin to slice away the skin all around them until she unearthed them, and blood was running down her face and onto her Abundacurve cleavage but she kept on picking and tearing at her skin with the pin until she knew that she had gotten everything out. The flies would have nothing to feed on now. She rubbed an ice cube on her face and felt the numbing chill.

September

THE ROOM SMELLED CRISP AND PINS STUCK THROUGH THE WALLS. They were pointing in at her quite sharp and menacing, and she suspected that her corporate sponsor had something to do with their appearance, since they seemed to be coming from outside the room and she definitely had no recollection of being outside. But the pins didn't matter, because the room had finally cooled off a bit. It had happened gradually at first—one day cooler and the next sweltering again—but something had finally shifted and she wasn't sure how or why, but she certainly wasn't going to question it. There was a sharp quality to the air that roused her from her lethargy, or perhaps it was the Happyam finally taking effect, but she was feeling an odd exhilaration lately, a sense that she had control over her life again. She had discovered from Rob's website that his next opening wouldn't be until October, which gave her lots of time to devote herself to the creation of a whole new level of beauty. She had been furious at Rob when he'd first told her about the wedding, but the more she thought about it the more she realized that marriages were hardly permanent these days, and she was rather confident that she'd be able to lure him away from Nevi before long. She wasn't too sure about the cooking and cleaning stuff, because nobody had ever taught her how to cook, and she never seemed to be able to keep things clean for very long, but she figured that if she could be transcendentally alluring he'd have no choice but to want to be with her forever. And so, she was determined to perfect herself by October. The only problem was that she couldn't stop picking her face and body, and it simply wouldn't do for him to see her all covered with cuts and scabs and swollen places. There wasn't any need to wear makeup inside the cube anymore, because Rob would not be visiting again for quite a while, so her face was always visible, always reflected to infinity in the many mirrors that surrounded her. She tried to convince herself not to pick, because it often made things worse, but she simply couldn't stop herself from removing things that didn't belong inside her skin. She had gotten very skilled with a pin, and she was often able to find the exact center of a blemish and push the needle in until she heard a pop, and everything would shoot out so cleanly from the little hole she'd made and she'd scrape the white bits from the mirror and roll them between her fingers and congratulate herself for removing something that had been so deep inside her skin. Her pimples seldom healed after the first puncturing and she had to go after them again and again and nothing seemed to heal properly and she was getting dark red scars all over her white skin, but at the moment of picking, it seemed to make perfect sense that it was the only thing to do. She had thought that wearing makeup less often would solve her problem because it would allow her pores to breathe, but she still kept getting pimples and clogged pores. She had tried every cream and treatment available on the web, but nothing so far had worked. Every time it looked like her skin was getting better, she'd see a whole new crop of pimples poking up and she'd feel like she wanted to kill herself. And then there was her body. Now that she was removing the hair from so many places on her body, she was getting ingrowns constantly and she had to make sure that she removed them or else they'd turn into huge red inflammations. She had decided against tweezing her legs and underarms because she already had enough hairs to worry about, but every day when she surveyed herself she saw more hairs growing back and more ingrowns to dig out, and the laser treatment hadn't done a bit of good. Rob would be horrified if he could see her without any makeup—her entire face and body were covered with red marks in various stages of healing. Whenever she looked at herself in the mirror, which was pretty much always, she wanted to die. If she expected Rob to find her transcendentally alluring when he visited her after his opening, she had to do something now to fix her problems. She had gotten to enjoy the ritual of plucking out her hairs every day, but she had read about a technique called electrolysis that killed the hair follicles one by one by electrocuting them. From what she'd read on the web, it seemed like it might actually be permanent, although the lasers had claimed that they'd be permanent also, and the Koremlu certainly hadn't said anything about blistering her skin. She was afraid of the pain of electrolysis, but she knew that she couldn't keep tweezing out her hairs every day and picking out ingrowns, and one morning she woke up and looked at all the hairs sprouting out and the new inflammations from ingrowns and she decided that electrolysis couldn't be more painful than having to spend all her time fighting against her hair. She went to the website where the laser robot and the anthrax robot had come from, and she found an electrolysis robot and selected all the body parts she wanted bare and sent the order off and felt exhilarated by the prospect of not having to worry about her hair ever again. She felt so optimistic that she began to search for something that might be able to help her skin. She finally found something that she hadn't tried before—a pill called Skindeep that claimed it would dry up all her facial oils from underneath by shutting down her oil glands completely. It was a very powerful drug with side effects ranging from muscle cramps to cognitive impairments to psychosis, and it caused such terrifying birth defects that you weren't even allowed to take it unless you were also taking a pill like Lunacede, but she figured that it didn't matter what it did to her as long as it cleared up her skin. She was already suffering from so many side effects that she didn't see how she could feel much worse. She ordered the Skindeep and stared at herself and tried to imagine all her oil glands screaming and choking as the Skindeep particles washed over them and killed them off forever.

Max was polite and very patient. She lay naked on the soft place while he inserted a needle into follicle after follicle and pulsed a current through the needle and then moved on to kill the next. She had requested that the music be rather loud so that she wouldn't be haunted by her thoughts, but she still found herself thinking about how it must be the most tedious job in the world to have to kill off people's hairs one at a time, and then she wondered if electrologists actually got a thrill from seeing every hair come out, and then she remembered that robot who told her a story and she got very sad and tried to focus on the music and not think about anything at all. The pain wasn't too bad—the electric current felt like a sharp sting, but it only lasted for a second and then she got a break while the robot slid the dead hair out with tweezers and inserted the needle into the next pore. He went systematically over every pore on her upper lip and torso, and he actually offered her a bit of advice when he got to her bikini line—he told her that she shouldn't touch the ingrown hairs if she got any more, and he would return every day and kill whatever hairs were sprouting out and remove all of her ingrown hairs without causing scarring. She thanked him and felt so cared for and asked him what it was like to live in Mumbalore and do this kind of work, and he told her that it was not within his duties to provide her with that sort of information, but he said it in such a resigned and kindly way that she could hear an actual person behind the script, which made everything okay. She lay there and thought about the Skindeep that would arrive any moment now and she was so excited that she was finally going to have smooth skin without any ingrowns, and she knew that she could get herself beautiful by October and Rob would come by again and he'd fall so deeply in love with her that he would gladly eat chocolate hazelnut spread with his fingers every day. She thought about that online world where she'd found Rob in a castle, and how she'd gone there for days afterwards but he seemed to have vanished and then she found his character up for sale on the auction site. He'd gotten a lot of money for it, which seemed to license him to buy more old phonographs and broken talking dolls than usual, and sometimes she went into the game with her orange skin and bulging codpiece and visited Rob's castle, which had gotten overrun by robotic rats, and she wandered around the vast virtual world and tried to figure out which of the hundreds of thousands of characters he had become. She never found him, at least as far as she could tell, but she did wonder if he had sold his character in order to avoid her. She didn't think she had done anything that wrong by looking for Rob inside the game, and she'd even sent him a warm email after she calmed down from ripping all those pomegranate seeds off the walls. She told him that she completely understood about his pragmatism, and she looked forward to many intimacies in the future, and in the next future and the next. She purposely kept the email short and easy to respond to, and all she had wanted was a tiny confirmation back, some sign that he actually cared about her, but he hadn't sent her anything at all. She didn't see why he couldn't send her just one little note, and she certainly didn't understand why he'd decided to abandon the castle so suddenly, but there was no way that she could email him again right now or ask him why he'd vanished from the game, so she tried not to think about all that and she focused instead on perfecting herself for October. He had told her explicitly that he wanted to see her again, and he wouldn't have told her such a thing if he didn't want to see her, so she figured that he'd ignored her email because that's just how he was with email, and he'd left the castle because he didn't want Nevi to look over his shoulder and notice him engaged in flirtatious banter with a large orange man. She felt the bursts of painful current working slowly over her pubic area and she tried to imagine how beautifully smooth she would look when the electrolysis was all complete. She tried to remember Rob's visit, but all she could summon from her memory was that flicker of him above her with his mouth so round, and the image was so powerful but so brief and she was overcome by sadness and tried to focus on the music and push the thoughts out of her head. How could he possibly spend his life with somebody as dreadful as Nevi? She was seized with the urge to email Nevi and tell her what had happened with Rob and let her know all the horrible things that he had said about her, and she tried to imagine what Nevi's reaction would be as she read the note, but she began to feel a bit of pity for Nevi just then and she figured that she didn't need to resort to such techniques—Rob would leave Nevi soon enough and then they would always be together. The electrolysis needle finally stopped, and the robot told her that he would return tomorrow and every day thereafter until she had no more hairs at all, and she pushed the golden button and he went away with a wave. She looked at the areas he'd treated, and she had small pink marks around the follicles, but nothing terrible at all. She supposed that it would be rather expensive to have daily treatments like this, but the grant people could hardly complain. After all, it was important for her to feel confident about herself so she could continue to make art.

She opened the package of Skindeep and was amused to see that they came packaged in a blister pack and every foil blister was covered by a tiny cardboard tab printed with a silhouette of a pregnant woman who had been crossed out with an ominous-looking X. She wondered what the Skindeep would do to a fetus, and she imagined an entire generation of children born with grotesque deformities and severe retardation and flawless skin. She peeled off a tab and popped a pill out of its blister with a satisfying click and swallowed the pill as she promised herself that she would never pick her face again. She checked her email and Rob's website and the auction site and Nevi's website, and the only new thing that she found was a link on Nevi's site to a wedding registry. She got furious as she looked at the items that Nevi had requested—forks and spoons and knives made out of silver in an elaborate swirling pattern, bone china plates with pink flowers on them and gold around the edges, sets of lead crystal glasses in different shapes for different kinds of alcohol, silk damask tablecloths and napkins, and a huge assortment of vases and candlesticks and serving plates and special spoons, all made out of silver or gold or bone china or lead crystal. Any pity that she might have felt before was replaced by fury and contempt as she looked at page after page of overpriced pretentious tableware and wondered what Rob thought about all this. What could possibly be the use of all these things? Not only were they absurdly expensive and unnecessary, but they were wholly unimaginative—if she had a gift registry that could contain anything, the last thing she'd do would be to fill it with clichéd items that were trying to imitate the tables of long-dead royalty. No, she'd find herself items of rare and obscure fascination: tortoise-shells inlayed with bloodstones and yellowed toenail clippings, succulent golden peaches imported from the Karakoram Mountains, lily pads so large that she could lie on them without sinking, sandbottles with mysteries sealed inside. Oh, she'd search the world and her imagination for all manner of delights, except for the fact that nobody was offering to buy her any gifts right now. Nobody except her corporate sponsor, and that didn't exactly count because she'd begun to suspect that she was giving them quite a boon in advertising compared to the paltry sums that she spent on Mumbalore robots and chocolate hazelnut spread and even errant air conditioners. Well, she was certainly entitled to a bit of fantasy in her life, and it was time that she treated herself to something that wasn't purely functional. She went onto the auction website and began to explore. Nothing quite caught her eye until she stumbled upon a Victorian choker that would encircle her neck with clusters of Bohemian garnets—round and deep red and densely crowded so that the patinated silver settings were barely visible between the shimmering clusters of red. She was mesmerized by the necklace and bid a price so high that she won the auction immediately. She felt strange about buying something so expensive and yet so frivolous, but she told herself that she was an independent woman and she could buy herself jewelry without guilt. She was so entranced by the fiery clusters of round garnets that she began to search for more pieces of jewelry in that style, and before too long she had acquired an entire collection of earrings and bracelets and rings, all encrusted with Bohemian garnets. She tried to picture the shimmering red stones against her pale skin, and she imagined that they would resonate so beautifully with the Golden Lotuses and of course with her nails and lips, and yes, the jewelry had been rather expensive, but the ads blinking at her as she bought the jewelry told her that she was worth it.

She woke up to see that Max had arrived in her cube again, wielding his electrolysis kit and greeting her politely. She put her sleepshirt on and took it off and lay back down on her soft place and prepared to have her hairs electrocuted. Sharp little pains persistent again, and Max told her that he could see she hadn't picked anything since he'd been there yesterday, and he was very pleased to see that. She felt so cared for and so excited that she was finally solving the problem of her hair, and she let her head float to the music and she pictured herself dressed all in black with brilliant red accents and the garnet clusters would be so transfixing and Rob would see her and realize that she was a woman of great taste and discernment, a woman who could not just be used and discarded like a character from a computer game. She imagined Rob emailing her as soon as his next opening was over, and he'd want to send her one of his new robots, whatever they were, and he'd come over again and this time she wouldn't be sick and they'd lie together and talk and talk and it wouldn't be too long before he'd realize that the eliminative materialists were wrong and he'd fallen in love with her and he didn't want to spend another moment living with that insipid Nevi. She would make herself perfect and everything would work out exactly as she wanted. The bursts of pain stopped just then, and the robot told her that he would return tomorrow and that she shouldn't pick in the meantime, and she pushed the golden button and thanked him and waved goodbye.

She looked at her face in the mirror and tried to see if the Skindeep was having any effect yet. She noticed that her lips seemed dryer than usual, so she slathered them with butterscotch lip balm, which tasted bitter like every other product that smelled so delicious, but it was probably a good thing because otherwise she'd lick it off her lips immediately. She didn't seem to have any new pimples forming, but there were several older ones that needed squeezing, and a number of clogged pores as well, and she fought with herself not to squeeze, because she'd only make things worse and the Skindeep was going to make her skin so clear and if she squeezed she'd end up with more scars that would take so long to fade. She clenched her hands and looked away from the mirror and sat down with her computer and felt such a strong urge to go back to the magnifying mirror and squeeze, and she didn't know why she couldn't control her urges, and her fingers were begging to move, to free things, so she tried to help her hands by looking for split ends to pick. She had read about lasers that would help fade acne scars, and if she could only get the pimples to stop coming she'd be willing to subject her skin to a laser again if that's what it would take for the scars to fade. She searched and searched but didn't find any split ends, so she twisted her hair around her fingers instead and pulled and twisted and pulled and twisted and kept telling herself that squeezing her face would be a very bad thing to do. She kept imagining what it would be like to squeeze certain pimples on her face, she pictured the exact pore that she'd insert the pin into and how deep it would go and the angle that she'd squeeze from and how much would come out and what it would sound like and what consistency and color it would be and how it would feel when she rolled it between her fingers, and she imagined peeling off the top layer of her skin and getting to the secret corrupted layer that held everything noxious, and there would be so many clumps of oil and pus and she would scrape every bit of it away and make herself clean. She twisted her hair furiously and told herself that she had to stop thinking about her skin, she had to stop tormenting herself like this, so she went online and looked at Rob's website and the auction site and Nevi's website and Panoptico's hands holding a soldering iron and she hoped that Panoptico would be going to the wedding so that she could watch the entire thing. She began to read about Bohemian garnet cluster jewelry and learned that it was very popular during Victorian times, and she looked at images of Victorian women and began to get an idea. The waist cincher had a delightful effect underneath a tank top, but a corset might be even more alluring. She doubted that corsets were available these days, because she remembered reading somewhere that they damaged the internal organs and made it impossible to breathe or move around very well, but she figured that maybe she could at least find a vintage one on that auction site and reinforce the old fabric herself. She did a search for corsets and was amazed to see that hundreds of sites sold them brand new and ready to be delivered instantly. She looked at the pictures of women all laced up and knew that this was exactly what she needed for her signature look. She wouldn't be able to wear the Abundacurve, of course, but the corsets seemed to push people's breasts up rather well, and that choker she'd bought would look absolutely stunning against her bare white throat without any tank top straps getting in the way. Yes, a corset would give her a graceful feminine form without any encumbrances at all. She was overwhelmed by all the different companies and styles and fabrics, and eventually settled on a company called Hysterical Reproductions that claimed to use extremely high-quality methods and materials, which she'd learned was extremely important if you wanted the corset to give you a breathtaking shape and stay firm around you through daily use. A lot of the corsets on the web were more decorative than functional, but she wanted a waist so tiny that Rob could fit his hands around it. She decided upon the simplest corset possible—no ruffles or other adornments because she wanted to provide a contrast between the simplicity of her clothing and the intricacy of her jewelry. She selected black silk for the outermost layer and silver hooks for the front and black laces for the back, and she selected a neckline like the top of a heart that was cut so low that her breasts would bulge out almost to her nipples. She decided that the bottom of the corset should extend down to her hips and end in a graceful curve, and the boning should be metal, not plastic, and the waist should be tiny, but not so tiny that her proportions would shift into the realm of the grotesque. She sent in her order with her specifications and her measurements, and she imagined herself putting on the corset and the jewelry and going outside looking more dazzling than ever before. She looked at herself in the mirror and saw that her hair was looking terribly frizzy and her roots were beginning to emerge brown and drab compared to the dramatic black, so she ordered a robot for a hairdye and a blowout and she read all the information on the Hysterical Reproductions website while she waited. There was a section where they said that they had received some hate mail for selling corsets, but they wanted to reassure their customers that just because they sold corsets didn't mean that they weren't feminists. The founder of their company, in fact, was such a militant feminist that she donated 2% of all profits to a fund to give makeup to the oppressed women of Arabia, and even after her tragic death from complications of liposuction, the girls at Hysterical Reproductions continued donating money to such worthy causes, and they just wanted to tell all the spoilsports out there that true feminism meant that every girl had the right to wear anything she wanted, even if that meant lacing herself into a corset. Anyway, just because studies showed that monkeys died when you put corsets on them didn't mean anything, because people weren't animals anymore and could make their own decisions. And besides, corsets were sexy, and when a girl wore a Hysterical Reproductions corset, she would be guaranteed to meet the Prince Charming of her dreams. And what feminist didn't secretly want to be a princess?

Max pulled her hair more taut than ever this time, but the blowout just didn't seem to be working very well. She didn't know if it was because she'd been getting blowouts so often that her hair was drying out, or because she'd been using too many antifrizz products on it, or because she'd been twisting her hair a lot recently, but even Max agreed that her hair was so frizzy that the blowout simply wouldn't take. She pushed the golden button anyway, because at least he'd been honest, and she proceeded to research treatments that she could get to make her hair sleek and smooth and straight again. She searched around a bit and finally stumbled upon a special thermochemical straightening process that came all the way from the Orient, where you'd be completely ostracized if your hair wasn't perfectly straight. She found a robot that would perform the procedure and ordered him to come at once. In the meantime, she began to open the boxes that had begun to arrive with her new jewelry inside. The garnets glowed, and the clusters were so intricate, and she put the choker around her neck and felt extremely sexy and exotic and of a different era.

Her cube was filled with a caustic chemical scent, but the robot assured her that the fumes were perfectly safe to inhale, in fact they were supposed to be good for the lungs because they would kill any bacteria that might have been growing inside. She stayed seated on the metal bench as the chemicals took effect, and she tried to make conversation with Max but he proved as reticent as most of the Mumbalore robots, so she listened to the music and tried not to breathe too deeply. The robot rinsed her hair and applied another chemical that smelled even worse than the first, and then he pulled out a flat curling iron and told her not to flinch, because it was so hot that it could give her third-degree burns instantly. She asked him why it needed to be so hot, and he told her that the heat and the chemicals inter-acted to change the actual structure of the hair, and she sat perfectly still as he pulled section after section slowly through the hot iron and she watched her hair as it gradually turned silkier than she'd ever seen it. When the robot was finished, he told her that she would need another treatment after several months as her roots grew in, but her hair would now be permanently straight. She pushed the golden button and he advised her not to wash it for three days or her hair would melt, and he waved at her and left while she admired her glimmering locks that didn't contain a single bit of frizz. Oh, she looked so beautiful again! She wished that the corset would arrive soon, because she was so excited to go outside and show Rob how devastatingly sexy she was. She put on all her makeup and the Mesmereyes and her skirt and stockings and all her jewelry and even the Golden Lotuses, and she sat on the soft place with her computer while she waited for the corset to come. She looked at Rob's website and Nevi's web-site and Rob had bought another vintage computer and Panoptico was asleep, and she began to read about laser treatments, and it was getting more and more difficult to type these days, with her long fake nails and now several large rings on her fingers and bracelets banging down onto the keyboard, and she found a good site with lots of infor-mation and she began to read and she stroked her hair, which felt so soft and silky, and she read about how the laser would burn off the top layer of skin and everything would grow back flawless, and she twisted a bit of hair around her fingers and screamed when she suddenly found herself holding a clump of hair that had somehow come off of her head. She felt sick with shock, and she looked in the mirror and saw that she now had a bald patch right in front, and she panicked and sent an email to the Mumbalore robot company demanding to know what was going on, and she was so disfigured now and she didn't know what to do. She should have known that the thermochemical treatment was much too good to be true. She stared at her bald patch in shock and kept wanting to touch her hair, but she was terrified that more of it would fall off, and she stared and stared and was interrupted from her staring by Max, who was ready to electrocute her hairs again. Had it been a day already? She took off all her clothing and jewelry and lay back on the soft place and tried to figure out what to do as she felt the little jolts of pain that she had come to like because they made her feel alive.

She got up from the soft place when Max was done and she glared at the clumps of hair that had broken off from the back of her head and she felt excited to go online and begin to assemble the next component of her signature look. A Scheherazade fantasy had begun to spin itself inside her head as she fell into a trance of pulses of pain, and she even giggled out loud a bit at her Orientalist vision and told herself that she would eliminate the need for ridiculous Oriental hair-destroying treatments completely. She would create herself a turban so magnificent that her hair would be irrelevant. She searched online for millinery supplies, and she bought a stiff mesh pillbox form that she would use as a base, and several yards of lustrous black silk velvet that would give a dramatic drape, and an enormous aigrette of dark red feathers that would rise up in a spectacular fan from the front. She searched and searched for a garnet hat brooch to hide the bottom of the aigrette, and she stumbled upon a set of fake eyelashes tipped with garnets that she simply had to have, and she eventually discovered a splendid brooch with a huge marquise-shaped onyx in the center and several rows of garnets all around. She broke off handful after handful of hair and it felt so liberating to be free of all this stuff on her head, and she envisioned herself hypnotically striking in her new turban and garnet-tipped lashes and she took a Lulliban and woke to find that Max was back again, ready to remove her sprouting hairs.

She felt her face as she lay there enjoying the little bursts of pain, and she was certain that her skin felt much less oily. Yes, the Skindeep was going to work so well and her turban and corset would look devastatingly sexy and Rob would definitely want to be with her forever. She asked Max how many more treatments it would take before they were finished, and he said that he was coming every day because he wanted to catch every hair as it grew back in from her tweezing, and her hairs grew at such a fast rate that he would be done with everything before too long. He explained to her that electrolysis was only effective on hairs that were in an active growth phase, and as long as he could kill the follicles while the hairs were actively growing, every hair that he removed would never come back again. She couldn't get him to talk about anything but the technics of electrolysis, but at least it was some company. She lay on her back with the perpetual cube lights upon her and listened to Max describe the lifecycle of a hair in meticulous detail. She wondered what he did when he wasn't working. She imagined a sad man in a tiny apartment with crumbling cinderblock walls. She imagined the smell of exhaust and rancid curry, and she imagined him trying to fall asleep every night to visions of tiny dark hairs creeping out of a woman's stomach one by one. She asked him what his real name was, because she knew it wasn't Max, and he said that it was not within his duties to provide that sort of information, and he let out a sigh so anguished that she wished that there was something she could do to help him besides pushing the golden button.

She looked at herself in the mirror as she assembled all her millinery supplies in front of her. She was now completely bald, with a faint tracing of stubble, and she knew that she could never go outside looking like that, but she secretly liked the way it looked—there was something fierce about having no hair. She had gotten an email back from the corporate headquarters of the Mumbalore robots, and it said that they were sorry for her inconvenience, but they were not liable for any damages that she may have incurred because she had checked a waiver box when she ordered the robot, and the corporation was officially registered with a small island far from anywhere and there was no way that she would be able to claim any reparations from them even if she hadn't checked the waiver box. But they hoped that they could incentivize her to continue to do business with them by accepting this token of their apology. And they included a coupon that was good for 10% off any service or combination of services that was offered by their newest generation of robots. She draped black velvet over the mesh form and told herself that she was done with services for quite a while, except for her daily electrolysis, of course. Her signature look was coming along beautifully, and her skin was finally healing, and she didn't have any hairs on her head to worry about anymore, and the fake nails never seemed to chip, so she wouldn't need another manicure until there was too much white showing at the base of her nails. She pinned the fabric into an elaborate mass of swooping folds that terminated at a central point where she would mount the brooch and the aigrette. She loved the depth and shimmer and softness of the black silk velvet, and she delighted in touching it as she stitched it carefully onto the mesh below. It took her a long time to get the folds of fabric to drape just right, and she concentrated on making little invisible stitches like her grandmother or perhaps her great-great-grandmother had taught her years before, when her fingers were still so tiny that they could learn how to do anything. Her long fake fingernails made the task especially challenging, but she worked gradually around and around until the velvet draped in sturdy graceful folds radiating from the center of the turban and covering the entire mesh form with a plush substantial surface. She put the turban on her head, just to make sure that the proportions of the velvet were right, and she was thrilled to see that the velvet swooped down perfectly—it covered her entire scalp and stopped just above her earlobes, which would be glimmering with dangling garnet clusters. She took the turban off and startled at her bald head, which was so jarring that she still didn't quite recognize herself in the mirror, and she proceeded to sew the brooch firmly onto the center of the turban, where all the folds converged, and she inserted the aigrette into a flat slot on the back of the brooch and stitched the aigrette into place from behind, and she stitched the brooch a bit more, just to reinforce everything, and she put the turban on her head and felt ecstatic. The velvet draped in lavish folds all around, and the lustrous red feathers rose far above her head and fanned out so dramatically, and the brooch provided a mesmerizing center point—the enormous onyx looked like a sideways eye in the middle of her forehead and the fiery garnets stood out stunningly against the black velvet. She couldn't wait to go outside again. She put in her Mesmereyes and applied a full face of makeup without even stopping to pick her skin, and she glued on the garnet-tipped eyelashes, which felt spidery but looked astonishingly glamorous, and she added an extra Egyptianate flourish to the outer corners of her eyes and made several Golden Mask corrections with different shades of concealer, just so she could look her best, and she brushed on a final dusting of Poudre Ophelia and she put on her leather miniskirt and arm stockings and leg stockings and unwrapped the beautiful silk-faced corset from its packaging and marveled at its weight and solidity and hooked herself in from the front and pulled the laces so tight in the back that she felt like she was wearing a straitjacket, and she put on her choker and earrings and bracelets and rings and she put the turban on her head and forced her feet into the Golden Lotuses and stepped back from the mirror as much as she could and stared and stared at herself in disbelief. She had finally achieved a level of beauty that she hadn't though possible. Her figure curved so magnificently, and her breasts curved out from the top of the corset just as she'd hoped, and the striped stockings and the turban and the Golden Lotuses and the Mesmereyes and the Egyptianate flourishes and the hints of glitter from her makeup and her jewelry and her eyelashes and her fingernails all resonated together to give her a look of otherworldly exoticism, of demonic fascination, of such searing hypnotic transcendence that Rob would never be able to resist her. She would have to figure out a way to keep the turban on her head during his next visit.

She moved her hands in arabesques and tried very hard to avoid the pins. They were sticking out from the walls and even from the ceiling, and some of the pins were extremely long and she flinched several times from bumping into them. It was a challenge to move gracefully while wearing the Golden Lotuses and wearing such a restrictive corset and still feeling dizzy from drugs, and she didn't like the strangling feeling of the choker around her neck or the way the earrings pinched her earlobes or the way the bracelets caught the little hairs on her wrists and jangled up and down, and most of all she hated the feeling of the rings encumbering the fluid movements of her fingers. Every time she bent her fingers even slightly, she'd feel a band of metal around them and she'd lose her concentration, but she knew that she looked astonishing so she tried to focus on how fascinating her hands looked with the striped arm stockings coming down and her fingernails so long and deeply lacquered and her pale fingers highlighted by glimmering garnet rings. Yes, these were the hands of a woman who got what she wanted.

She stayed outside until the Golden Lotuses and the corset got so uncomfortable that she kept tripping into pins, and she felt very relieved to see Max waiting for her with his electrolysis kit when she went inside. She took off all her clothing and jewelry and felt so free, and she lay down and asked Max to tell her all about hair while he worked. She lost herself in the details of the anagen phase of growth and the catagen phase of degeneration and the telogen phase of rejection, and Max finished all too quickly today and told her that he had gotten past a critical point and her hairs were going to be coming in sparser and sparser from now on, but she should still leave all the picking to him. She thanked him and pushed the golden button and she noticed as she waved goodbye that her fingers still had deep red indentations from the rings.

She looked at herself on the screen and was amazed at what she had accomplished. The walls looked strange with the eyes half-covered by glue embedded with dried-up bits of pomegranate flesh and pierced by pins, but her signature look had definitely become a thing of splendor to behold.

She looked just as beautiful as any of the women she'd seen on screens, and even more beautiful, she thought, because her look was so original. It was even hard to tell when she'd poked herself with pins inadvertently—she must have done a good job at covering up her missteps with avant-garde gestures. Yes, she'd done it. Rob would never be able to resist her now. She didn't have any email, but she checked her comments and felt so happy and alive as she read though pages and praises and everybody was more effusive than ever and she felt so successful and so loved. Everybody had such positive things to say about her new look. Everybody except that feminist, who was back from her August break with another barrage of criticism, undaunted by the fact that her critiques so far had gone completely unheeded. The feminist had a rather scolding tone today. She claimed that it was disgusting that the gynocidal tropes of androcentric pornography had made their way into contemporary fashion, that corsets were hideous symbols of submission and immobility and inequality, and it was just pathetic that women with unlimited clothing options would voluntarily constrict themselves into destructive garments that both symbolized and embodied the shackles from which women had fought for centuries to free themselves. The feminist then criticized her makeup, claiming that the massive cult of cosmetics was a sign of self-doubt and anxiety writ large and carcinogenic on the face of every woman who spends needless amounts of time and money making herself into a clown. And she didn't even have anything nice to say about her new turban and jewelry—she said that such ornaments were tokens of conspicuous waste that only served to reinforce the idea that women were merely decorative and delicate and overconcerned with trivial baubles and held no threat to male power at all. The feminist ended with a very direct challenge: she dared her to come out of the cube completely unadorned one day, wearing no makeup and only the clothing she had started with.

She read the comment and reread it and tried to think of why the feminist was wrong. Evolutionary psychology said that men liked women who were submissive and looked like clowns, or maybe it said that women who didn't wear jewelry would be miserable and alone, or maybe it said that men liked women who couldn't breathe or move around very well, but none of that sounded quite right, and she tried to remember what evolutionary psychology did say, exactly, but she couldn't quite piece things together, and she found herself wanting to send the feminist a note. She didn't know her email address because the comments were all anonymous, so she posted a comment on her own website and hoped that the feminist would notice. She wrote that she didn't know what to do, because if she stopped adorning herself she'd put herself at a disadvantage because she was really quite plain to look at, and she was only trying to survive as an artist in a world where appearances were everything. She submitted the comment and reloaded the page to see it with all the others, but her comment did not appear. She reloaded the page several more times, and there were new comments from several Zealots and a Provocateur, but her own comment was nowhere. She tried submitting it again, and she reloaded and reloaded and lots of people thought she was the hottest girl on the web, but her comment seemed to have vanished somewhere between her computer and the website. Where could it have gotten to? She imagined that cavernous building with rows of prim women sitting in front of enormous switchboards and moving their arms frantically from plug to plug, and she supposed that there were certain times when their arms got tired or a plug went into the wrong place, and she told herself that maybe it was better if she didn't post that comment after all, because it wouldn't do to have all her admirers see how vulnerable she really was. Anyhow, the feminist might be right about history, but she didn't seem to have a clear idea of how to live in the present world. And all she knew was that she'd gotten more praise since she'd started paying attention to her appearance than she'd gotten in her entire life, and if she wanted to get Rob to return, there was no way she'd ever go outside the cube without her signature look fully in place. She checked her email and found nothing from Rob, so she reread that email apologizing for her hair loss and clicked over to the website where the newest generation of robots resided.

The services on this site were extremely expensive and much more involved than any she'd seen so far. She'd been feeling rather insecure about her lips ever since she'd applied the Golden Mask to her face and noticed that they were thinner than the ideal, and she was intrigued to see that she could have a robot come and implant little pieces of plastic into her lips to make them fuller. There were lots of photographs of people's lips before and after the procedure, and it seemed so safe and easy, and her corporate sponsor couldn't object that much because she had a 10% off coupon, and anyway, wasn't there that artist who had made a postmodern commentary about the body and concepts of beauty by getting plastic surgery done on her face to look like a composite of famous paintings? There was no reason why plastic surgery couldn't be considered art, she reasoned, and she looked at her lips in the mirror and they were definitely thinner than all those plump pouty lips she saw on the screen, and if she could have beautiful lips within a click or two, why shouldn't she do it? She began to place the order and was then offered a special discount on a Double Lip Deluxe package, which included a simultaneous lip augmentation and labiaplasty for 25% off the entire thing. It had never occurred to her that there was anything wrong with her labia, but she looked at the before and after pictures and hers definitely looked more like the befores. The website said that it was a secret weapon to get your guy really in the mood. It seemed that men had gotten used to seeing porn stars with labia that were tiny and perfectly shaped, and all men secretly wanted their women to look like porn stars and now any woman could feel sexier and more confident in bed by getting their inner lips to look as small and perfect as their boyfriend or husband's favorite porn star. She didn't exactly have a boyfriend or a husband, but Rob did tell her that he would come back eventually and she certainly didn't want to repel him with labia that didn't look the way they should. It seemed like the procedure was rather safe, and that the only complication would be reduced sexual sensation, but ever since she'd started taking the Lunacede she didn't really have much sexual sensation anyway, and she had no plans to go off the Lunacede ever, since millions of women took it and it seemed like a necessity for every modern woman, so she looked at the before and after pictures of the labia again, and hers definitely looked too prominent, especially since she'd gotten all the hair removed from her pubic area, and she certainly wanted to be as sexy and confident as possible, so she sent off the order for the Double Lip Deluxe and hoped that it wouldn't hurt too much.

She covered her lips with butterscotch lip balm, because they'd been awfully dry ever since she'd started taking Skindeep, and she hoped that the dryness wouldn't complicate the surgery. She went to Nevi's page while she waited for the robot and she tried to figure out when the wedding would be. She realized with surprise that it was happening the day after tomorrow, and she didn't know where the time had gone, although she suspected that it had something to do with the fact that she was always sleepy, and she set her alarm to let her know when the wedding would happen and she wondered if Panoptico would be there. She still couldn't believe that Rob was actually doing this. At least he'd been honest to her about his pragmatism, but she still felt sick that Rob was neglecting her so much. She felt very dejected and didn't even know if he'd ever come back, and she tried to cheer herself up by reading her comments, but that only reminded her that she couldn't even comment on her own website, and she took a Lulliban and fell asleep clutching the little robot all wrapped up inside the cut stocking.

She woke up to two robots inside her cube discussing who would go first. The surgery robot said that he was entitled to go first, because his procedure was more prestigious, and the electrolysis robot said that he had a standing appointment with her and had been coming in for a long time now, so he should get to go first. She suggested that it would be hard to do electrolysis on her lip and pubic area for a while after she'd had surgery, and the surgery robot agreed glumly and stood there sighing while Max removed the smattering of hairs and ingrowns that had happened since he'd last been there. She felt hesitant to see Max go, because she at least knew that he wasn't going to hurt her, and she eyed the surgery robot with some distrust as he began to use his four arms to assemble a frightening array of knives and scissors and syringes. She asked him how he planned to anesthetize her, and he said that she could either have general or local anesthesia, and she opted to be put out completely because she was afraid that he wouldn't use enough local anesthesia and she'd feel the entire thing. He put a needle into her arm and attached a tube from somewhere deep within his body, and she was terrified for a moment that she'd never wake up again, and everything started to slip away and the next thing she knew her lips were stinging and her labia were stinging too and she felt so spinny and groggy and dizzy and she didn't know where she was, and it must have been a hospital because she seemed to be bandaged and in pain and the lights were bright and everything looked sterile and white, and she was so sleepy and she didn't know what had happened and she tried to bring her hand to her face to touch her lips and her hand was so heavy and there seemed to be things on the ends of her fingers, and the alarm went off but it couldn't be time to get up yet, so she closed her eyes and fell back asleep.

She woke up with a paranoid feeling that she had somehow missed Rob's wedding. She was in a bit of pain from the surgery, but she didn't stop to get some Numitol until she'd gone to Panoptico's website and saw that he seemed to be sitting in a crowded loft with lots of robots all around, and nothing much was happening. She must have missed the alarm, but she had set it for well before the wedding was supposed to start, so everything was still okay. Except for the fact that she was about to watch Rob participate in a ridiculous pageant when he should have broken up with Nevi already and it was only a few months since he'd been inside her cube and he was such a hypocrite and it was excruciating to be seeing this, but it was at least amusing to listen to Panoptico and his girlfriend discussing the situation. His girlfriend whispered to him that she hated weddings and she hated Nevi and she just hoped it would be over soon and she didn't understand why people had to make such intimate vows in public, and she really didn't want to be here. Panoptico apologized, and he said that Rob would have killed him if they hadn't shown up, because Rob had this subversive plan of assembling as many sloppily dressed people and robots in the audience as possible, and he said that he supposed that the public spectacle was so that Rob would be humiliated by the entire village if he reneged on his vows. Not that Rob would ever do such a thing, Panoptico added, with a sarcastic quality that made her wonder if Rob had told Panoptico about her. Panoptico's girlfriend went into a long rant about how Nevi was an embarrassment to everybody with two X chromosomes, how she herself wouldn't be caught dead wearing a big white dress, how these grotesque superficial displays were the stupidest waste of money that she could possibly imagine, and then some loud techno music started playing and her voice was drowned out and a line of women and robots started walking to the front of the room. The women were dressed in frilly pink dresses and the robots were also dressed in frilly pink dresses, and Rob came out wearing a worn white undershirt with sweat stains beneath the arms and a pair of rumpled khaki pants that appeared to have been splattered with ketchup or blood, and she was pleased to see that Rob looked miserable and then one of the robots in frilly dresses began to make electronic squeaking and squawking noises, and Rob said yes, and the robot turned and made the same sorts of noises in the other direction, and she couldn't see Nevi, but she heard Nevi's voice say yes, and she didn't understand why she couldn't see Nevi but she could hear her, and maybe she was still a bit loopy from the anesthesia, and the robot made more squawking noises and Rob leaned over and made a perfunctory kissing gesture into the air and she was absolutely baffled and Panoptico's girlfriend said that she knew that Rob was trying to be subversive about all this, but she still wanted to vomit, and Panoptico said that they only had to stay for a few minutes of the reception—he just wanted to have a cupcake or two, and his girlfriend laughed and said that she might as well try one of these infamous cupcakes now, since she gave the marriage three months at most before Rob came to his senses and broke up with Nevi for good. Panoptico started making his way through the squawking squeaking crowd towards the cupcake table, when all of a sudden Nevi screamed and told him to watch where he was going, and he apologized and told her that he hadn't seen her, and she told him that he must be blind with that computer on his head, and he told her that he could see just fine, it was just that he had programmed his computer with certain filters, and he had no interest in seeing billboards or ads or cultural clichés of any kind, and the image of a bride was definitely one that he'd filtered out a long time ago. Nevi told him that there was nothing more beautiful than a bride, and it was just too bad that he couldn't see the beauty in the world around him. And then her voice faded as she yelled something about a photographer and there were many cupcakes and robots and she listened to Panoptico chew, and his girlfriend said that she couldn't stay in that room a moment longer, and she watched the room recede and then a stairway and out onto the street, where Panoptico and his girlfriend burst out laughing and the screen went black and said *Private* and she closed her computer and her head was spinning and she tried not to think about what she had just seen. She noticed a pile of gauze and alcohol pads and surgical tape beside her, so she figured that she should use them to clean and dress her wounds. All of her lips looked surprisingly healthy underneath the blood-stained coverings, and she was very pleased to see that her lips looked plump and her labia looked tiny, and she dabbed them with alcohol and taped on some gauze and congratulated herself for being so resourceful and using a coupon to get not one but two useful procedures performed so well. Oh, she would be the loveliest creature that ever lived by the time she left the cube. These robots were really quite good at what they did. She carefully sipped a Dr. Tell's while she went to her website, and she was surprised to see that somebody had created a stylized drawing of her, complete with corset and turban and miniskirt and striped stockings and Golden Lotuses and garnet jewelry and white skin and red lips and oversized black eyes ringed with garnet-tipped lashes. The drawing showed up all over the site, and she noticed that there was a little trademark symbol next to it, which she supposed was to protect the artist who had drawn it, and she went into the *Press* section and found a new article about her that raved about how amazing she was—young, brilliant, talented, glamorous, exotic, with a look imitated by many but duplicated by none. She had put Golden Lotuses on the fashion map, brought garnet-tipped lashes and Mesmereyes onto faces everywhere, brought back clusters of Bohemian garnets, caused a run on striped stockings, and gotten women everywhere to stand up straight in corsets and cover their heads with elaborate turbans. Yes, she had become an icon, and millions of people daily were visiting her site, hoping to catch a glimpse of her in all her splendor.

She read the article and could only think of Rob. She thought of him scowling and looking so sad and vulnerable in his worn white undershirt, and she wondered what he was doing at this very moment, and she hoped that he was feeling miserable and that he would think of her and feel a solace and wish that she were there. Her lips were stinging and she looked at herself bald and bandaged with red spots still lingering all over her body, and she noticed a clump of her hair lying in the corner like a dead animal, and she picked it up and it was so silky and she started to cry and she told herself she mustn't cry, she had so much to look forward to, and she cried harder and began to play the *Swansong*

Serenade and it was so haunting and crackling and real and the violin cried with her and she thought of Rob and all the times they'd talked so deeply and she pictured his mouth round above her and he was so beautiful and she loved him and the music was too powerful so she stopped the song abruptly and threw the file away so she could never hear it again, and she threw the clump of hair down the trap door, and she didn't know why she was feeling so sad, because he said he would return to her, and even Panoptico's girlfriend didn't think it would last, and she felt so dizzy and so sick and she reached up to twist her hair but there was nothing left to twist, and she wouldn't pick at her face or her ingrown hairs, no she wouldn't, she was much stronger than that, and she opened up some pots of cream eyeshadow in green and violet and blue and began to paint a layer of arabesques over the one concealer painting that was already partially obscured by the yellow paint from the little robot, and she cried harder when she thought of the little robot but she continued with a dense tangle of arabesques, and when the layer was complete she opened up more pots and moved on to a new concealer painting, and she stumbled over her fingernails sometimes but she wouldn't let that stop her, and she loved the feeling of her fingers smoothing through the shadows and she became extremely focused on creating layer after layer so that the arabesques would interact between layers and hint at what was underneath, and she began to notice that there were certain shapes and configurations that she seemed to paint quite often without even realizing it, and she wondered if she was making a breakthrough with her language of images and she painted and painted and let her hands decide where the layers should go, and she loved the idea of covering and covering and creating a repeating set of abstract arabesques and she tried to decipher them as she painted, but she could only figure out that a certain set of squiggles meant that she was anguished and another meant that she was confused and another meant that she was scared, and she tried to clear her head and let her hands create the layers and she thought about her icon and felt rather jealous of its stylized perfection and she thought of all the other surgeries that she could get and she painted layer after layer and thought about what it meant to create a permanent alteration to the body and she told herself that nothing was permanent inside the mind. She moved her hands quite automatically and told herself that she could forget. Yes, she could forget.

October

THE ROOM GREW FETID WITH DECAYING SQUASH. She hadn't ordered any squash, but a huge shipment of them arrived in her cube one day and she decided to throw them out against the sharp walls as hard as she could. She didn't even leave the cube to throw them—she opened the door just wide enough to fit her arm and a squash, and she tossed and tossed until every squash was gone. The pins seemed unharmed by the ordeal, but the walls were splattered with orange flesh and the floor was piled with violently ruptured pieces of squash that were stringy with seeds and dark with rot. The pomegranate seeds had lasted for a while before they went bad, but the squash had started to smell almost immediately and darkened not long after. She had come to like the smell because it felt like someone was living with her inside the cube, even if it was only bacteria, and she was hoping that she could lure some flies to join her in the room again, because she was so terribly lonely ever since Max had electrocuted every single one of her hairs and told her that he would never need to return. She probably should have been ecstatic to hear that, but she was mostly just dejected because it meant that she would never see him again. He was the friendliest robot she'd ever met, except of course for the little robot and the woman who used to sit under mango trees, but they were both gone now, although she still liked to hold the little robot in its stocking shroud and stare at the yellow traces on the floor and imagine a day when Rob would surprise her with a charger. She tried not to think too much about Rob, but sometimes memories came into her head when she didn't even summon them, and she felt herself sad and filled with longing and she told herself that everything would be okay and she would see him again after his next opening was over. She still couldn't figure out what his next opening would be about—he hadn't emailed her in such a long time now, and he didn't go into detail on his website. But she did know that she had inspired it, which cheered her up a bit. She had recently begun to take two Happyams a day, because a single Happyam didn't seem to make her happy enough. Her misery was just an illness caused by a chemical imbalance, after all, and it was only a matter of taking enough pills to cure her illness and maybe her life would start to feel less miserable. The pills were rather beautiful with their scarlet luster and delicate gold lettering, and she always felt a little happier just looking at them every time she took one, and sometimes she even looked at them when it wasn't time to take one—she poured them out onto the floor and sifted them through her fingers and admired the richly gleaming little things and imagined all that happiness sealed up inside hundreds of little pills, just waiting to brighten someone's day. She had found a new occupation for her hands, which did make her a little bit happy sometimes— she had taken to picking her scalp. She had stumbled upon this hobby quite by accident; she had ordered a garnet hatpin because she was trying to figure out how to make the turban stay on firmly when Rob came by, but she realized as she inserted it that a hatpin expected a substantial mass of hair to anchor it in place. Her poor little hatpin went right in and found nothing but her scalp. She eventually tracked down a glue that could hold the turban to her head quite well, but she was more impressed by the scab that formed on her scalp where the hatpin had stuck in—it was rough and stiff and thick, and she picked it off and played with it and even chewed on it a bit and began scratching her scalp rather hard, in hopes that she would give herself more scabs to pick. Her experiment worked quite well, and soon she had an entire crop of scabs to pick and touch and chew on, and the scabs stood out so substantial and hard against her soft skin, and she could amuse herself for hours just rubbing her fingers over her scalp and seeing what she found. She didn't know why she chewed on all the scabs, but she remembered that once long ago she had watched a caterpillar come out of its skin and it ate the whole thing before going back to chewing leaves, so it was only natural to want to chew what came off of us and she did love the feeling of rubbing her fingers over her scalp and discovering a nice thick scab to chew upon. It also helped that she had gotten rid of those nasty fake fingernails—they certainly helped her through a difficult time when her nails were short and jagged, but her nails had grown back to a substantial length, and even though the polish did chip more easily on her natural nails than it did on the fake nails, the more frequent manicures were always nice, and the main thing was that she could feel her scalp again. The Skindeep had cleared up her face and the electrolysis had removed all hairs and ingrowns, so she had to have something to occupy her hands, and she especially liked picking her scalp because she could always cover it up with her magnificent turban. Not that she had any plans to go outside for a long long time, because she had big plans inside the cube, something that would definitely cheer her up while she waited for Rob to finish with his opening so he could visit her again. She had been reading about all the procedures that the next generation of Mumbalore robots could perform, and she had decided to get a lot of plastic surgery. Her labia had healed so beautifully and even though her mouth had some weird scarring around the edges of her lips, it was nothing that she couldn't conceal, and meanwhile they were much plumper than before, and she didn't see why she shouldn't look as perfect as possible, since all the technology was out there and her corporate sponsor was willing to pay. There were so many procedures on the website and she hardly knew which to choose, but she did know that she wanted to have a bunch of procedures done all at once so that she'd be able to heal as quickly as possible for Rob's next visit. Anyway, the website offered substantial discounts if you ordered their special packages, and she couldn't resist a bargain, and she was also intrigued by the idea of a robot with eight arms, all working simultaneously to make her into the most beautiful creature that ever lived. She was vacillating between the Porn Star package and the Sweet Sixteen package, but she was leaning more towards the Sweet Sixteen because even though the Porn Star included a chin resculpting, which the Sweet Sixteen didn't offer, it also included an extra-large set of breast implants, which she thought looked grotesquely huge, and a labiaplasty, which would be unnecessary since she didn't need her labia to be even smaller. The Sweet Sixteen seemed to cover the basic necessities—nose job, breast implants, and full-body liposuction. The only problem was that it didn't include toe reduction, which she'd been intrigued about ever since the Golden Lotus man mentioned it, or calf reduction, a procedure that was able to make over-muscled calves look more feminine by severing a nerve that would cause the muscles to atrophy. The website had a strict policy of no add-ons or substitutions, which was supposed to protect the client by making sure that the robot would be able to follow a precise script, and she measured her calves again and they were definitely more muscular than they should have been, but she really wanted to get the Sweet Sixteen, and she figured that she could always get her toes and calves done later in a Hot to Trot package, and if Rob came by right after the procedure she just wouldn't do much walking around. There was also a Smooth Perfection package, which offered laser skin resurfacing, but her face had healed surprisingly well since she'd taken the Skindeep and stopped picking, and the Smooth Perfection didn't include breast implants, which she definitely needed. The Golden Mask analysis had implied that her chin was too large, but only very slightly, and if she got the Porn Star she'd end up with breasts bigger than her head, which would make her proportions all wrong, so she settled on the Sweet Sixteen and entered her height and weight and blood type and current measurements and checked a waiver box and sent the order off.

She felt rather nervous as she waited, because the Double Lip Deluxe had been fairly minor, and all of these procedures were more invasive, and she really hoped that the robots knew what they were doing. She passed the time by looking at the same before and after pictures she'd looked at a million times before. Oh, it would be so wonderful to have a narrow nose and a slim cellulite-free figure and large round breasts. The website claimed that they used ultrascientific methods to determine everyone's ideal proportions, and she wondered what sort of nose and breasts they would create for her. All she knew was that ever since she'd applied the Golden Mask to her face, she'd hated her nose. And her breasts had been a source of much anxiety every since she'd started comparing herself to other women, and even though the Abundacurve and the corset gave her the illusion of large breasts, her breasts were nothing like the after pictures on the website, which she figured was what men really wanted. She felt like such a fraud wearing all that padding, and there was a picture of Nevi on her website wearing a bikini, and she definitely had breast implants, so that was probably what

Rob liked. Her own breasts were so small and they didn't bulge up round on top except with a lot of padding, and she couldn't wait to feel confident about her breasts the next time Rob came to visit. She lifted up her sleepshirt and said goodbye to her breasts, and they did look soft and healthy, but they looked so tiny and inadequate next to all those pictures she was looking at, and she felt a sudden chill, so she gave her breasts a farewell squeeze and lowered her shirt and put a pair of sweatpants on as well. She'd finally be slender after all the liposuction, and she'd never have to worry about her weight again. That stubborn flesh on her thighs and the backs of her arms and her stomach and her waist would finally be gone. And Rob would gaze upon her naked form in awe and rapture, and she would feel so beautiful, and she wouldn't have to drink any more of that disgusting Dr. Tell's. She looked at image after image of headless women with the fat removed from their bodies, and she reached down to her stomach and told it goodbye, she wouldn't be needing it any longer, and she felt very scared for a moment and shivered and hugged herself and thought about what that feminist would say about her transformations. Probably something about the expense and the risk and the fact that she was doing this to conform to heteronormative strictures of beauty, but what the feminist didn't seem to understand was that she was an aesthete and an independent woman and she was doing this for herself, for purely aesthetic reasons. She just wanted to create beauty, not to conform to any standards, and since her corporate sponsor would pay for her to make her proportions as harmonious as possible, there was no reason why she shouldn't be doing it. Maybe there was a risk, but there was a risk to doing everything worthwhile in life, and the results would certainly be worth it. She pictured herself with large round breasts and a perfect nose and a figure without any fat at all, and she thought of the icon on her website and told herself that she would look just as good as that icon before long. She reread the description of the Sweet Sixteen package, which said that several master surgeons from Mumbalore would control eight powerful arms to sculpt your body to perfection using the latest ultrascientific techniques to determine perfect proportions and the latest technological innovations to achieve perfect results. The Sweet Sixteen was all about providing a solid foundation for a lifetime of perfect beauty, because even if you didn't need to have anything lifted quite yet, you still needed to begin to correct your imperfections now. The Sweet Sixteen was an investment in a life of happiness and beauty, and you owed it to yourself or a girl you cared about to make the splurge, because every girl deserved to be beautiful. Every girl could benefit from larger firmer breasts and a more perfect nose and the removal of stubborn deposits of fat, and with the Sweet Sixteen, you'd be able to feel confident enough to know that you looked good both in and out of clothing, and you would never have to feel ashamed about yourself ever again. The Sweet Sixteen was the perfect gift for that special girl in your life, whether for a graduation or a prom or even a Bat Mitzvah, but it was also the ideal way to pamper yourself in high style, to transform yourself into a new you and free yourself forever. She picked a thick scab from her scalp and it tasted salty and she licked the rich metallic blood from her fingers and told herself that every girl deserved a bit of pampering.

The robot was enormous and he didn't even tell her his name. He told her to undress, and she shivered as she lay down on a sheet of paper on the soft place and he began to draw all over her body with a blue marker as he used his other eight arms to set up an elaborate array of equipment. His body contained so many flashing lights and tubes and wires and compartments, and she asked him what his name was and he didn't even respond. She felt terribly vulnerable lying there naked and chilly and scribbled upon like an animal about to be butchered, and she tried to breathe deep and relax and the robot reached down to her arm and inserted a needle and then a tube and she heard a beeping and she felt so cold and she glanced at the blue graffiti covering her breasts and felt so terrified and floaty and all the metal knives were shimmering and the room was spinning and everything went black and she woke up to such violent pain that she didn't know what to do. Her head was hurting worse than it ever had and her nose was stuffed full so she couldn't breathe and her throat was sore and swollen and she was suffocating and it felt like a boulder was crushing her chest and her entire body hurt and she felt like she was about to vomit and she turned and tried to reach the toilet, but there was a robot in her cube who held out a basin and she vomited black and choked and her head was full and her nose was completely packed and she felt like she was going to die, and the vomit came again and she couldn't breathe and the robot told her to lie down again, and she told the robot that she couldn't stand it, she was choking and the world was closing in and her throat was burning and her body was in so much pain, and the robot put a little chip of ice inside her mouth and gave her some pills to swallow and she asked for more ice and the robot gave it to her and she told the robot that she couldn't breathe, and the robot gave her another chip of ice and stroked her forehead and the world got blurry and she felt herself falling asleep.

She woke again to a terrible pain everywhere and she tried so hard to breathe out of her nose but she couldn't, and she gasped for breath and her throat was so sore and there was a robot next to her putting an ice chip in her mouth, and her chest was burning and tight and hurting so much and her head was about to explode with pain and she told the robot that she needed more painkillers and she asked the robot why it was hurting so much and she couldn't even cry because her head was packed full, and she was going to suffocate like this and why had she done this, why had she tortured herself like this, what could she do to feel better except take more painkillers and sleep? She knew that she was going to choke and die and her body just couldn't stand this much pain, and she felt so cold and the robot fed her ice chips and pills until she fell asleep again.

Oh, she was choking! Somebody was strangling her throat and her nose was full and there was a robot next to her and she was so cold and her chest was hurting worse than anything she'd felt before, and her breasts were red and huge and tight and burning and stinging and she was covered with bandages and her whole body was burning and hurting and why had she agreed to this, and her throat was burning and she gasped out that she needed help and the robot fed her an ice chip and some pills, and the ice chip felt so soothing on her throat and she told the robot that there must have been a mistake, because she couldn't breathe out of her nose and her throat was mostly closed, and the robot said that everything would be okay and fed her ice chip after ice chip and she didn't think that she would ever fall asleep again because she was in such agony and she could barely breathe, but she felt herself drifting down to sleep.

What was wrong with her head? She strained as hard as she could and she couldn't breathe out of her nose and her throat felt raw and she was freezing cold and her chest was in such agony, and there was a robot standing next to her, so she told it that she was choking and she needed to get something done about her nose, and her chest was burning and hurting so dreadfully, and the robot put icebags on top of her breasts, which felt a little better but made her even colder, and she told the robot she was freezing and he pulled a blanket out of his torso and draped it over her, and she begged to get her nose unclogged but the robot said that it needed to stay packed or otherwise her nose would collapse, and he gave her an ice chip and then another and another and she was in such pain all over her body, and this had to have been the stupidest thing she'd ever done in her life, and she asked the robot for painkillers and he gave her some and she couldn't sleep because she felt like she was drowning so she asked for more and the robot agreed and she was out.

She opened her eyes and her head felt so full and she was in so much pain and she asked the robot for more ice chips and painkillers because she simply couldn't live this way. She gasped for breath and asked the robot how long she needed to keep that stuff inside her nose, and he said he didn't know, he was only the nurse. She told him that she was freezing, and he put another blanket on top of her, and she asked him how long he was going to stay with her and he said that he didn't know, he was only the nurse, and she asked him if he could please tell the doctor to come and take that stuff out of her nose, because she felt like she was choking to death, and her told her that he was only the nurse, and she asked if he could rub her forehead at least, and he conceded and rubbed her forehead mechanically while feeding her ice chips at regular intervals and finally the painkillers kicked in.

She woke up because she felt somebody poking around inside her nose. Everything hurt and the robot nurse was pulling gauze out of her nose with forceps, and there was so much gauze inside and it hurt when he pulled it out but she knew that she would be free so soon, and she could deal with all the other pain if only she could breathe again, and the gauze was stained with red and yellow and it kept coming and coming and finally she had her nostril back! Oh, she felt so free that she didn't mind the pain of the forceps in her other nostril, and she breathed deep and her throat was still so sore but she felt like her world had just expanded because she could breathe again, and it was stinging inside her nostril but she didn't care, and she watched as all the gauze came out and she felt something ripping from deep inside her head and it was painful but finally her head was clear again! She told the robot thank you so much, and she inhaled and exhaled and inhaled and exhaled and her chest was killing her and her whole body felt as though she'd gotten beaten, but it didn't matter because she could breathe. The robot pulled the blankets back and took the icepacks off her chest and began to change her bandages. They were mostly soaked through with blood and pus, and her body was extremely bruised and swollen and her breasts looked like bloated balloons covered with tight red mottled skin, and everything was stinging and burning and she felt so weak and tired and the robot put fresh bandages on all her wounds and told her that she shouldn't get wet for two weeks because her sutures would melt and he put a box of bandaging supplies and painkillers by her side and he told her that the Sweet Sixteen was officially over. She asked him what to do if something went wrong, because she wasn't feeling very good and she could use somebody to take care of her a little longer, and he told her that he didn't know, he was only the nurse, and she said that there had to be somebody she could contact if she wasn't healing properly, and he said that he hoped she would take the time to submit a positive testimonial to their website, and she said that she was going to submit an outraged comment if he couldn't even tell her who she could contact for help, and he said that he wished her a speedy recovery and he hoped that she would call upon them for all her future beauty needs. And he put the blankets and the icepacks inside his metal body and left without even waving goodbye.

She looked at herself in the mirror and felt bewildered. Where had she gone to? She was staring at a battered bandaged creature with huge hard breasts and two black eyes and a bald head covered with scabs, and her nose was swollen and her lips were scarred and her body was blue and purple and swollen and it hurt even to lean over and look at herself, and she was so cold and her head was throbbing and she wanted somebody to take care of her and why had she done this to herself and her throat was dry and painful and she needed more painkillers but she didn't have any water or ice, so she reached over to the refrigerator and it hurt so much and she found some ice chips in the little freezer compartment and put a few in her mouth and swallowed some pills when the ice chips melted and tried to breathe deep and told herself that the pain would be over soon enough.

She woke up feeling wretched and foggy and her entire body was hurting but at least she could breathe again. She turned to look at herself in the mirror and her nose was swollen but she could see that it was definitely narrower than before. Her breasts still looked like foreign objects straining to escape from her chest, but their size was quite remarkable and she told herself that they'd settle down before too long. And her body was still rather swollen but its contours were different and slimmer and if she could only get through this terrible pain and swelling and bruising she might actually end up looking good. She pulled herself up to the sink and was horrified to hear the booming scale announce that her weight was higher than before, and she figured it was all the swelling and she drank several handfuls of water and felt so weak that she had to lie down again. She heard an odd sloshing noise when she lay down, and she didn't know what was causing it so she moved a bit and there it was again and it was coming from her chest and she realized that she had big bags of salt water inside of her, and she reached down and touched her breasts ever so gently because her body felt so delicate that she was terrified of breaking it, and the skin stung and her breasts felt so tight and hard and her nipples were numb and she wondered how long it would be before everything felt better, and she was so chilly but the robot had taken the blankets away, so she put on her sweatpants and sleepshirt with much effort, being extremely careful not to bump her nose as she pulled her shirt over her head, and her breasts strained against the fabric but all of her other shirts were much smaller, so she found a pair of scissors and carefully cut several slits in the front of the shirt, and she was so worried that she'd pop her implants but she didn't, and she gathered up all the clothing she could find and piled it behind her and draped several shirts across her chest and made a nest of clothing around her and on top of her, and she put her computer on her lap and it felt so nice and warm and she realized that she needed to take some more painkillers because everything was hurting, so she reached over and got some ice chips and some pills and covered herself up completely and put her computer on her lap and she was going to check her email but she must have fallen asleep.

She woke up with a clarity that she hadn't felt in quite a while. She was still in terrible pain, but everything felt lighter and sharper and she smelled the rotten squash and suddenly remembered that it was October and Rob would have his opening and then come over, and she hoped she hadn't missed it because she had been asleep forever, and she looked on Rob's website and his show was called *TerraRob-ots* and it was supposed to open tomorrow, and she was so happy that she hadn't missed it and she'd still have a bit of time to heal before he came, and she set her computer to chime when it was time, and she reached over for some ice chips and painkillers and the clothing was soft and her computer was warm and she would be beautiful soon.

A chime and she opened her computer and went to Panoptico's website. He seemed to be on the subway and people were looking at him oddly, so she checked her email, which she hadn't checked since before her makeover, and she was so hopeful but Rob hadn't sent her anything at all. He must have been quite busy lately, and that was okay, because she'd send him email after his opening and he would want to collaborate and see her and she'd be so beautiful with her new nose and breasts and figure and he wouldn't be able to resist her. It was interesting to see the subway with blank spaces where the ads should be. Panoptico's computer had put a metal background in the spaces to match the rest of the subway car, and she giggled when she thought about how nasty he was to Nevi and she wondered what Panoptico would see if he looked at her website with all those cicada ads around her. She picked a huge scab off of her head and chewed it while she watched Panoptico climbing the steps and walking down a crowded street and then a less crowded street to get to the opening. There were so many buildings out there and so many cars, and not even the taxicabs had ads on top of them, and she wanted to talk to Panoptico and tell him not to be bothered by all those people on the street who looked at him so oddly.

The gallery was extremely crowded, and she tried to hear

what people were saying, but Panoptico was walking too fast towards the food. He began helping himself to the same robot cookies as last time, and nobody else was eating any, and a woman with piercings all over her face came up to Panoptico and told him that she didn't know how he could eat anything, and she wrinkled up her face in disgust and her piercings made a clinking noise, and Panoptico told her that he'd gotten used to the smell since he'd been helping Rob retrofit his robots for the show, and the smell was the least of Rob's problems right now and he'd be very surprised if these robots actually worked at all. She said that she didn't know how long she'd be able to tolerate the smell, and she was seriously going to throw up if the show took too long. Panoptico told her to pretend that she was using a public restroom, and she smiled and showed off a gleaming pair of fangs and a split tongue and told him that at least public restrooms have deodorizers and perfumes and stuff, and she didn't understand why Rob couldn't have been more considerate of everyone and at least provide some cans of air freshener that people could spray around. Panoptico said that considerate and Rob didn't really belong in the same sentence, and she laughed and her fangs looked rather sharp and she said that she was going off to find the wine, because she'd definitely be needing it tonight. Panoptico took a few more cookies and walked towards the front of the room, and there were only seven robots this time and they were much larger and Rob's scruffy assistants were making adjustments and the lights dimmed and Rob came out into a spotlight and everybody cheered. Rob looked intense and beautiful as always, and he said that before he started he just wanted to explain about the smell—these were the true Rob-ots of the future, and they didn't even need batteries because they made their own fuel, and he purposely didn't try to hide the smell because he wanted everybody to be reminded of what kept these

Rob-ots going. And he explained that they were called TerraRob-ots because the future was all about the earth and being sustainable, and he'd found these awesome guys who were making robots that lived on flies, and when he discovered them he knew that this had to be his next generation of Rob-ots. He described how the TerraRob-ots started out with some raw sewage inside, just to attract the flies, and once the flies got trapped inside they'd drown in the sewage and the bacteria would break them down and release electrons that would create a current, and as long as there were enough flies around, they could theoretically keep going forever. He said that the TerraRob-ots had neural network brains just like all his other Rob-ots, and he was going to apologize in advance because the TerraRob-ots were a little slower than most of his Rob-ots, and the show might not be quite as fast-paced as some of his others, but he liked to think of the TerraRob-ots as more than just inanimate robots, they were almost like living creatures attuned to the deep rhythms of nature. And he waved out his arm with a flourish and the scruffy assistants put the robots on top of canvasses and the loud techno music started playing and his assistants came out with jars of flies and released them and they started buzzing everywhere. People in the audience were cursing and making slapping noises and Panoptico seemed to be trying hard not to keep from laughing, and the robots started moving ever so slightly, but they were mostly just making puddles of paint on the canvasses. The assistants brought out several more jars and opened them directly over the robots, but the flies flew away in the other direction and Panoptico started walking towards the cookies again and they were crawling with thousands of flies, and he shook the tray but they landed back again, and he groaned and made his way to the bathroom and took a plastic bag out of the trashcan and went back to the cookies and dumped the entire tray into the bag and tied the bag up, and flies were buzzing all around him and he took the bag into the bathroom and put it in the trashcan and came back and looked at the stage again, and the robots were moving slightly faster now and the flies seemed to be staying around the stage and getting lured into the robots, and Nevi came up to Panoptico and told him that he was a fucking bastard for throwing her cookies away, and he said that the cookies were luring all the flies and he had to throw them out, and she said that it wasn't her problem if the cookies were so good that the flies couldn't stay away, and he told her that he was just trying to help, that these robots needed hundreds of flies just to move a short distance, and the show would take all night if the flies kept going over to the cookies. She told him that he was an ugly useless cyborg and she was going to make sure that her husband had nothing to do with him ever again, and he told her that she was ridiculous and he turned away from Nevi and stared at the robots again. They were moving so slowly that the assistants kept having to hold the jars of flies right over the robots, and the flies were still buzzing all around the room, and Panoptico knelt down and started to collect fly bodies from the floor and she watched his fingers carefully picking up each dead fly from the stained concrete floor and he walked up to the stage and beckoned to one of the assistants and handed him the flies and the assistant thanked him and dropped the flies into a robot and everybody cheered and Rob came up to him and they discussed what to do and Panoptico said to get bug spray to kill the flies in the jars and dump them directly into the Rob-ots, because the flies had a mind of their own tonight, and Rob ran off to an assistant and the assistant ran out of the gallery and the other assistants kept trying to coax the flies into the robots, and Rob came back to Panoptico and his face was so beautiful and he told Panoptico that he was a total lifesaver, and Panoptico said rather snidely that his wife didn't think so, and Rob said that Nevi was just angry because he wanted her to make fudge in the shape of little turds to go along with the cookies, and Nevi thought it was gross and wouldn't do it, so he ordered the fudge himself from a rival of hers, but she flushed it down the toilet before the show because she didn't want people to think that she had made it, and he told her that he was going to break up with her as soon as his opening was over, and she was still really angry about that. Panoptico said that he didn't understand what Rob saw in her, and Rob said that he didn't see much, and then the assistant came running back in with a bag and Rob ran over and went backstage and the assistant and Rob came out with jars of dead flies and poured them into the robots and everybody cheered, and the robots began to speed up and started making patterns and not just puddles, and there was jar after jar of dead flies and the robots were moving methodically around on their canvasses and making the usual sorts of patterns and eventually the assistants stopped bringing out flies and the robots moved around a little longer and then went still. And the music turned off and Rob came out and said that there were no more flies, and he appreciated everybody coming out for this exciting interlude with nature, and everybody cheered and the assistants lined the robots up next to him and he waved his arm out to coax everybody into a cheer for the robots, and they cheered again and he bowed deeply and left the stage. Panoptico tried to walk over to Rob and talk to him, but there were so many people crowded all around him shaking his hand and hugging him and patting him on the back that Panoptico just stared for a while and left. It was dark outside, and she saw Panoptico dialing his cellular phone and he began to tell his girlfriend that he'd just had the most surreal experience of his life, and the screen went black and said *Private*, and she sent Rob an email telling him that TerraRob-ots was brilliant and breaking up with Nevi was brilliant too, and she'd been busy with some other robots lately but she'd love to see him when he got the chance. And she closed her computer and left it on her lap because it was so warm and she took some painkillers and fell asleep to flies buzzing all around her.

There were no flies when she woke up, although the room still smelled of rotten squash. She checked her email and Rob hadn't sent her any sort of response. It had only been a day, or however long she'd been asleep, so there was nothing to worry about. Just more time for her to heal. She surveyed her nose and breasts and body and even though she still looked like she'd been attacked, the swelling was definitely going down and her breasts were less red and her nose was getting narrower every day. She was still in some pain, but it was more of a tenderness and an achiness and a general dizziness and weakness, so she decided to take a pause from the painkillers and stay awake for a bit. She draped herself with shirts and shivered and began to read about people's experiences with plastic surgery. She found an entire site about breast implants that had thousands of personal accounts, and she read through them one by one and was struck by all the sadness behind them—so many women out there feeling so inadequate about themselves, so many tales of seeing huge breasts on screens everywhere and feeling unlovably small and yearning for surgery and going into credit card debt and having all sorts of complications afterwards and having to go back for second and third and fourth operations, and so many women out there feeling hideous and it didn't seem right somehow, and she read about implants contracting and rippling and turning around and she read about losing sensation in the nipples forever and she read about infections and hematomas and sudden ruptures and she stopped reading when she came across one woman whose breasts turned blackish purple and smelled like rot. She hugged her computer closer to her and shivered and ordered herself a heater and a down blanket and lots of warm clothing. Oh, it would feel so good to snuggle up underneath a fluffy down blanket while she healed. She took some painkillers and fell asleep clutching her computer below her stinging chest.

She woke up to find that nothing had been delivered except a bouquet of flowers from the Mumbalore robot corporation thanking her for being such a valued client. The flowers wouldn't exactly keep her warm, so she tossed them outside the cube and felt a sharp pain on her chest and sat down and saw that something was bleeding underneath one of her breasts. She started crying and her nose swelled up inside so that she couldn't breathe and she peeled off the blood-soaked bandage and pressed a piece of gauze to the bleeding and held it there until it seemed to clot. She taped on a fresh bandage and told herself that she would have to be very careful in the future. She was very delicate now, and if anything went wrong, she was very much alone. She huddled up under the clothing with her computer and checked her email and told her corporate sponsor that she was freezing inside the cube, and the cold was hindering her productivity and she would very much appreciate it if they would turn the heat up or send her a heater and some blankets. She remembered what had happened with the air conditioners and she wondered if they would even listen, and her fingers were so numb and if only she could get the orders to come somehow, and she ordered all the heaters and blankets and thick jackets she could find and her breast was hurting where it was bleeding before and Rob still hadn't sent her any email and she was too weak to move or to think, so she took another dose of painkillers and told herself that she'd wake up to a wonderful soft blanket.

There had been nothing delivered at all while she'd been sleeping. It was definitely getting colder in the cube and she checked her email and Rob hadn't sent her anything and the grant people hadn't sent her anything and she huddled underneath her covering of stretchy shirts and tank tops and told herself that there had to be a way of getting warm again. She could place an order for a heater or a blanket and instead of using the corporate account, she could use her own, except that she had no credit cards of her own and she couldn't remember her name. Had she always been inside the cube? It was so cold in here, and if she took a warm bath she'd bleed to death because her sutures would melt, and she picked at her scalp with numb fingers and checked her email and why wasn't Rob writing her back and why was she in so much pain, and she hadn't created a new installation in so long now that people must be saying terrible things about her, and she looked at her comments and she was surprised to see that everybody thought that the squash and the flowers were brilliant, but they wanted to see her outside again. There was no way that she could possibly go outside right now. And even if she did, the feminist would have such terrible things to say to her and she wouldn't even be able to defend herself. She went back to look at the last comment that the feminist left, and she didn't know why she couldn't find it, and she looked and looked and went back further and she was determined to find the comment and she went back so far that it seemed like the feminist's other comments must be missing too, and she looked and looked and went through every single page and even rediscovered that weird guy who wanted to play chess with her, whose comment had been directly adjacent to the feminist's first long rant, and there were thousands of comments but they were no match for her compulsiveness and she read through absolutely everything several times and none of the feminist's comments appeared anywhere. Could she have imagined them all along? That was impossible, because the feminist often told her things that she hadn't really thought about before. And yes, she'd been feeling dizzy and tired for a while now and she couldn't remember Rob's visit very well, but if she remembered something then she knew that it really happened, and the feminist had been talking to her for a long time now and she definitely hadn't imagined it and she wondered where the comments went to and she imagined that cavernous building with prim switchboard women wearing headsets over perfect bouffants of hair, and their purses were tucked neatly behind them in special metal cages attached to their chairs, and she supposed that there were certain times when they heard mysterious voices whispering into their headsets and they pulled this plug instead of that one and something vanished. Well, maybe it was for the best if she couldn't read those comments again, because they'd probably just upset her, and she checked her email and noticed that the grant people had finally emailed her back, and she opened the letter eagerly and was disappointed to see that they didn't say anything at all about the cold. They were pleased that she'd been bettering herself lately, and that she was doing some very successful work, but they felt that it was time for her to return outside again, and they just wanted to send this gentle reminder to let her know that she had millions of audience members who would love to see her soon. She looked at herself in the mirror and tried to figure out how she could possibly go outside. She was covered with bruises and bandages, and her breasts were red and her face was still swollen and there was a drip pad underneath her nose that was perpetually stained with orange fluid. She figured that she could put concealer and Poudre Ophelia on everything that was discolored, but there was no way that she could hide the drip pad or the swelling, and her body was less swollen and she could probably just squeeze it into a corset, but she simply couldn't imagine showing her face right now. If only her turban were one of those big floppy hats with a veil in front, then she could hide her face behind it, and she thought about veils and didn't see why she couldn't sew one onto the front of her turban and go outside that way. It would even add additional mystery and intrigue to her persona, and she wouldn't have to worry about trying to contour away the swelling on her face with concealer. She huddled underneath the layers of clothing and looked online for a veil. It had to be opaque enough so that nobody could see her face at all, but translucent enough to see through so she wouldn't trip into the pins, and most of the veils looked so gauzy and ineffective until she came upon an old Victorian mourning veil made of thick silk crepe. It looked like nobody would be able so see anything except her faintest silhouette through the crimped black fabric, and she ordered it immediately and began to think about how she would attach it to the turban. She held a tank top to the front of the turban to gauge the way the veil would fall against it, and she was so cold because the layers of clothing fell off of her, but she got the idea to alter her shirts so she could wear them over her slashed-up sleepshirt and keep herself warm. She didn't have to do a careful job—she just wanted to give enough fabric to the breasts because they still felt sensitive and it would be too painful to stretch her tiny shirts over them. She set about with her numb fingers cutting and stitching and splicing extra material from several sacrificed shirts to make altered shirts that were actually comfortable to wear. Her arms felt weak and she stumbled over her fingernails a lot, but she kept stitching and stitching and putting on each shirt as she finished it. She was finally beginning to feel warm again, and she found a pair of baggy drawstring pants in the pile of clothing that she was using and she had forgotten about them completely and she put them on over her sweatpants and looked at all the old splatters of paint and felt wistful and kept stitching and stitching until she was wearing a thick layer of flimsy low-cut shirts, and she even used some extra material to make herself some armwarmers and a cowl that covered her chest, and she didn't need any stupid heaters anyway because she was so resourceful, and she still had a pile of shirts that she could alter if she needed to be warmer, and she would go outside when her veil came and Rob would see her and get so intrigued that he would email her back at once. She ordered herself a manicure, because she'd noticed while she was sewing that her polish was chipped and her cuticles were encrusted with dried blood, and while she waited she watched Panoptico looking at trees whose leaves were yellow and orange and red. She couldn't tell where he was, but there weren't any buildings around or any cars and all she saw were trees. She wondered who'd painted all the leaves and she watched as he walked along with his girlfriend and talked about how good the air smelled and how quiet it was and how maybe it was time for them to move out of the city. And his girlfriend laughed and said that he'd go crazy without ads to block and surveillance cameras to thwart and cultural abominations to criticize, and he said that it might be difficult, but he'd seriously like to try, that lately he'd been blocking so much of the urban environment that all he saw were pigeons and the occasional bit of sky. He'd recently started blocking everybody in a suit or a uniform, because he figured that they were just automata who couldn't be trusted, and he'd been bumping into so many people lately that he was afraid he was going to get arrested. Maybe they could just start over and he'd start recording his life in sonnets instead, and they'd plant pumpkin seeds and peaches and walk naked in the sun. And his girlfriend laughed and said it sounded wonderful, except for the fact that the semester had just begun and there were several hundred students who would be devastated if they were deprived of her blinding insights into Biology 101, and Panoptico laughed and said that they could both teach somewhere else, somewhere without anything to block, and she asked him where that would be and he said he'd teach the wild rabbits all about robotics and she could teach biology to the trees, and she hugged him and said that she never imagined that she'd be spending her life with a luddite cyborg, and he said that all he wanted to do was remember every moment of his life so he wouldn't lose anything, and they started kissing and the screen went black and private and she felt such longing and she stared at the dark screen until the manicure robot arrived.

The robot stroked her hands with the massage routine that she'd memorized completely, and she sat there hoping that the robot would add an extra stroke or squeeze or anything to show that there was actually a person controlling those soft metallic hands. She watched her fingernails and cuticles become perfect again, and she pushed the golden button carefully and she even knew the precise moment when the robot would wave goodbye. The veil had arrived during her manicure, and she was eager to open it, but she needed to let her polish dry, and she sat down on her soft place with her hands immobile on her thighs. She looked over at the black cut stocking with the little robot inside, and she felt so sad and she looked at the layered painting with little glints of yellow paint peeking through and it was splattered with tiny red spots on top and she looked at the painting next to it and it had the same little red dots and she looked around at all the paintings and they were all splattered with a fine misting of red and she looked around her cube and there were little red spots everywhere that were much darker than the lingering spots from the henna and she realized with horror that nobody had ever cleaned up her blood from the Sweet Sixteen. She forgot all about her fingernails and she began to scrub the soft place as hard as she could and her arms felt so weak and her chest was hurting but the faint stains of red remained and she scrubbed and scrubbed and she eventually stopped scrubbing when she realized that there was no way that she could scrub the blood from her concealer paintings without destroying them. She stared at her wrinkled ruby fingernails and her hands were shaking and she told herself that she had to calm down somehow before she went outside. She realized that she hadn't taken any Happyam for a while, and she decided to increase her dosage to three Happyams at a time because two Happyams had still left her feeling miserable. She swallowed the beautiful little pills and tried not to look at her ruined paintings and she told herself that she had important work to do outside the cube, and she mustn't get distracted by a few spots of blood.

She opened the box with the veil and was glad to see that it would be perfect—the thick dull crepe would hide her face completely, but if she held it up to her face she could still see through it quite well. She stitched it onto the front of the turban using a loose running stitch so that she'd be able to remove it easily when her face was better again, and she tried the turban on and it was a bit uncomfortable because the mesh felt rough against the sores on her head, but she'd tolerated much worse pain before. She took the turban off and began to peel off all the layers of altered shirts, and they really looked ridiculous but they worked well all together to keep her warm, and she finally got to her slashed sleepshirt at the bottom and took it off and looked at her new breasts. They were still red and high and tight on her chest, but everything she'd read on the web said that they would take at least a month to settle down and sit more naturally. She still couldn't believe that she actually had breasts this large, and her waist and stomach were definitely slimmer and the contrast between her chest and the rest of her body was certainly more dramatic than she'd anticipated, but it made her look almost identical to her icon, which she supposed was a good thing. She took off her drawstring pants and sweatpants and she was so cold, but her hips and thighs were so much slimmer now, and she zipped up the leather skirt and was pleased to see that it wasn't nearly as tight as it had been before. She put the corset around her torso, and it was difficult to fasten the top hooks, but she let out the laces at the top of her back and closed the hooks and arranged her breasts so that the nipples didn't show, and the corset was hurting her breasts so much that she made the laces as loose as she could, and she was still feeling very weak and everything hurt and it didn't help to be immobilized inside a corset, but she persevered because she had to go outside or she didn't know what her corporate sponsor would do. She felt like an arthritic 90-year-old as she inched her stockings up her legs and arms, and she painfully bent to dab her thighs and cleavage and upper arms with enough concealer to hide her bruising and the redness on her breasts. She dusted everything with Poudre Ophelia and startled at the juxtaposition between her perfect body and her head, which was nearly bald and covered with scabs and scars and bruising and swelling and ornamented with an orange-spotted drip pad. She put all her jewelry on, and it felt like the choker was strangling her today because her neck must had been a little swollen, and maybe she didn't need the choker because the veil would cover up her neck anyway, but if there was a breeze her neck might be exposed for a moment, so she decided to leave the choker on just in case. She glued the turban onto her head with the special adhesive she'd found, and she crammed her feet into the Golden Lotuses and lifted the veil from her face just to make certain that she hadn't forgotten anything, and everything was hurting but she did look perfect, as long as she kept the veil over her face, so she brought the veil back down and opened the door of the cube slowly and dramatically and stepped outside to the overwhelming stench of rotting squash.

It was difficult to avoid befouling her Golden Lotuses with rotten squash flesh, but she did her best, gesticulating in strange theatrical bursts and trying hard to hide the fact that she was freezing cold and in terrible pain and incredibly weak, and she hadn't stood up for this long in quite a while, let alone in Golden Lotuses, let alone with a labyrinth of rotten squash to avoid. She moved her hands in erratic patterns and got a sudden flashback to Rob's face above her and felt terribly sad, but at least she was hidden behind a veil and nobody could see her face, and she didn't know why he hadn't been in touch with her for so long now, and his opening was over, and she had so much rotten squash that the flies would love it here, and maybe he would bring over a terrarobot and a jar of flies and they would set it up together and they'd laugh together in the cube while the robot ran around outside and they'd hold each other and he would find her so beautiful and he wouldn't mind that she kept the turban glued to her head the entire time, and maybe they'd move out of the city and grow organic robots and squash covered with arabesques, and the air would smell good like an air freshener and he'd tell her that he loved her and they'd hold hands and spin until they were dizzy and they'd feed each other the most beautiful pills and she'd create an installation as large as the world itself and he'd never need to find a screen. She waved her hands and tried to remember what it felt like to stare into Rob's eyes, but all she could see was a doll, and she remembered a picture she'd seen of a hostage somewhere in Arabia who had been photographed dead but propped up to pretend that he was alive, and she shivered and felt rather sick and she was in so much pain and she knew that she would slip on the squash if she stayed outside any longer. Her nice warm shirts would be waiting for her and she could take this accursed corset off and maybe she'd warm up her feet in the bathtub and hold her computer on her lap and read all sorts of glowing comments, and she made a final gesticulation with her hands and walked back to the door undulating her arms so that nobody would notice she was limping, and she opened the door and screamed because all of her clothing was gone.

She lifted the veil and looked around and there was not a single garment left on the floor or on the shelves and she didn't know what could have happened and she pushed the button to open the trap door, because maybe her clothing fell inside somehow, and the door wouldn't open, and she didn't know what was wrong because it always opened when she pushed the button, and she pushed it again and again and the door still didn't open and she pounded on the button until she felt a sharp pain on her chest, and she felt very scared all of a sudden and all she had to wear was this ridiculous uncomfortable outfit, but at least she could still soak her feet in warm water, and she turned on the faucet and pried off her Golden Lotuses and peeled off her stockings and sat on the edge of the tub and put her feet into the water and screamed because the water was freezing. She turned the faucet in both directions and there was no hot water at all, and she tried the sink and it was cold as well, and she pushed the button again but nothing happened and she felt so trapped and she huddled up on her soft place still wearing her turban and corset, and she put her stockings on again and held her computer on her lap for warmth but she was still so cold and she suddenly noticed that the little robot inside the cut stocking was gone. Her tears felt hot and her nose swelled closed inside and she gasped for breath between her sobs. Her computer was warm and purred so softly on her lap. She stroked it and held it tight.

November

The room was filled with smoke which lent an ashy cast. She sat by the bathtub and added another crumpled piece of paper to the fire and poked it with a pencil and tossed the pencil in as well. The good thing was that she'd ordered hundreds of sketchbooks and pencils and packages of matches before they caught on to what she was doing. The bad thing was that she didn't know what she was going to do when everything ran out, so she was rationing the paper and pencils as best she could and hoping that her corporate sponsor was just playing a little game with her, maybe testing her to see how resourceful she could be, and that once she was completely out of stuff to burn they'd finally turn the heat back on. She'd tried ordering every heater and blanket and jacket that she could find, and when that didn't work she tried other clothing, and even raw fabric, and when nothing arrived she got concerned and started stocking up on things to burn. At first she was able to get everything she ordered that wasn't an obvious source of warmth, and she had a lovely supply of wooden canvas stretchers and wooden easels and wooden artist's models as well as the sketchbooks and the pencils and the cardboard from all sorts of things that she ordered just to use the boxes. But somebody must have noticed the smoke one day, because all deliveries stopped abruptly and she wasn't able to order anything else at all. She thought that she had found the perfect secret source of warmth when she ordered a manicure and realized that the robots gave off a lot of heat and proceeded to keep a manicuring robot around at all times, but after several days of wonderful warmth the robots stopped arriving too. The wood was all gone now, and there was absolutely nothing left that she could order, no matter how much she begged her corporate sponsor to help, so she rationed her paper and pencils and Dr. Tell's and stayed perpetually dressed in her turban and corset and Golden Lotuses and hoped that the game would be over soon.

She hadn't left the cube ever since she went out in a veil and returned to find that all of her clothing had been stolen. She was terrified of what they might take from her while she was gone. She was especially worried about her computer vanishing, because it was her only reliable source of warmth at this point, and it was also her only link to the outside world. Rob still hadn't sent her any email, but his website said that he'd been rather busy with his new robots, so she figured that he was just waiting until things calmed down a bit before getting in touch with her again. She imagined that he was still trying to get the robots to move faster and the flies to behave better, and she wondered if he'd surprise her one day by sending over one of his terrarobots. Meanwhile, she'd been spending a lot of time sitting by the bathtub with her computer in her lap. The corset made it difficult to sit comfortably, but it was her most substantial garment of clothing and she'd be absolutely frigid if she took it off. She kept reading about blankets and heaters and trying to order them, but nothing ever came. She had picked off the glue attaching the turban to her head, which made it easier to reach underneath it and see what she could find. Every time she slept she tried to huddle up in a fetal position for warmth as much as the corset would allow, and every time she woke up she was completely numb because the fire had gone out. She had her computer set to check her email every minute, and sometimes she checked it even more often than that because she knew that her life would change when Rob emailed her back. He had certainly purchased a lot of old electronics in the meantime, and Nevi had put up pictures of herself in a big white dress, and Panoptico had been keeping most of his activity private lately, so she wasn't really sure what he'd been doing. All she knew was that it was freezing in the cube and she had to get warm and even if only one little heater or ski jacket managed to arrive, her life would be transformed. It was hard to think in this numbing cold, and she often found herself forgetting what website she wanted to look at next. She couldn't even scowl properly because of the anthrax, and every time she looked at her face, all she could see was that her nose was narrower but now it tilted slightly to the left. She had tried to order more Mumbalore robots to come and fix it, but nobody came. Nobody ever came anymore, and her corporate sponsor ignored her when she complained, and Rob was out there somewhere but he might have forgotten all about her. She checked Panoptico's website again, and there was a new declaration right at the top that said he was boycotting all fascist airlines, and she clicked on the link and found a number of articles about an incident that must have happened to Panoptico when he was flying home from his trip to see the painted trees. He was trying to go through the security gate at the airport, but the security people told him that he wouldn't be allowed on the plane with his cyborg apparatus on. He showed them letters from his doctor and from the university where he taught and he even showed them magazine articles about him, and he told them that it would be very dangerous if he took the apparatus off because he'd been wearing it for decades and he'd gotten used to seeing the world rotated ninety degrees and through his own personal filters, and he pleaded with them to let him fly intact but they took him and strip-searched him and tore electrodes from his body and made him bleed and broke his special glasses and kept most of his equipment, and he fell and hit his head and passed out while they were searching him and he was so disoriented that he couldn't even walk without his girlfriend guiding him, and after he got home he was feeling dizzy and ill and having trouble concentrating and he'd finally cobbled together a new apparatus but he was still feeling shaky and confused and he vowed never to fly again. She imagined Panoptico being tortured by sadistic security guards and feeling so vulnerable and wobbly and she felt so sad for him and wondered if he'd ever go again to see the trees. She shivered and put another piece of paper on the fire and decided that she would email Rob about Panoptico. A double email would be okay in this situation, because she could begin with the premise of wanting to know more about how Panoptico was doing, which was certainly a valid thing to ask about, since Panoptico was sort of a mutual friend, and she rubbed her hands together to warm up her fingers slightly and it was difficult to type with her fingers so numb, but she managed to write that she had heard about Panoptico's airport ordeal, and she wanted to know if he was doing okay, and she was also wondering how his TerraRob-ots had been going and if maybe he'd like to come and visit soon, and if he could bring a blanket with him when he visited or maybe a little heater because it had gotten chilly in the cube and she was afraid that her warm hospitality wouldn't be quite enough to make him comfortable. She sent the note off and congratulated herself for thinking to include a plea for a heat source, and she felt so sleepy but it was so hard to fall asleep because she was shivering so much and she opened the bottle of Lulliban and realized that she only had one pill left. She had been trying to order refills on all of her pills, but nothing ever arrived anymore, and she was completely out of painkillers and she tried to sleep without the Lulliban but her mind was racing and she kept having to check her email and she eventually decided that if she took the last Lulliban now, the game would end tomorrow.

She woke up numb and checked her email even before she started a new fire in the tub. Rob had finally written her back! He said that Panoptico was fine and that his show had been going really well lately. Her idea about feeding the Rob-ot flies was so cool that he'd looked to see whether anybody was doing that sort of thing, and he'd found these guys with robots powered by shit and flies, and they said that the future was going to be all about sustainability and being green, so he figured that he couldn't go wrong turning the robots into TerraRob-ots, since he wanted to be on the cutting edge and all. Everybody loved his show, and he'd already gotten an award from an environmentalist group and he was doing a segment for a documentary about the future and he hadn't gotten a single bad review this time—he'd been worried about people getting bothered by the smell, but everyone just said that it was so brave of him to let nature into a gallery space. He was really excited because the guys who invented the robots had come up with a way to make the robots go even faster on fewer flies, so he was going to retrofit those with Rob-ot brains and give them a try. And he was also excited because he'd recently tried out a new cellular phone that could also work as a handgun, and it was really cool because everybody on the street had a cellular phone anyway, so nobody would know how well protected you were until it was too late.

She reread the note again and again and tried to read between the lines for any glimmerings of passion and interest, but all she could see was technology. He didn't even seem that concerned about Panoptico. The only thing that she could think of was that maybe he hadn't read her entire note, or maybe a few of her lines got lost somewhere inside that cavernous room of switchboards, or maybe he'd written more and his lines were the ones that got lost, but whatever it was, they weren't communicating very well, so she sent him another note telling him that she'd love to see him again, and it was really cool about his robots and all, but they really hadn't talked for a long time now and it would be great if he could visit her in her cube one of these days, because she'd really like to see him and she missed him and he'd promised to visit after the wedding and the opening, and she'd been really looking forward to it and she was getting very lonely in the cube and it would be so wonderful if he could come to call. She sent the note off and told herself that he would have to visit her after a note like that. She realized that she was freezing, so she leaned into the bathtub and made a little fire of pencils and crumpled paper and put her computer on her lap and began to check her email. He had to write back soon this time—he would probably realize that they hadn't communicated properly last time, and he'd email her back apologetically, and he would tell her that he'd be over so soon, and everything would be perfect. He'd see her new enhanced body and he wouldn't be able to neglect her ever again. He'd sent her email, after all, which he didn't have to do if he wasn't interested in her, so he was probably ready to resume the relationship, and she reread his note and lingered over every word and checked her email again and again and she finally got a note and she was so excited, but it was only from her corporate sponsor, and they said that she must be fully recovered from her surgery by now, and they urged her to go outside without the veil. She figured that it was probably even colder outside the cube, but if that was what she needed to do to get the heat turned on again, she'd be more than happy to oblige. Yes, she'd go outside in all her splendor and Rob would see her and he'd be enraptured by her beauty and he'd definitely come to call before she even knew it.

She stood up and pains shot through her feet because she'd been wearing her Golden Lotuses continuously to retain a bit of heat. She pulled back her veil and looked at her face and determined to create the most perfect beauty that the world had ever seen. Perhaps her nose tilted a tiny bit and her chin was still slightly too big, but she could fix all that with concealer and she would be even more beautiful than her icon when she'd finished. She began with her eyebrows, which she hadn't plucked in quite some time, and she got rid of all the little hairs that didn't belong and marveled at how narrow her eyebrows looked when she was done. Her skin didn't have any pimples anymore, but there were still a few dark red acne scars, and the boundaries of her lips were also scarred from the surgery and she still had dark circles underneath her eyes, so she went to work with her concealers and foundations, blending and shading and mixing colors until she had an absolutely perfect canvas. Perfect except for her nose and chin and the fact that her eyes were still a trifle too close together, so she blended and shaded some more until she'd changed her contours to conform to the Golden Mask. She dusted everything with Poudre Ophelia and delighted at her velvety white face. Her fingers seemed to be warming up, and she felt a certain energy burning through her as she put in her Mesmereyes and smoothed her brows with tinted gel and went around and around her eyes with kohl and gilded her lids with silver shadow and glued her garnet-tipped lashes on and finished with Egyptianate flourishes more dramatic than ever before. She had already concealed the scars around her lips, so she spread on a bit of lip sealer to prevent her lipstick from bleeding, and the pink of her lips was now erased completely but she marveled at how plump they were. She recreated her lip contours with liner, drawing on a cupid's bow where she thought most appropriate, and she filled her lips in with the liner and put on a layer of burgundy lipstick and blotted the excess oils onto one of her last tissues and perfected the contours with another layer of liner and added shine and depth with another layer of lipstick and dusted a bit of shimmering gold powder in the middle of her lower lip, and she stared at her face and she put some eyedrops in to kill the redness and she gave herself a sultry wink and knew that she had created perfect beauty. She took the turban off and startled at the scabby mess and snipped the veil off and tossed it aside. A bit of glue to hold the turban on her head, and she stepped back and looked at herself and realized that her corset was covered with ashes. She brushed them off the black fabric as best she could, and she looked at herself from every angle in the mirrors and tried to understand how she got to be inside this ravishing creature. Her breasts had finally recovered from the surgery and their skin was white again and they curved so beautifully out of the top of the corset, and she pulled the laces tighter through her waist and was amazed at how narrow she was, and Rob's hands might well be able to fit around her waist and he'd be so drawn to her, and her hips and legs were so slim now and she stared at herself as she put on her choker and bracelets and rings, and her nailpolish had gotten slightly chipped, but it didn't matter because she was the most demonic creature who had ever lived, and she would hypnotize everybody outside and she would sear them and she would transcend them and she would fascinate them with her perfection.

She hadn't shown her face to the world since she'd gotten her lips and nose redone, and she knew that she had to make a dramatic entrance as she left the cube. She also planned to take her computer outside with her so that nobody would take it while she was gone—it was silver, after all, so it wouldn't interfere with her look. The only problem was that she didn't want to anger her corporate sponsor by making them think that she didn't trust them not to take her computer, so she had to figure out a way to make it seem perfectly natural that she was bringing her computer outside with her. She shivered and hugged her computer close and decided that she would hold it open in front of her face when she went outside and then she'd do a slow reveal. That would heighten the drama and mystery that she'd created with the veil, and hopefully her corporate sponsor wouldn't suspect the real reason why she was bringing her computer outside with her. She unplugged it from the wall and stood up and opened it and held it to her face and opened the door and stepped out slowly and imagined millions of eyes upon her as she gradually raised it over her chin and lips and nose and finally her Mesmereyes and she stared at the cameras so intensely that she hoped they'd turn to stone, and she closed her computer and put it down carefully and began to dance. She waved her hands in arabesques so bold that she almost fell over, and she tried to avoid the squash and the pins and especially the eyes. She danced to the smell of the rotten squash and she danced to the feeling of the pins against her skin and she danced to the songs inside her head that she could no longer remember. She danced and moved her hands and felt everybody's eyes upon her swollen lips and breasts and she turned to show her curves from every angle and she talked to the mottled walls with elaborate arabesques. Eventually her feet begin to hurt so much that she had to try not to cry, and so she picked up her computer and opened it and moved it slowly over her chin and her lips and nose and finally her Mesmereyes. She turned and went inside, quite pleased with her performance, and she surveyed her cube with a paranoid eye and realized that they'd taken her mourning veil away.

She put down her computer and looked everywhere and the veil was definitely gone. What could they possibly have wanted with a mourning veil? She searched and searched and the trap door still wouldn't open and she didn't have any clothing for the veil to hide in, and she certainly wouldn't have tossed it into the bathtub to burn because she could have used the extra layer of fabric to drape over her shoulders, and she couldn't remember where she'd put it, exactly, but she did know that it had been in her cube when she left and now it was missing and this was getting ridiculous. She sent a note to her corporate sponsor telling them that she'd put up with enough—she was bringing in so much ad revenue and the least they could do was let her have a veil. She'd been sitting in the cold forever now, and she'd put up with it when they took her clothing away and when they wouldn't send her heaters or anything warm, but they'd gone way too far this time and she was going to stop this project right now if they didn't give her the veil back, and maybe a heater or a jacket while they were at it. She'd had quite enough of them and their prim switchboard ladies and their incessant cicadas, and she only wanted to make art in a pure environment and they were acting like fascists and she wasn't going to tolerate this sort of treatment any longer. She was sick of being ignored, and if she didn't hear back from them soon, they'd have to find themselves another artist to exploit. She sent the note off and fumed as she knelt over the bathtub and began to light a fire and almost singed her face from an oily blast when she used a lipliner pencil instead of a lead one.

She sat and read through her comments, which calmed her down a bit. Everybody thought that she was beautiful, and a number of Aficionados thought that the juxtaposition of the natural decay of the room with the artificial perfection of her beauty was utterly brilliant, especially since the room was inherently artificial and she was inherently natural, and they went on and on about nature and artifice and she scrolled through all the comments and looked for any sort of sign that someone cared about her. Even a comment from the feminist would have been welcome, but the feminist had likely been silenced by the prim switchboard ladies with their ridiculous bouffants, and she read and read and it seemed like everybody was getting Sweet Sixteens and Double Lip Deluxes now, and the Provocateurs wouldn't stop talking about her new breast implants. She looked at her press, and there were so many glowing articles that she didn't know where to start, and she began to read one that said she was a goddess and a celebrity and that her look had become popular even in online worlds, where people could buy an avatar that looked just like her, but she stopped reading immediately when she noticed that she'd gotten an email back from Rob. She opened it and read it and sat there in shock. *Chill*, he said. Chill. That was all he said to her. Chill. Just one word. Chill. He was never coming back. He was never coming back again. A formal feeling came over her and she huddled numb and couldn't even cry, and the paintings on the walls began to talk to her and she told them she was so so sorry she'd been neglecting them, and she got out her plastic palette and broke off every lipstick that she owned and determined to overwhelm the splatterings of blood. She crushed the lipsticks all together between her hands and kneaded them until the oils softened from her warmth, and she dipped her fingers into the dark red mass and began to paint. She fell into a trance of hands and fingers moving fingers moving soft red oils layers fingers moving soft and the arabesques fell faster than her head could tell and pain paint pain paint pain and her fingers moved and the arabesques told her new words that she couldn't understand and she tried to talk back to them as best she could and they talked about despair and loneliness and terror and she rocked back and forth and her fingers told stories that she had forgotten long ago and her head could only nod along numb with pain paint pain paint pain and when she'd finished with the lipstick she tore into the concealers and foundations and shadows and mascaras and liners and layer after layer and the papers all were full and thick with paint but she had to finish everything and she ended with a black nub of kohl in each of her hands and a layer of arabesques so intricate that she began to understand. She saw herself wild and painted in the mirror and she found her tubes of acrylic paint and she began to make arabesques all over her face. She moved down to her arms and such lovely large canvasses on her bosoms and she layered arabesques of paint around her thighs and moved up again to her face and created a layer of black patterns that even overwhelmed her Mesmereyes. She grabbed her computer and went outside and waved her arms frenetically and danced around as best she could until her feet were hurting her so much that she got faint and almost fell, and she waved her arms once more and stared fierce into the cameras and picked up her computer and collapsed on the floor of her cube laughing and crying maniacally.

She lay down on her soft place shivering and agitated and drained and she tried so hard to calm her mind, but it wouldn't stop racing, and she checked all her bottles of pills just to see if maybe some Lulliban had made its way into a different bottle, and she shook each one and everything was empty except for the Happyam, and she didn't know what she was going to do because she couldn't sleep, and she opened the bottle of Happyam and there were only four pills remaining, so she cupped them in her hand and stroked them and told them that they were so beautiful and she loved their scarlet glimmerings and she hadn't gotten happy yet but if they could please please help her she'd be so grateful, and she swallowed them all with a sip of icy water and lay back down and waited for something to happen. She was so exhausted, but her mind kept going and dredging up all sorts of things that she had to push back into the folds of her brain and her hands kept wandering to her scalp and picking off scabs no matter how many times she told them to stay folded in front of her, and she simply couldn't fall asleep no matter how hard she tried, and she wasn't even getting any happier, so she made a fire and sat by the bathtub sipping a Dr. Tell's and reading her latest comments. The Aficionados all loved her latest creation, although the Boosters and Zealots seemed slightly less enthusiastic than usual and the Provocateurs felt that the arabesques interfered with the view, but the Aficionados were the only ones whose opinions she really cared about anyhow, and the fire was warming her up a bit and she fed more paper and pencils into the flames until she felt a lovely warm glow, and she watched herself on the screen all covered with arabesques, and perhaps she was really getting somewhere with her art, and she continued to read through her comments until she noticed that her corporate sponsor had sent her a very odd note. It said that she needed to wash that mess off of her face and body immediately, that she was supposed to look sexy and not like a freak, and that she had committed trademark infringement by altering their product in a manner so as to create confusion for potential customers. If she didn't comply with their request, they would be forced to pursue legal action. She read the note several times and felt a searing hatred and they couldn't do this no no no and she would beat them at this game and she opened her tubes of acrylic paint and used her fingers to make bold eyes all over her body. Some were small and some were larger and she tossed *Milady's Book O' Tips* and the Golden Mask into the fire as she painted an enormous eye on each of her breasts. She kicked off her Golden Lotuses and felt a terrible relief as her feet felt solid underneath her again and eye and eye and a row of eyes all up her thighs and pain paint pain paint and her fingers wet and strong and sure of color and form and eye and eye and never never again and she stared at herself staring back piercing and she laughed and grabbed her computer and ran outside and danced wild and maniacal and the squash soft underfoot and her hands stabbing into arabesques of manic frenzy and she stared at the eyes on the walls obscured with glue and dead pomegranate flesh and they were no match for her evil eyes and she waved her arms and leaped and pirouetted and her feet were hurting with an exquisite pain of freedom and she felt her forceful gait returning and she no longer had to move her arms to compensate for her feet and everything poured out of her and she twirled and stayed far from the pins and her fingers fluttered and she got an idea all of a sudden and raced into the cube and grabbed all of her paints and gesso and a plastic bucket and a wide brush and she ran back out and sat on the floor with the rotten squash and emptied every tube and bottle into the bucket and stirred and stirred until everything was brown, and she began to paint scathing notes on the walls saying that everyone should boycott her corporate sponsor and ignore the advertisements all around her. She painted large and triumphant over the pins and filled every space she could with caustic words and when her paint ran out she made an obscene gesture into the cameras and threw her paintbrush against the wall so hard that the plastic handle cracked.

They had taken all her paper away and all her pencils and all her Dr. Tell's. She hugged her computer tight and her pulse was racing and she looked at her website and the words looked so striking and strong and she laughed and laughed and imagined the impact she would have on millions of viewers, and she went back to the archive of what she'd just done and she cackled as she watched herself wild and primitive and possessed of an energy and intensity she didn't even know she had, and the eyes on her breasts were perfect and nobody could control her and she watched herself paint messages in bold brown letters all over the room and she watched and watched and all of a sudden the messages were gone. She thought that maybe she had gone back to an earlier archive by accident, but she still had the eyes all over her body and her hand still held a paintbrush, it was just that nothing went onto the walls as she painted. She looked at the current view of the room and her broken paintbrush was still lying on the floor but the messages had been erased somehow. She felt frantic and grabbed her computer and went outside and the messages were still there, and she looked at the screen and she saw herself standing there with her computer and looking at the screen and seeing a room without any messages on the walls, and inside the room she was standing there and looking into a screen and no messages and room and screen and room and screen and scream and scream and scream and she unhooked her corset in a fury and unzipped her skirt and peeled her stockings off her arms and legs and ripped off all her jewelry and threw it hard against the walls and garnets flew everywhere and she tore off her turban and scabs came off with the glue and she danced around and moved and moved until she was dripping with sweat and wet and blood on her head and squash soft on her feet and arabesques and eyes and scars all over and she twirled and crouched down and leapt up and rolled in the rotten squash and cold and wet and stench and garnets in the rotten flesh and handfuls of pulp against the walls and slippery and soft and scream and scream and writhe in pain paint pain paint pain and the garnets scraped her and the pins stuck in and she stood and held her arms above her head and howled as loudly as she could.

This time they hadn't taken anything away. She scraped off the excess squash with trembling hands and flushed it down the toilet and watched the shimmering red dots disappear. A piercing chill and she laced herself back up into her stays and zipped up her skirt and pulled on her stockings and put her turban back onto her head. The feathers had gotten rather crushed, so she ripped them out and threw them into the bathtub. She lit the feathers on fire for a moment of warmth and looked at the archives and she had been entirely covered up by a large black square. Her email was full of angry messages from her corporate sponsor talking about obscenity and nudity and fines and losing advertisers and there was even a ridiculous note about how they'd warned her twice about trademark infringement and they would be forced to seek legal redress, which would result in the impoundment and destruction of all goods bearing infringing trademarks, and she sent them back a note saying that she was an artist and she could do what she wanted and they were supposed to pay for anything, including fines from stupid prudes who were more offended by a naked body than by crippling garments that made women into fragile ornaments, and she sent the note off and felt giddy and terrified and she stared at herself covered by a large black square and she was shaking and the squash smell was making her nauseous and all she wanted was a Lulliban, and she curled up on the soft place with her computer and it was so cold in the cube that the soft place wasn't even very soft and she tried to breathe and she didn't know what she had done and her head was screaming and everything was shaking inside and she tried to breathe deep but the corset wouldn't let her and she picked at her head and chewed on the scabs embedded with glue, and she was so tired and the scabs stuck to her teeth and pick pick chew scab pick no no no hands on chest fold hands breathe deep breathe warm computer warm breathe stop shaking stop mind racing eye eye eye pick chew glue bitter no no no eye squash eye Rob no no no no no stop breathe breathe deep stop pick thick scab chew scab oh oh no so tired so hungry so so so hungry stomach numb numb stomach no food must eat must sleep nose numb no no no.

She woke up to a strange mummified feeling and she was afraid that they had done something terrible to her body until she looked in the mirror and remembered everything. Arabesques and eyes and dried squash pulp and her body was definitely her own. But she was hungry, very hungry, so she looked everywhere inside her cube for perhaps an errant bottle of Dr. Tell's. All her chocolate hazelnut spread was long gone, and she remembered the days when she'd eat fingerful after fingerful and it was so sweet and rich and she couldn't find any Dr. Tell's but she opened up her jar of chocolate ganache neck gel and sniffed it and held her nose close and it smelled so good and she licked it just a bit and if she tried very hard she could taste a hint of chocolate underneath the bitterness, and she stuck her finger in and took a gob and licked it and smelled the jar while she swallowed and if she concentrated very hard on the smell she could almost get it to taste good. Yes, this would be a fine solution to her hunger problem—she still had so many jars and tubs and bottles of all sorts of delicious products, and if she could ration them out and focus on the smell she'd be just fine. Maybe she didn't have anything else to burn, but she still had her little silver computer that purred at her and sat warm in her lap, and she didn't need to be that warm anyhow, and she shivered and held her computer close and stuck her nose into the jar of neck gel while she swallowed down another mouthful. That extra layer of paint and squash gave her even more warmth, and her corporate sponsor would probably be so impressed by her recent boldness that they'd be sure to turn up the heat very soon now. She had told herself that the game would definitely end with her last Lulliban, so she just had to wait and enjoy her splendid confections and all would be well. Oh yes, she had pushed her work so far yesterday that her corporate sponsor must be very proud of her, and they were probably just testing her with all those silly emails and alterations to her room. They were fervent believers in freedom of creative expression, after all, and they probably just wanted to see if she'd stand up to petty restrictions because they had a wonderful surprise planned for her at the very end of the project. She shivered and her hands were numb and she could see her breath condense into a faint white cloud in front of her. She stumbled over the latch to open her computer and she could barely push the keys to read her email. Her face was burning from the cold and nobody had sent her anything at all, and she looked at the large black square moving around the room and she looked at Rob's website and he was still showing off his terrarobots and Nevi was still showing off her dress and Rob had bought a broken talking doll without a head and Panoptico hadn't added anything since the airline fiasco and she went to the place where she could see through his eyes and she was startled to hear a woman sobbing and all she could see was a sterile white ceiling overhead. She had a sickening feeling that something was very very wrong, and she searched for news articles about Panoptico and she started to cry when she saw the headlines. A coma. Brain-dead. No chance of recovery. He had been hit by one of those billboard trucks with a tiny cab and an enormous narrow billboard dragged along behind it. The truck company denied all responsibility because Panoptico was the one at fault for blocking out all ads. It was only a matter of time before they pulled the plug. Acute hemorrhaging. Vital signs absent. No chance. His girlfriend sobbed and the ceiling loomed above and she closed her computer and held it tight and she felt so sick and terrified and her computer wasn't warm enough and she lit a match and held it in her hand until it almost burnt her fingers and she lit another and another and her breath was white and her lips were numb and she looked around for something to burn and she suddenly noticed her paintings all around. They pleaded with her not to burn them, and she said that she was freezing to death and she couldn't help it and they said no no you mustn't and she said she would freeze otherwise and she was so so sorry so so sorry and she sobbed as she pulled the paintings down one by one and tossed them into the bathtub and she needed warmth so badly and she was so cold and she saw the painting with the yellow traces underneath and no no no and cold and cold and pain paint pain paint pain and lit a match and hot black smoke and pictures fading blast of flame and pain paint pain and smoke so thick choke smoke open door must open door must open door smoke choke black push hard door closed room closed pins closed squash closed eyes closed no no no door no no no closed no.

December

THE ROOM BEGAN TO FILL WITH BLISTERING SNOW. She couldn't feel a thing. There was a robot in the corner of her cube who stared at her as she stared at herself dancing around on the screen. She had pounded on the door for days and even tried to break the glass, but she was trapped inside the cube and she had no idea how they got her double to dance around the room. She couldn't hear anybody outside—all that she could hear was the loud electric whirring of the snowblower that they'd somehow installed in the corner of the room. It looked like it would be a lot of fun to be frolicking in the snow, but she didn't quite understand how her double could spend so long out there in a corset and miniskirt and not get cold. Her double was dressed exactly as she had been when they designed the icon of her, but her double's arabesques were sadly inadequate—she waved her arms haphazardly without any sense of pattern or design. It was difficult to watch her double bastardize her work, and it was even worse to look at her comments and see that nobody even noticed that she had been replaced. Her admirers were still leaving comments about how beautiful and brilliant she was, and the Provocateurs were urging her to take it all off and make naked angels in the snow. She was not at all surprised to find that the comments held no trace of her earlier escapades involving body paint and nakedness and defamation of her corporate sponsor, nor was she surprised to see that the feminist had definitely been silenced.

She had tried everything to get out of the cube. When it was clear that neither the trap door nor the room door would open, she spent a lot of time banging on the glass and trying to break it with her Golden Lotuses, but all that happened was that her Golden Lotuses broke and little red crystals flew everywhere. She tried slathering herself with vanishing cream, but all it did was make her greasy and heighten the smell of the rotten squash that was still dried all over her body. She tried emailing the Time Travel Trust and telling them that now would be a great time for her to leave, if they could facilitate such a thing, but she never heard back from them. She even tried emailing Rob, using Panoptico's tragic accident as a pretext and hoping that if she could only get him to come and visit her somehow, then he could help her to escape, but all he said was that it sucked about Panoptico, and that he had always told Panoptico to look into cryogenic preservation, but now it was too late. She couldn't think of anybody else who would be able to help her, so she was stuck inside the cube until the end of December with this silent robot who did nothing but stare at her. He did take the edge off the cold, though it was still rather chilly inside the cube, and he also offered her several bottles a day of a sweet warm milky drink that reminded her of cambric tea. The bottles were labeled Dr. Mitchell's Celebrated Tonic for Increasing Flesh and Soothing the Nerves, and she didn't really want her flesh to be increased, but her nerves were definitely jangled and she didn't have anything else to eat, so she figured that a few bottles a day couldn't hurt. She didn't like to be stared at all the time, but at least the robot wasn't playing any music, and if he kept giving her bottles of Dr. Mitchell's and warming up the cube a bit, she supposed that she'd be able to tolerate the remaining days until she was free. She was terribly uncomfortable inside the corset, and she hated the fact that she couldn't order anything or go outside, but she knew that she could make it through. And when she got out of the cube, she'd have a new life. She had been reading a lot lately, and she was getting glimmerings about what she wanted to do after they let her free. It was difficult to read anything completely because web pages kept vanishing as she tried to read them, but she had been trying to figure out what came after postmodernism, because she knew that she'd had quite enough of living in a cube surrounded by mirrors and staring into a screen. She had found one website that talked about a movement called neonaturism, but almost as soon as she had begun to read it, the screen went blank and told her that the page was nowhere to be found. She couldn't get the first sentence out of her head, which read: *Realism frames the mirror, modernism breaks it and mourns, postmodernism celebrates the shards as it bleeds, and neonaturism stares into a pond instead and sees through to its depths.* She didn't know what that meant, exactly, but she did know that she wanted to understand, so she sat and tried to ignore the robot's stares and tried to discover what sort of world she might want to inhabit. She was becoming terribly frustrated because her searching was growing increasingly impaired—it seemed that everything she did resulted in a *Page Not Found* message, and she took a large gulp of Dr. Mitchell's and kept trying to search and search until she realized that it was futile to keep trying. She looked at her own website, and she was still able to view her inept double bouncing around blithely in the snow, and she tried Rob's website, hoping so much that he would still be there for her, and she found herself staring at Rob's beautiful face staring at a robot. There was nothing new on his site, but she looked at all the pictures that she had already pored over before, and she noticed that her vision must have shifted because all those women by Rob's side who had previously looked so beautiful to her eyes now looked like corpses. There was a dead and artificial quality to them, and she became acutely aware of the fact that most of the men in the pictures looked so much more natural and the women were plucked and colored and contorted into masks. She looked and looked through all the pictures and she couldn't find one woman whose face was completely unaltered by some sort of artifice. Were all these women so insecure that they didn't want to be looked at without masks? She supposed she knew the answer. She thought about Rob and wondered what he had really wanted from her all along, and she began to write a note to him. She told him that it was cold inside her cube and that she had burned her secret drawings and that not even an Omniscope could bring them back. She'd gotten sick of being watched and she was going far away when this was all over, far away where nobody had even heard of the web except in terms of spiders. She was going someplace where her appearance didn't matter, someplace where she could be naked and nobody would care, someplace where she could make art for the trancelike playlike joy of it and not for accolades or show. She was going someplace where she could invent new words in her language of images, words for feelings that she could only discover when she was free. She told him that there might not be nanotechnology in this place, or the hope of cryogenic preservation, but that she craved a different kind of immortality, the kind you feel each moment when you're living connected to yourself and to the earth and to real people around you. She told him that she hoped that they could be together in this place one day. And then she reread her note and something odd happened. She started to imagine a response from Rob and she decided not to send the note quite yet and she began to type his answer. He would tell her that he'd been really busy and that her next project sounded cool. He would tell her that he was working on his next show, which involved TerraRob-ots that went really fast because they ate mice instead of flies, and that he'd recently won an award for being one of the hottest young artists of the year. He would tell her that he had found a new memory drug that he was convinced could make him remember twice as much. And he would tell her that he had won an auction for yet another silent talking doll. She read her note again and savored every word of her response and realized that she didn't have to send the note at all. It suddenly hit her that there was nothing more to him than what she could imagine. She had fallen in love with an image. An image that was dead inside. She peeled off her Mesmereyes and bit off her long chipped fingernails one by one.

She accepted a warm bottle of Dr. Mitchell's from the robot's metal body, and her fingertips felt so sensitive and free as she rubbed her hands over her broken scalp and determined to stop picking. She sipped at the warm sweet liquid and thought about how rough and substantial her scalpscabs felt in contrast with her silky hair which was growing back sparsely in patches, and she thought about how satisfying it would feel to pick a scab off and if it was dry and fat enough it might even crunch between her teeth before it stuck to them, and her hand kept going up to her head to pick and she kept having to pull it away. She checked her email so that she could give her hands something to do, and she was glad to see a note from her corporate sponsor, because they hadn't responded to her email for such a long time, and she'd been pleading with them to let her out early, but they seemed content to send her a robot and make her wait, and she opened the note and choked on her Dr. Mitchell's as she read *Congratulations! You have won a lifetime in here.*

She stared at her scarred and painted body in the mirror and took a bar of soap in each hand and began to fill the mirrors with bold white arabesques that spoke of things that she might never understand. The scale began to announce her weight in a booming voice as she saw her face gradually vanishing in the mirror above the sink, and she heard another voice coming from the robot and asking her to please sit down and rest, and she ignored the cacophony and she kept painting the mirror until her face was entirely obscured by arabesques. She moved on to another mirror away from the sink and the booming voice was still unrelentingly announcing her weight and the robot was demanding that she please sit down right now, and she didn't know why the scale was still going or why the robot cared what she was doing, so she kept painting and painting and they couldn't keep her inside here and this had to be a joke and she wanted to work and grow and live and she had to get out of this cube and her arms moved in a frenzy and the voices grew louder and more insistent and the robot started to come towards her and no no no this could not be this could not be and she kept on painting and the robot grabbed her wrists with two of his arms and took the soap away with his other two arms and his grip was so tight and it was hurting and she struggled but he was too strong and pain paint pain paint pain and the robot pushed her down and the scale stopped yelling and the robot's voice grew calm and said that she had to stay inside her cube and rest like a good girl and she mustn't trouble herself with such wearying activity, and all of that nasty wallpaper was burnt up now and we didn't need any more of those horrid patterns; they did tire the eyes out so frightfully to look at them. She told the robot that she needed to keep painting and he told her that he would take such good care of her, and he was here to provide her with a deluxe Melt-O-Pak body wrap that would purify her body and take all the toxins away. And he turned on the water in the bathtub and told her not to worry, that all she needed to do was relax and he would take care of the rest. He gave her another bottle of Dr. Mitchell's to drink and two of his hands were still holding her down and she tried to get free and he told her that she needed to relax and he held her down even more firmly while the water filled the tub. She was already chilly and she didn't want a freezing cold bath and she didn't trust this robot at all and she didn't know what was going on, and she screamed *Let me go!* and he told her that she had to be a good girl and he had such a lovely body wrap in store for her, but first he had to wash all that filthy paint off of her skin, because nice girls didn't paint themselves, and she struggled and struggled and the bathtub was full and the robot told her that a proper girl didn't wear her stays in the bath, and he began to unhook her corset with two of his hands while she tried to get free, and she saw her ridiculously large breasts fall out of the corset and the robot unzipped her skirt and peeled off her stockings and the rest of her body was so skinny that she barely recognized herself, and the robot told her to drink down the Dr. Mitchell's and get into the tub, and she refused and he told her that he knew best, and she said that she wanted to leave the cube and she didn't want to wash the squash and eyes and arabesques off of her body, and he told her that she had to learn to follow orders and he would hurt her if she didn't listen, and she still refused and he put his hands around her neck and began to close them and she relented and gulped down the Dr. Mitchell's and climbed into the tub and she was shocked to see that the water was delightfully hot. She felt the hot water melting her chilled flesh, and it had been so long since she felt this good and the robot began to rub her with soap and she was finally warm and the robot's hands felt wonderful as he scrubbed her gently with a soft brush that he had pulled out from somewhere deep within his metal body. He let the dirty water drain as the tub kept filling and filling with clean hot water, and he scrubbed her and scrubbed her until her skin was smooth and new again. He told her that she was such a good girl and he gave her another bottle of Dr. Mitchell's and she drank it down and the hot water felt so soothing that she didn't want to come out, and the robot told her that it was time to dry off and prepare for the body wrap, and he pulled out an enormous white fluffy towel and she climbed out and he wrapped her in it and dried her off so gently, and she felt so enveloped and warm and she didn't know what was happening and he pulled out a soft white ruffled flannel nightgown and matching cap and told her that she would look so pretty in her new outfit and he dressed her and encouraged her to lie down on the soft place. He gave her another Dr. Mitchell's and she drank it down as he swaddled her in a puffy white blanket, and she was feeling more relaxed but she still didn't know what was happening, and she reached over for her computer and the robot restrained her and told her that she mustn't trouble herself with work and she needed to relax and let the nice Dr. Mitchell's soothe her nerves, and he fed her another and another and she was beginning to feel calm and floaty and the nightgown and the blanket felt so soft and warm and the Dr. Mitchell's did taste sweet and the robot began to massage her over the blanket and nightgown and he massaged her arms and legs and shoulders with long melting strokes and it felt so good and she asked the robot when she could leave the cube and he said that he would tend to her forever and she said she wanted to come out and he asked her if his massage didn't feel relaxing or his blanket wasn't warm enough, and she said that they felt fine but she wanted to go and he told her to be a good girl and drink another Dr. Mitchell's, and she drank it down and felt so calm and his mechanical touch felt lovely and she pulled her arm out of the blanket and started to reach up under her nightcap to pick a scab that was itching and he pulled her arm down and told her that a proper girl should stop picking and let her pigtails grow out nice and silky and he swaddled her more tightly and fed her another Dr. Mitchell's and kept massaging her with his four Shivaite arms and she memorized his entire sequence of movements but it didn't matter because it felt so good and her mind was dancing and frolicking through piles of soft warm snow and she thought about Panoptico's camera staring at the sterile white ceiling while his girlfriend sobbed by his side and she felt so sad and she tried to forget about Panoptico and the robot fed her another Dr. Mitchell's and she remembered the crackling sobs of the *Swansong Serenade* and the little robot with the yellow paint and Rob's mouth gaping round above her and she tried to forget and tried to push those memories back into her brain but they were just too powerful and she tried to concentrate on relaxing into the massage but her brain wouldn't cooperate and her eyes started to cry and the robot told her that a nice girl shouldn't look so troubled and he fed her another Dr. Mitchell's and she struggled to get free and he wrapped her even more tightly and she suddenly remembered what had really happened in those monkey studies that she was trying to read about months or perhaps years ago—the monkeys were reared in isolation in a strange laboratory filled with tiny cages and there were hundreds of studies and they weren't faked by luddites at all and the monkeys had cried and cried and rocked and mutilated themselves by biting and scratching their skin and when they were finally let out of their cages they were unable to interact with any other monkeys at all. She screamed to be let free, and the robot said now now, a pretty girl like you needn't be making such a fuss, and he fed her Dr. Mitchell's after Dr. Mitchell's until she felt floaty and didn't know where she was except that she was on top of such a nice warm soft lily pad and the lotus flowers smelled so sweet and Mommy was getting her special pampering spa treatment and she would bake such lovely cupcakes and everybody would clap when Daddy finally came home.

She lay on her back in the light and the robot unrolled the blanket and took off her nightgown and she protested and said that she was cold and he said that she would be warmed up so deliciously in a moment because it was time for the Melt-O-Pak body wrap now that she was clean and soft and all relaxed. There were such funny white balloons on her chest and she reached up to touch them and the robot put her arms back down by her sides and said that nice girls didn't touch themselves like that, and he began to rub her all over with warm lotion that smelled like sugar cookies and he told her that it was Vita Cream and it would prepare her skin for the wax and she suddenly had a memory of terrible pain and she told him that she didn't want any wax and she liked her hair the way it was and the robot told her that this wax would leave her hair intact and it was special wax that would draw out all her toxins and he fed her another Dr. Mitchell's and told her that he was going to take such good care of her and nothing would hurt and the wax would take out every-thing bad, and he turned her over gently and rubbed the warm lotion into her shoulders and back and legs and she began to feel a warm thick substance being painted onto her feet and it was stiffening as it cooled and she felt so enveloped and cared for and she felt the wax on her legs and the voices in her head began to sing of mango trees and cicadas and blades of grass and she would never be lonely again and the robot turned her over gently and the wax was so stiff that she couldn't move and she was warming up again and she felt the wax on the front of her legs and the robot explained that nature abhors a vacuum and there would be a vacuum between her body and the wax which would fill with toxins and impurities and she was such a good girl and he fed her another Dr. Mitchell's as she felt her legs become immobilized and she tried to tell herself a story in a singsong voice, but all she saw were fragments of a veiled woman walking through a labyrinthine medina with whitewashed walls and turquoise doors and minarets rising up beyond, and she followed the woman into a narrow doorway into a warm round room blurred with steam and lit with pillars of light that streamed in through tiny star-shaped holes in the high domed ceiling. There were naked women everywhere talking softly and laughing and reclining on a wide marble platform, and there were ornate basins overflowing with water all around, and the veiled woman turned to her and helped her to undress and an enormous naked woman bathed her with bowls of warm water and laid her down on the warm marble platform and began to rub her body with a small coarse cloth and layers of dead skin rolled off and finally her body was clean and the woman began to massage her and the platform was so warm and the woman was so strong and she lay between the woman's solid legs and looked up at the stars of light. She felt so warm and loved and the robot told her that it was time to wrap her head in special silk from spiderwebs to make her hair grow out so soft and pretty, and she couldn't move and she was getting hot and she tried to open her eyes but they were covered with something filmy and sticky and her body was sweating and itchy and there were spiders coming out of her pores and they were terrified and she told them that everything would be okay and she would keep them nice and safe inside the wax and she tried to think of how to breathe and she couldn't see and she felt so hot and cannot see you cannot see me cannot breathe cannot recall cannot remember anything at all.

LaVergne, TN USA
07 December 2010
207781LV00001B/50/A